HEARTSTRINGS

ALSO BY ALI NOVAK

My Life with the Walter Boys
My Return to the Walter Boys

The Heartbreak Chronicles:
The Heartbreakers
Paper Hearts

HEARTSTRINGS

ALI NOVAK

Copyright © 2025 by Ali Novak
Cover and internal design © 2025 by Sourcebooks
Cover art and design by Maeve Norton
Internal design by Tara Jaggers/Sourcebooks
Cover images © DeawSS/Shutterstock, dr-interior/Getty Images

Sourcebooks and the colophon are registered trademarks of Sourcebooks.

All rights reserved. No part of this book may be reproduced in any form or by any electronic or mechanical means, including information storage and retrieval systems—except in the case of brief quotations embodied in critical articles or reviews—without permission in writing from its publisher, Sourcebooks.

No part of this book may be used or reproduced in any manner for the purpose of training artificial intelligence technologies or systems.

The characters and events portrayed in this book are fictitious or are used fictitiously. Any similarity to real persons, living or dead, is purely coincidental and not intended by the author.

Published by Sourcebooks Fire, an imprint of Sourcebooks
1935 Brookdale RD, Naperville, IL 60563-2773
(630) 961-3900
sourcebooks.com

Cataloging-in-Publication Data is on file with the Library of Congress.

The authorized representative in the EEA is Dorling Kindersley Verlag GmbH. Arnulfstr. 124, 80636 Munich, Germany

Manufactured in the UK by Clays and distributed by
Dorling Kindersley Limited, London
002-355725-Oct/25
10 9 8 7 6 5 4 3 2

To Flynn,

This series is about so many things—music, fame, friendship, and first loves. It's also about sisters and the different bonds they share, so thank you for being the best sister out there. You let me read my stories to you when I was too scared to share them with anyone else, and for that I'll always be grateful. (Also, I'm sorry about throwing that Polly Pocket house at you when we were kids. Can we forget about that now?)

CHAPTER 1

I couldn't remember the last time my dad graced me with his presence, so when he strode into the kitchen Saturday morning, his ever-present Bluetooth headset clipped to his ear, I nearly choked on my bagel.

"No, the contract is already signed. Has been for weeks now," he said, talking in sweeping arm gestures. "I'm sorry, King, but it's my job to do what's best for Violet, end of story." Dad was so dialed into his conversation he didn't notice me sitting in the breakfast nook.

The fact that this was my first father sighting in a week—even though we lived in the same house—spoke to his status as an expert-level workaholic. I was used to having my sister's beachfront property all to myself, so it was jarring to see him standing in the kitchen as if this were his natural habitat.

"Absolutely not! We've been over this a million times, and I'm done arguing about it," Dad exclaimed. "Call my lawyers if you have a problem." He hit End without so much as a goodbye and jammed a fresh K-Cup into the Keurig.

"What'd the coffee maker ever do to you?"

Dad spun around at the sound of my voice. "Indie, I didn't see you there."

"And that makes it okay to manhandle the most important appliance in the kitchen?" I teased.

"Sorry, it's been a rough morning."

I brushed a few stray crumbs off my shirt and slid to the end of the bench. "Everything okay?"

"You know how King Williams is." He rubbed his forehead. "The man's an overbearing control freak who throws temper tantrums when things don't go his way. But don't worry. It's nothing your old man can't handle."

As I carried my dirty plate over to the dishwasher, I tried to imagine the CEO of Mongo Records having a toddler-esque hissy fit but couldn't conjure the image. Then again, I hardly knew the man. The Williamses were family friends, but King was too busy expanding his music empire to have time for potluck dinners or camping trips with us. I was totally okay with that; there was something about his icy demeanor that gave me the creeps.

"Well, good thing you get to spend all day tomorrow with yours truly." In one not-so-graceful hop, I planted my butt on the island countertop, heels banging against the lower cabinets. "What time are we leaving?"

To celebrate the start of October, our local theater was hosting a Halloween marathon, starting at noon with *The Exorcist*. I'd inherited my love of scary movies from Dad, so the following fifteen hours of monsters, gore, and jump-out-of-your-skin scares would be the perfect father-daughter bonding time.

All the essentials were piled on the counter next to me: gift cards to buy popcorn and soda, five different boxes of candy I planned to smuggle in using my purse, a bottle of caffeine pills to keep us awake, and oversize sweatshirts in case the theater was chilly. My excitement level was so far off the charts that I hadn't been able to sleep last night.

"Leaving?"

My stomach dropped at the question. "For the horror marathon at Cinépolis, remember?" I forced myself to sound upbeat, but it was never a good sign when I had to remind Dad of our plans.

"Sweetie," he started, and I knew I wouldn't like what he said next. Dad only used that particular endearment when he felt guilty. "You know I can't take the day off. What with Violet's promotional work for the final season of *Immortal Nights* and her new career direction, I'm swamped."

Surprise, surprise.

Dad was picking her over me again.

I should've known better. Violet's priorities always eclipsed everything else. It hadn't always been this way, although it was getting harder to remember our lives before my sister was famous. We used to be a happy family—Mom, Dad, Violet, and me—but then my sister decided she wanted to be an actress. On my thirteenth birthday, she was cast as vampire princess Lilliana LaCroix in the MTV series adaptation of *These Immortal Nights,* the wildly popular young adult trilogy.

That was five years ago, but it felt like a lifetime.

Pressing my lips tight, I counted to ten. I would *not* lose my shit. "Dad, you promised."

"Are you sure?" His eyebrows gathered together as he studied his phone. "I don't see you on my calendar."

I gripped the edge of the counter as my entire body tensed. Ever since he quit his job as a bank director to be Violet's manager, Dad had become increasingly unavailable, but this was beyond ridiculous. "My bad," I snapped. "Didn't realize I had to schedule an appointment to hang out with you. Should I email your assistant so he can pencil in my birthday?"

Welp, so much for not losing my shit.

"Indie, don't be a brat," he said, shooting me a disapproving look over the rims of his glasses.

"Hey, just calling it like I see it." Dad was right, of course. It was a bratty thing for me to say, but I couldn't help it. This was the third time he'd bailed on me for Violet since the start of the school year.

"*Indigo Josephine Mitchell-Jamiolkowski.*"

Oh crap. The full name. I only heard that pretentious mouthful when I landed myself in dangerous waters. Letting out a frustrated sigh, I pushed back my bangs. "I'm sorry, Dad, but this sucks. I've been looking forward to spending time with you."

The scowl on Dad's face softened. "I know, Indie. I'm sorry. Violet's schedule will get less hectic soon, and then we can do something together, just you and me. I promise." The Keurig let out a long beep, and he turned to collect his mug as steam rose in lazy tendrils from the freshly brewed coffee.

"Yeah, sure," I replied, swallowing back my disappointment. There was no point in arguing with him, not when it involved Violet's career. Work always came first.

Dad beamed. "That's my girl." His phone buzzed less than a second later, and he punched the Talk button. "Hi, this is Edward Jamiolkowski… Ah, Courtney! So good to hear from you. I've been meaning to call so we could discuss the lineup for…"

I heaved a sigh as Dad swept out of the room. A small part of me thought he'd change his mind, but when his office door slammed shut, the hope flickering inside me petered out. For a moment, I considered calling Sofia, but even watching action movies freaked her out. There was no way she'd make it through a horror long haul. I could always text some friends from orchestra, but I doubted anyone would be up for a fifteen-hour commitment on such short notice.

Guess that meant I'd be attending the movies solo.

Whatever. More popcorn for me.

☆ ☪ ♪

Waking up Monday morning after the marathon was brutal.

That being said, Freddy, Jason, and Michael were well worth the lost shut-eye, and somehow I made it through the day without falling asleep in class. By the time I got home, all I wanted to do was pass out, so when I reached my bedroom, I ignored my violin case resting in the corner and collapsed face-first onto my mattress.

You should practice right now, the voice inside my head chastised. Because that was my routine: three hours of violin every day after school. I only had two months left to select and perfect my repertoire before my college application was due.

A knock interrupted my guilt trip. "Indie, you in here?"

"No," I muttered into my pillow, because I didn't currently have the mental capacity to deal with my sister. Maybe if I ignored her, she'd go away.

No such luck.

When I lifted my head a few seconds later to see if Violet was gone, I found her standing in the doorway.

"You need something?" I asked. Aside from acknowledging each other's presence around the house, she and I rarely spoke. What could Violet possibly have to say to me?

She took a hesitant step into my room. "Yeah, do you have a minute? There's something I want to run by you."

"Nope," I replied, flopping back down and locking my hands behind my head. "Kinda in the middle of something right now."

Violet gave my postschool sprawl a once-over before crossing her arms. "Really? You don't look busy."

"That's because I'm not."

"Oookay—you seem irritated. Did I do something to piss you off?"

Ding! Ding! Ding! We have a winner.

"Dad was supposed to go to the movies with me yesterday," I said, glaring up at the ceiling. A cobweb stretched between the fan blades, and I tried to remember the last time I'd dusted.

"But…he didn't?"

That she had the audacity to sound confused pissed me off even more. "Of course not! He was too busy doing stuff for *you*."

Sighing, Violet ran a hand over her ponytail. "Haven't we gone over this before? I don't set Dad's hours."

"Yeah, whatever." I turned away and curled onto my side, hugging the duvet against my chest.

"Indie, I'm sorry. I had no clue he canceled on you. I'll talk to him about it, okay?" she said, but I didn't bother responding. Why should I when I was never considered a priority in this family?

A tense silence stretched between us. It lasted so long I momentarily thought Violet had walked away, but then the mattress dipped as she sat down beside me.

"Aren't you sick of always being mad at me?" Her question sounded weary, so I flipped over to face her.

"Vi," I said, not unkindly, "what do you need?"

"Well, about that... I know this isn't the best time to ask for a favor, but I have a major crisis on my hands. Lydia called last night. Poor thing broke her leg, so she can't come to New York with me this weekend. Obviously I feel terrible, but her timing is awful."

I rolled my eyes. Lydia was Violet's personal assistant. Heaven forbid she went one day without someone to fetch her nonfat, unsweetened café au lait. Always the drama queen, my sister.

"Gabe promised his assistant, Sadie, could help me out on Friday," she continued, which made sense. Whenever Violet made a promotional appearance, Gabe, her *Immortal Nights* costar, was always there with her. "But I know she'll be too busy on Saturday to lend a hand."

My brow inched up in speculation. Despite the absurdity of its direction, I had a feeling where this conversation was heading. "And what does any of this have to do with me?"

"Well, I was hoping you could fill in for Lydia."

Ha! Over my dead body.

On Thursday, the doors to the East Coast's largest and most kick-ass gathering of geeks, fangirls, and pop culture aficionados would open—New York Comic Con. The cast of *Immortal Nights* would have a busy schedule packed with autograph signings, press interviews, and, of course, a panel. No doubt my sister would run me ragged if I took Lydia's place.

Had Violet planned on leaving for New York Wednesday night, I might have considered assisting her so I could meet Chelsea Hirano, the creator of *Lady Phoenix*, my favorite comic book. As soon as Dad told me Violet was making an appearance, I'd looked up the convention schedule to see if I could beg her to get my favorite issue autographed. Unfortunately, Chelsea's panel was scheduled for Thursday morning before Violet's flight even took off. The fact that I would miss her appearance by half a day made the thought of attending with Violet even less appealing.

For a moment, I wondered if I could see my mom. Baltimore was only a few hours away from NYC by train, so maybe she could come up and visit, but then I remembered that she would be out of town on a girls trip.

"Not going to happen." If I wanted a good dose of torture, I'd stick my hand down the garbage disposal.

"Just hear me out before you say no." The alarm in her voice made me pause, and she seized the opportunity to keep talking. "I only need your help on Saturday. I'll pay you five hundred bucks for the entire day, and you'll get to skip school on Thursday and Friday. You can do whatever you want with your free time—sightsee, check out the convention, maybe take a tour of Juilliard? Please say yes. I'm desperate here."

I had to give it to Violet, she made an enticing offer. I'd been dreaming of Juilliard since picking up my first violin. Throw in a get-out-of-school-free card, cash to spend, and a weekend trip to New York, and any normal teen would jump at the opportunity. Then again, most kids my age didn't have a celebrity for a sister. If I did this, I was in good conscience agreeing to participate in the Violet James show, which meant screaming fans, paparazzi, and watching everyone and their mother kiss my sister's ass. The thought made me cringe.

"I don't think so, Violet. I have a test in calculus on Friday and—"

"That makeup artist you like," she interrupted. "What's her name?"

"Melody Nguyen?"

"Yeah, her. She's on a panel called Behind the Prosthetics. It features a bunch of Hollywood's top special effects makeup artists. If you help me out on Saturday, I'll give you a break to go see her panel."

I pursed my lips. I hadn't thought to check if Melody was making an appearance. Violet must have saved her as a trump card in case I refused her offer. Because we both knew there was no way I'd pass up a chance to meet one of my idols, even if it meant spending time with my sister. The question was, how much did Violet need an assistant?

Studying my nails, I tried to appear as uninterested as possible. "Make it a grand and you've got yourself an assistant."

Violet's lips curled in a triumphant smile. "Done."

☆ ♭ ♫

"So…" Violet said, twisting her hands in her lap.

"So…" I said back.

As of five hours ago, the two of us were New York bound. Violet had explained my duties for Saturday on the way to the airport. Essentially, I was a glorified errand girl who was also in charge of manning her business phone.

But now that we were trapped at an altitude of thirty-five thousand feet? Violet was struggling to come up with a conversation starter. Neither of us knew what to say to each other, almost like we were distant relatives forcing small talk at a family reunion.

Maybe that was because we hadn't felt like sisters in years. We used to be best friends, but ever since getting her big break, Violet never had a free moment. If she wasn't in New Orleans filming *IN*, then she was off promoting the show or on the set of whatever side project she was working on. Bottom line—she was too busy to be my big sister.

Violet cleared her throat. "Did you schedule a campus tour?"

"I tried."

When I didn't elaborate, she shot me a look. "*And?*"

I glanced at the comic resting on my tray table, the latest issue of *Lady Phoenix*, and ignored the urge to start reading. "All the slots were full."

"Oh, that sucks. I'm sorry, Indie." She tucked a curl behind her ear and glanced over at me. "Have you finished applying yet?"

"No," I said, sighing inwardly. "I'm done with all the easy stuff like my essays and letters of recommendation, but I'm stuck on what to do for my prescreening." As part of the application process, I had to submit a video recording of my proposed live audition. Problem was I'd developed a nasty case of deer-in-headlights when it came to selecting what pieces to play.

"What's the issue? Maybe I can help."

Raising a brow, I turned in my seat to stare at Violet. She was joking, right? When we were kids, Mom wanted both of us to learn to play violin, but Violet gave up after a handful of lessons. "No offense, but I doubt that."

She crossed her arms. "Oh yeah? Try me."

"Okay, any idea what Paganini caprice I should pick? Or how about which movement from a Mozart concerto I should play? I also need two movements from a Bach solo sonata or partita, so if you have any suggestions, I'm all ears."

The confidence faded from her face. "Ah…"

"Yeah, that's what I thought."

"Jeez, I was only trying to help."

Realizing my response had come out sharper than intended, I let my breath go in a quick huff. "I'm sorry. It's just…this audition is really important."

"I know," she said, reaching over the armrest to briefly squeeze my wrist. "When's it due?"

"December first."

"Well, you have some time left. You're the best violinist I know. I'm sure you'll figure things out."

That wasn't saying much. Who did Violet know that played besides me and Mom?

"Yeah, hopefully."

We fell quiet again. As the silence mounted around us, it

occurred to me that this conversation was one of the longest we'd had in months. And that meant we weren't due for another exchange until New Year's Eve at the earliest. Perfect. I turned my attention back to the comic in my hand, but before I could start reading, Violet perked up in her seat.

"Hey, guess what?" She didn't wait for me to respond. "I'm almost done recording my album. I just need one or two more tracks, and then we can decide which to use for my first single."

Now that *IN* was ending, Violet wanted to take a break from acting to start a career as a recording artist. At first, she considered signing with Mongo Records because of our friendship with the Williams family. Not only was Mongo one of the top music labels in the industry, but they were responsible for superstars like Jenna Ocean, Diego St. James, and Starlight Summer, just to name a few. But it only took one business meeting for Violet to realize that King didn't care what her music sounded like as long as her millions of fans bought the album. So Violet did something risky: she walked away from her deal at Mongo and partnered with King's son, Alec, who was launching his own label.

Alec Williams was so unlike his father, I often wondered if there was a mix-up at the hospital and he'd been switched at birth. He was quiet but loyal, the kind of person who'd drive hundreds of miles to help a friend in need. Our moms were college roommates turned BFFs, so Violet and I grew up with Alec and his sister, Vanessa, as if they were our cousins. Play dates, birthday parties, Fourth of July celebrations—the Williamses were there for it all.

Until they weren't.

Like most of the good things in my life, the era of Mitchell-Jamiolkowski/Williams family get-togethers came to an end when Violet's career took off. Around the same time, Alec joined a garage band that later became the Heartbreakers, arguably the most famous boy band of my generation. Things were never the same after that.

"That's awesome. Still glad you signed with Alec instead of King?"

Violet's entire face lit up at my question. "A hundred percent! He's such a natural, you'd never guess this was his first time producing a record. Speaking of, Alec might be at Comic Con this weekend."

"How come?"

"Jewel wanted one of the boys to make a guest appearance during our panel. Drum up excitement, you know? Dad's been coordinating with their manager, and since he's known Alec forever, I'm guessing he'll be the one attending."

Oh, right. God only knew how I managed to forget the three-episode arc the Heartbreakers filmed for *IN* earlier this summer. In the months leading up to the shoot, it was

Dad and Violet's sole topic of conversation. MTV thought having such a popular band on the show would help boost ratings for the final season.

"Since we're on the topic of Saturday," Violet said, looking me up and down, "I'm assuming you brought more appropriate clothes? Something more…"

I glanced at my outfit. Fishnet stockings under a pair of distressed jeans, a black lace kimono over my *Hocus Pocus* graphic tee, and Doc Martens. Then there was my amethyst pendant, which was a permanent fixture around my neck no matter what I was wearing.

I grinned at Violet. "Something more what?" I asked, rolling the crystal between my fingers.

Her mouth twisted as she tried to think of an adjective that wouldn't insult me. Violet never approved of my fashion sense or, as she referred to it, lack thereof. She was forever trying to give me a makeover, and while I didn't mind her style, the designers she preferred didn't make clothes for girls my size. Well, screw that. I'd keep my comfy T-shirts, plaid flannels, and jeans, thank you very much.

"Something more professional," she said at last. "As my assistant—"

I cut off her excuse with brutal precision. "Absolutely not. I never agreed to that, and we're going to Comic Con, not an award ceremony. Tons of people will be dressed in cosplay. Nobody will think twice about my wardrobe."

Violet's mouth flattened into a thin line, but after one tense moment, she flicked her gaze heavenward and exhaled slowly. "Fine, I suppose you're right. But please, for the love of God, no black lipstick."

"Miss James?" a flight attendant interrupted.

I jerked my head toward the woman in surprise. It always startled me to hear people call Violet that. She'd taken James as a stage name because the show's executive producers thought Mitchell-Jamiolkowski would be too hard for people to pronounce. Five years later, and I still wasn't used to it.

"Yes?" Violet replied, glancing toward her.

"We'll be starting our descent momentarily. Is there anything I can get you beforehand?"

"No, thank you." Violet turned back to me and, despite our disagreement moments ago, smiled. "I'm really excited you're coming with me this weekend. I cleared some of my schedule so we could hang out. We have dinner reservations tonight, mani-pedis at the hotel spa tomorrow morning, and I even got you on the list for one of the industry parties I'm attending on Saturday. How cool does that sound?"

Me at some hipster nightclub packed with Hollywood stars? This wasn't the deal we'd agreed to. Violet promised

I could do whatever I wanted with my free time, and playing at being sisters didn't fall under that category. Did she feel bad I'd be spending most of the weekend by myself? If so, my sister had reached new levels of obliviousness—with Mom gone and Dad and Violet constantly working, I was *always* alone.

"Violet, you don't have to worry about entertaining me. I already have plans."

"Oh. Are you sure? Because it's not a prob—"

"Trust me," I said, making a show of opening my comic to signal our conversation was over. "I'm positive."

CHAPTER 2

The last time I'd visited New York, I was six—maybe seven?—and not old enough to appreciate a trip to the city, so after we landed and checked into the hotel, I used the rest of the day and all of Friday to do touristy things. While Violet was busy with a photo shoot, I took a ferry out to see the Statue of Liberty, rode the elevator up to the observation deck at the Empire State Building, and spent hours wandering the Met.

Although I tried to enjoy myself, Saturday loomed over me like an execution date. Especially after Friday morning, when Sadie, Gabriel Grant's uptight personal assistant, stopped by the hotel room to give Violet and me our Comic Con registration badges. The first thing I'd noticed about Sadie was the permanent scowl on her face. That and the way her hair was raked into such a tight ponytail, I thought her scalp would peel away from her skull. Before handing over my badge, she made me promise not to lose it.

"This is a professional pass," she'd said, holding it out of my reach as she explained its importance, like she was talking to a child. "Not only does it come with great responsibility, but it's your lifeline this weekend. It gets you into restricted areas and lets event staff know that you have an important job to do. Do not, under any circumstance, remove it. Am I clear?"

Being trapped on a plane with Violet had been uncomfortable enough. How excruciating would it be to spend an entire day with her *and* people like Sadie?

As it turned out the next day, "excruciating" wasn't really the right term to describe working for my sister. The more appropriate word was "draining." Violet wasn't the total diva I feared she'd be, but I wasn't prepared for a day in the life of Hollywood's hottest TV star. Hair and makeup arrived bright and early to help her get ready, followed by breakfast in the car on the drive to the Javits Center since there wasn't time to eat. I didn't even get a chance to look around before Violet was hustled off to her first appointment, a one-on-one sit-down with a prominent entertainment reporter. For the next five hours, Violet had back-to-back interviews with a variety of different media outlets. By the time she finished, I was dead on my feet and it was only noon. I didn't understand how she hadn't collapsed from exhaustion, but I supposed this was normal for her.

Thankfully, Violet and the rest of the cast had a break before their panel. Everyone was lounging around a private greenroom while I worked her business phone and tried to answer the constant stream of emails flooding her inbox. After finishing one more message and hitting Send, I slumped back against the couch cushions in defeat.

"Hey, Vi? Behind the Prosthetics starts in forty minutes. Mind if I take off? I wanna get a good seat."

Before she could answer, Ryan Klein, one of my sister's costars, cocked his head and asked, "Who are you again?"

We'd met on multiple occasions, but he never remembered my name. Which was beyond irritating. Ryan had joined the cast of *IN* two years ago. Granted, he wasn't the sharpest tool in the shed, and I rarely visited the set, but still. Most people found my name memorable. Indigo, like the color, because Mom loved naming her kids after different shades of the rainbow. If Violet and I had more sisters, I was positive that they'd be named Scarlett or Jade or some other color-themed moniker.

"Seriously, Ryan?" Violet glanced up from the magazine she was browsing. "I've introduced you to my sister at least three times."

A lumbering grin stretched across Ryan's face. "Oh, right. You're Izzy."

Wrong, but I didn't bother to correct him. He'd forget in a few minutes anyway.

"Indie, not Izzy. Come on, man. How can you forget her name when it's paired with such a pretty face?" Gabe, Violet's on-screen love interest, punched Ryan on the arm before flicking a tousled black lock out of his eyes and winking at me. He probably expected a giggle or blush in response to his compliment, but I was immune to the gravitational pull of Gabriel Grant. He used his looks like a weapon, aiming an icy blue smolder at whichever girl caught his attention before obliterating her with a dazzling, movie star smile.

Can you say gross? Arrogance was not my cup of tea.

Besides, I knew Gabe wasn't interested in me. No guy was once they met my sister.

The two of us were complete opposites. With her fair locks and petite frame, Violet reminded me of Tinker Bell, albeit a badass, butt-kicking version. She was in top shape, her muscles tight and toned from hours spent choreographing *IN* fight scenes. In comparison, I was tall and big-boned with ample curves, and my wavy hair was a dull, dishwater blond. If not for our eyes, a light-brown, almost golden color, nobody would guess we were related.

My jaw clenched. Gabe was using me to get Violet's attention, and it worked.

"Can you not hit on my little sister?" she asked, her nose wrinkling up.

Gabe dropped an arm around her shoulders. "Babe, you

know I'd never do anything to jeopardize Luliana," he said, using the ship name Nighties coined for their characters, Lilliana and Luca.

Ugh, gag me.

"I'm not your babe," Violet said, shrugging him off.

I bit the inside of my cheek to keep from grinning. It was comical, really. Gabe could get any girl he wanted with the exception of the one he was interested in. He'd been stuck on Violet for years. During the early days of *IN*, the two did so many appearances together that they were rumored to be dating. Even though they maintained they were just friends, the speculation still created enough of a buzz to boost the show's ratings, and for months, Violet and Gabe couldn't go out in public without being photographed and winding up on the front page of every tabloid magazine. But over the course of their public are-they-or-aren't-they relationship, Gabe developed feelings. Feelings he had yet to get over. I wondered if he knew that he'd never be Violet's type. For now, only a few people in her life knew this, but no guy ever would.

"Violet, you wound me," he said, clapping both hands over his heart in dramatic fashion. Everyone laughed at Gabe's antics, and had I not been staring directly at him, I would have missed the split second of hurt that flickered in his eyes. An exasperated sigh hissed past Violet's lips, but she didn't respond.

"Um, Vi?" I interrupted before Gabe could put his foot in his mouth again. My original question had yet to be answered.

She flipped the page of her magazine. "Mm-hmm?"

"I'm taking my break now."

Her eyes snapped to mine as I stood up from the couch. "Wait, hold on. I need you to run back to the hotel before you leave."

"Why?"

"It's Jewel's birthday next week. Everyone here"—she gestured at the rest of the cast—"chipped in to buy her a present, but I left it in my suitcase."

"Can Sadie go get it?"

Gabe shot me an apologetic look. "Sorry, but she just left for her lunch break."

"Can't this wait until after she gets back?" I asked, glancing over at the clock.

"No," Violet said. "We plan on giving it to her during our panel."

"Why didn't you tell me before?" I complained. There'd been two hours for me to go back to the hotel during the cast autograph session earlier in the day. "You promised I could attend this panel. If I don't leave now, I'll get a crap seat at the back of the room. There's no time to run an errand for you."

A look of guilt rose on Violet's face—clearly Jewel's present wasn't the only thing she'd forgotten about—but she quickly masked her expression. "Of course there is. The hotel isn't that far away."

"But, Violet—"

"Indie, I'm paying you to do this, remember?" she said, her tone gentle but firm.

"Fine," I snapped. Every moment spent arguing with her was time wasted.

I stormed out of the green room, made my way down to the lobby, and hailed a cab outside the convention center. Which turned out to be a major mistake. Traffic was crawling at such an agonizingly slow pace that I could have jogged back faster. There was only half an hour until the panel started, and as the seconds ticked by, my anxiety inched up. If I missed an opportunity to hear Melody speak because of Violet… It went without saying: there would be hell to pay.

A bead of sweat trickled between my shoulder blades. I shifted in my seat, trying to escape the sun that was beating down on me through the window. Despite the unusually warm weather, my taxi driver had the heat cranked high, and by the time we arrived at the hotel, I was dripping.

Two minutes, I decided as I rushed through the lobby. That was my allotted time to get cleaned up. I tossed my bag on the nearest armchair when I reached the suite Violet and I were sharing and went to find Jewel's present. Once I located the brightly wrapped box, I peeled off my top layer and barreled into the bathroom, where I took a hasty sink bath to wash away the smell of BO and panic. One liberal application of deodorant and an outfit change later, I was out the door. By some miracle, I reached the Javits Center with enough time to deliver the gift and make it to Behind the Prosthetics.

"Badge?" a muscled security guard asked when I stepped inside.

"Huh?" Okay, not very eloquent of me, but I was momentarily distracted by the fact that he was wearing sunglasses indoors. They were black Gargoyles, like the ones from *The Terminator*.

"Your badge," he repeated. "I need to scan it if you want to enter the convention."

"Right." I unslung my bag from my shoulder and unbuckled the clasp. It was one of those purses that doubled as a small backpack, because carrying a handbag made me feel like my mom. I dug around inside, my fingers scrambling across my wallet, a half-eaten pack of peanut M&M's, and my hairbrush, but nothing else.

The guard cleared his throat as I continued to rummage. "Miss, you're holding up the line."

"Just give me a sec." I unzipped the large inner pocket only to find a tube of Burt's Bees and a few bobby pins. "It has to be here somewhere," I muttered to myself.

After all, I'd sworn up and down to Sadie that the all-important pass would not, *under any circumstance*, leave my neck. But less than an hour later, I'd yanked it off.

I know, I know, how irresponsible of me, but the lanyard was beyond itchy, and despite my broken promise, I made a point of putting it in my backpack where I couldn't lose it.

So where the hell was the damn thing?

"I'm sorry, miss," the guard said, pointing at the exit, "but I need you to leave until you locate your badge."

My chest tightened, and I scrambled for an excuse to get me in the door. "Look, sir, you don't understand. I'm Violet James's assistant. I need to deliver an important package before her panel starts. If I don't..." I trailed off, hoping he'd fill in the blank with a consequence worthy of sympathy. "I'm in a jam here. Any way you could help a girl out?"

The man crossed his arms. "Lady, I don't give a shit who you work for. No badge, no entry."

"Jeez, you don't need to be a dick about it," I shot back. Before he could respond, I whipped around and threw the door open with more force than necessary, bursting out into the golden afternoon light.

There was only one person who could help me now, so I

pulled out my phone and muttered a quick prayer. Violet answered after two rings.

"Hey, I was just about to text you," she said. "We have to leave for the panel in five, and I need Jewel's present. Where are you?"

"Stuck outside the convention center," I told her, wedging the phone between my shoulder and ear. With my hands free, I searched my bag one last time. "I can't find my pass, and there's this huge, Arnold Schwarzenegger–looking dude who won't let me in."

"Well, where'd you last have it?"

I stopped for a second to think. All Comic Con attendees were required to scan in *and* out of the convention. "When I left the convention center for the hotel," I said, and two seconds later, a terrible thought occurred to me. "Oh God! What if I lost it in the cab?"

"Indie, relax. I'll send someone to collect the present, and then you can retrace your steps."

"Retrace my steps?" I choked out. "I don't have time to traipse across New York City. Melody's panel is about to start."

There was a pause, but then my sister said, "What exactly do you expect me to do about it?"

"You're Violet James, for crying out loud! Tell them to let me in." The moment the words left my mouth, I realized how childish I sounded. Never in my life had I sunk as low as leveraging my sister's fame to my advantage.

"It doesn't work like that, and you know it." Violet's tone wasn't snarky, but there was a definite, matter-of-fact edge to her response. "I'm really sorry, Indie, but I have to go. Stay where you are, and someone will be down shortly."

"Wait, Vi—"

But the line went dead. I wondered for a moment if this was actually happening—if I was about to miss the main reason I'd come to New York in the first place. Maybe my apprehension about working for my sister had manifested in the form of this ridiculous nightmare, and in reality, it was late Friday night, and I was fast asleep at our hotel.

A cool voice roused me from my musing. "Hello, Indigo."

"Jesus!" I exclaimed, slapping a hand to my heart when Sadie popped up beside me like a malevolent Whac-a-Mole. "How'd you get down here so fast?"

She ignored my question. "Where's the gift?"

"Right here." The holographic wrapping paper flashed in the sunlight when I held it up for her to see. "I was hoping you could help me—"

"No," she replied, not waiting to hear the rest of my question. Her mouth pinched together as if the mere act of standing in my presence was painful.

"I—what?"

"No." She seized the box from my hands. "I don't help people break rules, especially those with no regard for them."

"You've gotta be joking."

"Have I done anything in the short time we've known each other to indicate I'm the joking type?" Sadie replied, and I had to admit, she had a point. She looked like the kind of girl who'd be typecast as the stereotypical punitive librarian. Or a drill sergeant.

"What's your problem with me?" I finally asked.

She sniffed. "My problem? You're a disgrace to personal assistants everywhere."

"You know I'm not actually a personal assistant, right?"

"That's exactly my point."

"Okay, fine," I said, coming to the conclusion there would be no reasoning with her. "I'm a shitty PA. I promise I'll never assume such a lofty position again, but please—there's a panel starting in"—I glanced at my phone—"two minutes ago that I'm dying to see, and I could really use your help."

Sadie studied me. From the way her head was cocked in calculation, I knew she could do it—she could get me inside. After another moment, she straightened up and brushed her ponytail over her shoulder. "If attending meant so much to you, then you shouldn't have removed your badge." Her mouth twisted into a not-so-polite smile. "Enjoy the rest of your day, Indigo."

HEARTSTRINGS

Throat tight, I watched as she slipped back into the convention center, Jewel's present tucked snuggly under her arm.

☆ ♡ ♪

The green room was deserted when I finally returned, my Comic Con badge hanging around my neck.

Despite all the trouble a piece of plastic and lanyard caused me, my pass hadn't been hard to locate. My first guess was that it was riding around Manhattan in the back of a taxi, but since I had no clue how to track down said taxi, I went to the hotel in hopes of finding it there. Sure enough, it was lying underneath the armchair I'd dumped my bag onto. All I wanted to do afterward was crawl in bed and put my miserable day behind me, but Violet's business phone was still in my pocket, so I had to go back to the convention center and return it.

Exhaustion settled over me as I dragged myself toward the couches, tossing my bag on the coffee table as I passed by. My aim was off, and it hit the floor, spilling its contents across the carpet. At that exact moment, my cell buzzed with an incoming text.

VIOLET:
> Hey, find your badge yet? Our panel just finished, but we're doing a signing, and I'd really appreciate a FIJI Water.

"Seriously?" My entire body felt drained, like a phone on two percent battery. The last thing I wanted was to deal with my sister, especially after today's events. It wasn't her fault I lost my pass, but she hadn't helped me either. "You know what I'd really appreciate, Violet?" I said, dropping to my knees to clean up my things. "If you took your goddamn FIJI Water and shoved it up your bony, stuck-up—"

"Um, are you okay down there?"

At the sound of someone's voice, I jerked in surprise, slamming my head against the underside of the coffee table.

"Crap, I'm sorry! I thought you knew I was here."

I looked up to see who was talking, but the pain at the back of my skull was blinding. All I could make out was the blurry frame of someone tall. "Ow," I groaned, rubbing the tender spot that I hoped wouldn't become a baseball-size lump by tomorrow.

Once the sharp throbbing faded to a dull ache, I blinked the tears from my eyes and focused on the culprit responsible for scaring me to death. Standing above me was a lanky guy with messy, strawberry-blond hair in desperate need of a cut.

"Where the hell did you come from?" I asked, still grimacing.

Mystery guy pointed at the opposite couch. "I was napping."

"And I knew you were here *how*?" I muttered, more to myself than him. From the door, it was impossible to see anyone lying across the cushions. He arched a brow at me, and I sighed. "Sorry, I'm having a craptastic day."

"Here," he said, squatting down beside me. "Let me help." He swept a pile of spare change together and pushed it in my direction. With our new proximity, I was able to get a better look at him. He wasn't handsome in the standard context of the word—his nose was a bit too long, and his jaw was slightly crooked—but there was something endearing about his boyish looks and freckles. His eyes, however, were breathtaking: a soft green that reminded me of new growth in spring surrounded by thick, blond lashes.

I know this guy, I realized. *How do I know him?*

As I shoved the last of my belongings into my bag, mystery guy rose to his feet.

"Are you all right?" he asked, offering me a hand up. I blinked but placed mine in his, and he hauled me off the ground. "You sounded upset before."

Great, he'd heard me bitching. What a wonderful first impression. "Oh, that? I'm fine. I was just venting. Nothing to worry about."

"But you mentioned someone named Violet. You weren't talking about Violet James, were you?"

"Unfortunately, yes."

He grimaced. "She your boss or something?"

"I'd rather taste test dog food for the rest of my life than work for Violet. I'm Indie, her sister."

"Dog food, huh," he said, his face relaxing. "Even the wet kind? That stuff makes me think of chemically processed barf."

"Especially the wet kind," I told him.

The corner of his mouth twitched in an almost smile, and he held out his hand in greeting. "I'm Xander. It's nice to meet you."

"Likewise," I said, and as we shook hands, realization plowed into me with the weight of a three-hundred-pound lineman: *this* was Xander Jones, lead guitarist for the Heartbreakers. Without his usual square frames, he was surprisingly unrecognizable. My mouth went dry, and I took what I hoped was an inconspicuous moment to collect myself. "Are you here for the *Immortal Nights* panel?"

Xander stiffened. "Um, yeah," he said, gaze dropping to his feet. "I am."

I frowned, caught off guard by his sudden mood change. Had I insulted him somehow? Or maybe he was disappointed I hadn't gushed over meeting someone as famous as him? Before I could figure out what was wrong, my back pocket vibrated.

VIOLET:

> Everything okay? Haven't heard back from you and I really need that water.

Unbelievable. Was she incapable of going two hours without me? There had to be someone else who could help her. Someone like Sadie. Surely the world's greatest PA was able to fetch Violet a drink; she'd probably gnaw off an arm or sacrifice her firstborn for the opportunity. Chances were, even if I left now, the signing would be finished by the time I located a damn FIJI Water and—

Wait a minute. The signing wasn't over yet. What the hell was Xander Jones doing up here with me?

"Shouldn't you be with the cast right now?" I asked, narrowing my eyes. "Their panel ended a few minutes ago, but you were already in the green room."

"I'm supposed to," he said, kicking at an imaginary speck on the ground.

"And you're not because…?"

"It's complicated."

Wow, because that clarified everything. Hint taken.

"Okay, well, I'll be out of your hair in a second," I said, strolling over to the minibar at the back of the room. Maybe if I brought Violet her water, she'd give me details about what was going on with Xander. "You can go back to napping or whatever."

"You don't have to leave."

"No offense," I replied, opening the refrigerator door, "but it seems like you want to be left alone." Inside, I found a row of Coke, Red Bull, Snapple, and Dasani, but no FIJI. Oh well. Violet would have to deal.

"Look, I'm sorry," he said, rubbing his chest as if he was in pain. "I wasn't trying to be a dick, but today's been shitty for me too." He offered me a hesitant smile and gestured at the couch. "Wanna sit down and compare notes on whose was worse?"

I turned the water bottle over in my hands, deliberating. Violet had yet to pay me, and I was afraid that if I ignored her, I wouldn't get my money. But I was also intrigued by Xander. Boy bands weren't usually my thing, but I bought the Heartbreakers' first album out of loyalty to Alec. No one was more surprised than me when I wound up loving it. Sure, some of the tracks were cheesy, but there were just as many songs with beautifully written lyrics about grief and growing up and disillusionment. When would I get another opportunity like this?

"All right, sure." I crossed the room and sat down before I could change my mind.

"Do you know Jewel Peck?" Xander asked, plopping down beside me.

"Yup. She's the executive producer of *IN*. Known her since I was thirteen."

"Oh, right." Xander grinned sheepishly and scratched his cheek. "You probably know more about the show than me, don't you?"

"Let's just say that if there's ever an *Immortal Nights* edition of Trivial Pursuit, I'd kick your ass." I wasn't an expert by choice, but after five years of Violet's job consuming my life, I'd picked up a thing or two.

"Duly noted. Anyway, it was Jewel's idea for one of us to make a surprise appearance today," Xander said, and by *us*, I figured he meant the Heartbreakers. "When I heard, I immediately asked Courtney if I could—"

"Wait, who's Courtney?" I interrupted.

"Our band manager. As soon as I heard about the panel opportunity, I volunteered myself. Appearing at Comic Con has been a dream of mine since I was eight."

"That's an interesting dream for an eight-year-old."

He laughed. "My parents are huge Trekkies, like so obsessed they named my brother Scotty after Montgomery Scott. When I was a kid, our family vacations consisted of traveling to different fan conventions. My favorite thing to do was wander through Artist Alley in the exhibit halls and look at all the cool art. Can't do that anymore, you know? I'd be mobbed."

"Yeah, I get it. I was with Violet when she was swarmed once." The two of us had been Christmas shopping when a fan spotted her and posted the sighting on social media. One minute, we were making ourselves nauseous by smelling every bottle of perfume in Sephora, and the next, we were pinned against the back counter by a horde of teenage girls begging for pictures and autographs.

Xander's entire face lit up. I had a feeling he didn't expect me to understand his situation—how fame made everyday life complicated—but because of Violet, I *did* understand. "The fans mean well, but every once in a while, things get dicey."

"More like terrifying. I don't understand how you guys do it."

"Do what?"

"Handle everything. The constant attention, the lack of privacy, the media scrutinizing your every move." Violet's life was a nightmare. Just thinking about swapping places with her made me feel as if I'd eaten something rotten.

He shrugged. "You get used to it. I'm not saying there aren't days when all you want to do is shut the world out, but I've learned to deal."

"Is that what happened today?" I asked, steering the conversation back to the original topic. I still didn't understand why Xander Jones had been napping when he could've been onstage addressing thousands of excited fans.

A line appeared between his brows. "What do you mean?"

"With the panel. Did something happen that you weren't up to dealing with?"

"Oh, no." He raked a hand through his hair, then sighed as if the simple action was exhausting. After several silent moments, he said, "The truth? I didn't go because I got cut from our cameo. Jewel broke the news to me earlier today."

"Wait, what?" I gasped. "You're not in *any* of the episodes you guys filmed?"

"Well, there're a few scenes where the four of us appear as a group. We're some sort of vampire-hunting gang? I'm not entirely sure. The point is I had zero lines in those scenes. All I did was stand in the background and wave a pistol in the air. The script literally read, 'Vampire Hunter Number Three waves pistol tauntingly.' The frustrating thing is I filmed this really sick chase sequence with Gabe Grant where I almost capture Luca, but apparently it wasn't good enough to make the cut."

His explanation made my heart sink.

"I'm sorry, Xander. That blows."

He shrugged. "It is what it is."

At this, I frowned. Extra material—even full scenes—got axed from the final cut of an episode all the time. What I couldn't wrap my head around was how Xander had been treated. "So let me get this straight—Jewel didn't want you on the panel anymore because of your lack of screen time?"

"She never came out and said that, but when Oliver showed up..." Xander trailed off and shook his head.

The Oliver he was referring to could only be Oliver Perry, the lead singer of the Heartbreakers, which confused me even more. "I don't understand. I thought you guys were based out of LA. What's Oliver doing here?"

"We are, but his girlfriend, Stella, goes to school in New York, and he's visiting her this weekend. He dropped by to say hi. As soon as he showed up, Jewel started making comments about how he'd be perfect for the panel since he played the biggest role on the show. I got the message, so I pretended I wasn't feeling well and let Oliver take my place."

"You're mad," I realized.

Xander scrubbed a hand down his face. "Not at him specifically. It's just... I'm disappointed, that's all. I'll get over it." He pasted on a smile and changed the subject. "So what's the deal with your sister? You seem pretty angry at her."

It was clear he was done talking about what happened, so I forced myself to ignore the geyser of questions welling up inside me. "Violet needed an assistant for the day. I agreed to help her, but only if she gave me a break to see a panel I was excited about," I explained, trying not to scowl. "*That* turned out to be a major mistake."

"I'm assuming you missed the panel?"

"Yup."

"What was it about?"

"SFX makeup."

"*What* kind makeup?"

"Special effects," I said. "It's basically where you use prosthetics to create cosmetic effects in movies and stuff."

"So like Mystique from *X-Men*?" he asked, referencing one of my all-time favorite Hollywood makeup transformations.

"Exactly," I replied with a grin.

My interest in special effects makeup stemmed from my obsession with Halloween. I loved everything about October 31—from its roots in ancient Celtic harvest festivals to trick-or-treating, because who didn't enjoy free candy? There was always a palpable excitement in the air during the days leading up to the holiday: families carving jack-o'-lanterns to display on their front porches; little kids deciding if they wanted to be princesses, superheroes, pirates, or ghosts; friends scaring each other shitless at haunted houses. Like horror movies, Halloween was an ode to the macabre and monsters that went bump in the night, terrors we could experience one day a year without ever being in real danger.

But if I had to pick my favorite part about the holiday, it was the process of crafting the perfect costume. You wouldn't catch me dead in a sexy nurse getup or devil's horns. I relished the challenge of coming up with a concept that was original or clever or whimsical, which was how I discovered Melody. I'd been searching for the perfect DIY costume when I stumbled across her evil mermaid makeup tutorial on YouTube. The contrast of gore and glitter immediately caught my eye, and I was able to transform myself into a creepy version of Ariel using everyday items from around the house. The only thing I'd had to purchase was latex paste. After that, I was hooked.

"I was really pumped to meet Melody Nguyen. She's this amazingly talented makeup artist who was on the panel. I watch all her YouTube videos religiously."

Xander cocked his head. "The Melody who just won an Oscar for that indie film? What's it called again?"

"Yes! *Midnight Slips By*," I said excitedly. "She's the youngest person to ever win an Academy Award for Best Makeup and Hairstyling. No surprise though. Her attention to detail is stunning. And don't get me started on her prosthetics. They're mind-blowing." A small smile crept onto Xander's face, and I realized I was rambling. "Sorry, Melody is kind of an idol of mine."

"Hold that thought." Xander pulled out his phone and scrolled through his contacts before hitting Call. "Hey, long time no talk. How are you?" he said when someone answered. "Yeah, so I've heard. I'm here too... Well, I was supposed to, but that fell through, and now I have some free time. You wanna meet up? There's someone with me who's dying to meet you."

My eyes went wide. Holy shit. Was Xander talking to who I thought he was?

"Yeah, sounds like a plan," he said with a nod. "See you in five."

"What was that all about?" I asked, trying to sound calm.

"It just so happens that I know a certain makeup artist." He leaned to the side so he could shove his phone into his back pocket. "Have you seen the music video for our song 'The End of Love'?"

I beamed. Of course I'd seen the video—it was the band's first single and largest hit off their debut album. "The apocalypse one."

"Yeah, where we turn into zombies. Melody did all our makeup for it. Would you like to meet her? Obviously her panel is over, but she's still here."

"Are you serious right now?" I exclaimed. "I'd legit sell my kidney to meet Melody."

"One hundred percent serious. No internal organs required."

"Oh my God, yes!" I wanted to explode off the couch, whoop with joy, and dance around the room, but I forced myself to rein in my excitement by taking a deep breath. "Thank you so much, Xander. This is beyond amazing."

"Does this help make your craptastic day a little bit better?"

"So much more, you don't even know."

A crooked smile appeared on his face. "Then it's my pleasure." Standing up, he stretched, then nodded at the door.

"Ready when you are."

My phone buzzed again.

VIOLET:
> Seriously? If you're going to ignore me, you should turn your read receipts off.

"Give me one second," I said, holding up a finger. Knowing she wouldn't be able to answer in the middle of a signing, I called my sister. As expected, it went straight to voicemail, and I left a message. "Hey, Vi. Just wanted to give you a heads-up that I'll be taking the rest of the day off. Good luck finding someone to replace me, but if you do, give them my regards. I have an overwhelming amount of sympathy for them."

Xander whistled when I hit End. "Wow. You're seriously pissed, aren't you?"

"Actually," I said, a smile tugging on my lips, "I'm feeling pretty good right now." After all, I was about to meet Melody Nguyen. Giving my sister a figurative middle finger was an added bonus.

CHAPTER 3

"You know Alec, right?" Xander asked as we made our way through the convention center's tangle of back corridors.

The area was restricted to everyone without a professional pass, and while the public floors of the building were enclosed in glass, allowing an ocean of natural light to sweep inside, the guts of the operation were undressed and gloomy: the ceiling was exposed, revealing ducts and pipes and steel beams that crisscrossed each other like a network of roads; the floor was sealed concrete, shiny and unforgiving to dirt and scuff marks; and the fluorescent overhead lights cast the space in a sickly white glow.

"Yup. Violet and I grew up with the Williamses. They're kind of like our unofficial cousins."

"How come we've never met before?"

I shrugged and tucked a strand of hair behind my ear. "It's not like Alec and I hang out on a regular basis. If you haven't noticed, his life is kind of hectic."

Xander grinned. It was the adorable lopsided kind where one side of his mouth lifted up higher than the other. "Okay, fair point, but hasn't he invited you to one of our concerts?"

"We're talking about the same Alec Williams, right? The most reserved, modest person I know? He'd never assume someone was interested in seeing him perform, even if that someone is important to him."

"That's true, but what about you? You've never asked for tickets?"

"Um…" I opened my mouth, then closed it as I tried to formulate a response.

When I didn't answer, Xander froze in the middle of the hallway, the tips of his ears bright red. "God, I'm being a complete ass right now. Sorry for assuming you like our music."

"No! That's not it at all," I said in a rush. "I love *Dance Till Dawn*. Seriously, I know every song on it by heart."

"So if it's not about our music, then why?"

I tugged on my amethyst as I quickly organized my thoughts. "What you have to understand is I've seen the way fame ruins relationships. The more popular *IN* became, the more people in Violet's life—acquaintances, friends, even family—expected things from her. They wanted to cash in on the perks of knowing a celebrity, something I'm sure you've experienced, and I refuse to be that person. I won't put Alec in a position that compromises our friendship."

As I spoke, a hint of a smile appeared on Xander's face. "I get what you're saying. That's commendable."

"There's obviously a but coming."

"Alec is a smart guy. He can tell the difference between a freeloader and someone who actually cares about him. I think he'd be thrilled to have a friend like you supporting him backstage."

He was probably right, but before I could say so, a small assembly of people poured into the hall, filling the quiet space with a blast of conversation and laughter. At the head of the pack was a woman with a clipboard and headset. As they passed by us, I did a double take, my head whipping around so fast I put a kink in my neck. Without thinking, I grabbed Xander's arm and sucked in a sharp breath.

"You all right?" he asked, glancing down at my hand and then up at me. "You look like you've seen a ghost."

"That was Chelsea Hirano," I explained, heart racing.

"Who?"

I shot him a dirty look. "You did *not* just say that."

"Is she from a movie or something?"

"No, she created *Lady Phoenix*." Xander looked at me with a blank expression, so I added, "The comic? Come on, it's only the bestselling series by a female cartoonist in the past decade. She must be making a surprise appearance for something. There's this rumor going around that Netflix is interested in doing a TV adaptation. Now that I think about it, Comic Con would be the perfect place to make an announcement. Oh my God, I hope it's true."

He gave a half shrug. "Never heard of it."

"I'm seriously offended right now."

"Between recording new music and our touring schedule, I don't have a lot of leisure time." Xander paused to study a map posted on the wall. After locating the red YOU ARE HERE dot, he pointed us in the right direction. "What's the comic about?"

"I could spend the next twenty-four hours trying to explain it to you, but the basic premise? There's this girl named Hotaru who discovers she's a phoenix, and she uses her powers to protect the mortal world from demons, monsters, and evil spirits. Next time you get a break, check it out. You won't regret it."

"I'll put it at the top of my list," he promised before nodding at a nearby stairwell. "We need to go this way."

"When you do, remember to let me know what you think," I said, pushing open the door.

"How does a full briefing of my thoughts and feelings after every issue sound?" he joked, not realizing there were well over a hundred.

"As long as you don't ship Soshi and Emerald together, I want to hear every detail." Phoenix fans either loved or hated the pairing, and since the couple grossed me out, I fell into the latter category. Over the course of what felt like a never-ending storyline, readers were tortured with a sexually charged enemies-to-lovers romance, only to discover the characters were twins separated at birth. Very Luke and Leia, but with a lot more than kissing.

His brows knitted together as we started up the stairs. "Am I supposed to know what that means?"

"Nope," I said, laughing. "Let's keep it that way. I don't want to be responsible for corrupting your young, innocent mind."

Xander snorted. "Believe me, that ship sailed a long time ago. Besides, aren't I older than you? You're what—seventeen?"

"Eighteen, but age has nothing to do with it. The average *Phoenix* fangirl can reach levels of smut that would shock the devil," I replied with a wink.

"My life comes with a built-in fandom, remember?" he said, shooting me a pointed look. "Once you read an X-rated fanfic about yourself, there's no going back."

I grinned at him. "You read fan fiction about yourself?"

"Not voluntarily, but last year, our tour bus got stuck in a traffic jam. JJ decided to pass the time by doing a dramatic reading of a few stories he found online."

"That's gold," I said, choking back laughter. "I need more details."

"Apparently, there's a lot of slash fiction written about JJ and me." He paused, and a flush crept across his cheeks. "That's all I'm going to say on the subject."

My grin was uncontrollable. "Okay, you're right. Your innocence is long gone."

"Glad that's been established," he grumbled, his face ten shades of red. "New subject please?"

☆ ♭ ♪

"I think this is it," Xander announced when we finally arrived at our destination.

I hesitated outside the door as a wave of nerves flooded my system. *Someone pinch me*, I thought. I was about to meet *the* Melody Nguyen.

Xander knocked. "Hello?"

"Come in," a familiar voice responded. After watching hours of makeup tutorials, it was impossible not to recognize Melody's cheerful tone.

Xander pushed open the door, revealing a green room identical to the one provided for the *IN* cast. Perched on the armrest of the nearest couch was a woman wearing a cyan leopard-print jacket, a pink butterfly T-shirt, and leather pants covered in rhinestones. Melody was known for her eccentric, vibrant wardrobe, and I was glad to see today was no exception.

"Hey, you!" she exclaimed, throwing open her arms. "Get over here."

He strode across the room, and I slowly inched after him, unsure whether I should follow or wait in the doorway until I was introduced. "It's good to see you," he said, wrapping her in a hug.

"You too." She pulled away to look at him. "I almost didn't recognize you without your glasses. What's with the contacts?"

"I've been attempting to go glasses-free whenever I have a public appearance. Not a huge fan of putting anything in my eyes though, so I don't know how long I'll keep this up."

"Well, I like the contacts. Makes it easier to see those gorgeous green eyes of yours." She turned to me with a smile. "Who's this?"

"Oh, sorry!" Xander said, glancing between the two of us. "Indie, this is Melody. Melody, Indie."

That he didn't introduce me as Violet James's little sister made me want to fling my arms around him in gratitude.

Melody nodded at me. "Nice to meet you."

"You too, and can I say that I'm, like, your biggest fan?" The words tumbled out of my mouth before I could stop them, but I didn't care. I wasn't embarrassed to fangirl over her. "I've followed you on YouTube since forever, and I've attempted at least ninety percent of your tutorials. I nearly cried when you won your Oscar this year."

"Aww, thanks. That means the world to me." A pink the

color of Melody's shirt flooded the apples of her cheeks. "So I take it you're an aspiring makeup artist?"

"Actually, it's more of a hobby for me."

"Hey, that's still cool. Have anything to show me?"

"Oh my God, of course. Hold on." With trembling hands, I pulled out my phone and scrolled through my camera roll until I found the picture of me from Halloween freshman year. "This one's my favorite," I said, handing her my cell.

"Oh, hey! This is from my evil mermaid tutorial. You did a kick-ass job!"

I could've died and gone to heaven right then. Melody Nguyen had complimented *my* work. "Thanks. I wish the line wasn't so obvious where I attached the tentacle to my collarbone, but it was the first time I made my own prosthetic, and the edges turned out too thick."

"Yeah, it's always hard when you don't spread the latex thin enough," she said, nodding her head in agreement. Suddenly, her eyes lit up, and she glanced back at me. "Hey, I have one of my makeup kits with me. Want me to teach you a trick that will help with blending?"

"Holy hell, yes! That would be amazing."

Melody hopped off the table and grabbed Xander's wrist. She yanked him over to an armchair and forced him down onto the cushion. "You sit here," she instructed. "You're going to be our model."

Xander's eyes went wide. "What?"

"I need someone to demonstrate on. Remind me—are you allergic to latex?"

"Well," he replied, cocking his head in consideration. "I've never tried to eat it before, so I'm not sure."

"Don't be a smart-ass," Melody said as she rolled a huge professional makeup case over to the armchair. The organizer had eight drawers and was almost as tall as she was.

His mouth twitched, hiding a grin. "No, I'm not allergic."

"Awesome. Nearly all the products I plan on working with today I've used on you before, so they'll be safe, but we should check the ingredient list of this new foundation I've been dying to test out."

"What do you mean by safe?" I asked as Melody rifled through one of the drawers and produced a small bottle.

"I have a lot of allergies that I need to be careful about," Xander explained. "Most people aren't aware that some makeup products are made with ingredients that trigger allergic reactions, like nuts, dairy, and eggs."

"Wow," I said as Melody scanned the tiny print on the back of the foundation. "I never realized that."

"What's *Arachis hypogaea*?" she asked.

Xander pulled out his phone and typed it into Google. "Peanuts. I can't use that."

"Not a problem. I'll just have to test it out a different time."

Melody placed the bottle back in her organizer. "Okay, now be a good boy, and don't move." Opening the top drawer of her case, she revealed a collection of premade prosthetics. There were everyday body parts like noses, ears, and chins, but there were also gills and horns and scaly skin.

"Whoa." I shook my head in amazement as she pulled out supplies. "These are awesome."

"This is nothing. You should see what I have at home. My boyfriend thinks my studio looks like some kind of twisted morgue or the den of a serial killer. There are fake body parts and life casts everywhere," she said, grinning as she fastened a black barber cape around Xander's neck to keep his clothes clean. "Anyway, let's get started. Can you grab a bald cap? They should be in the bottom drawer."

Xander shifted nervously in his seat. "A *what* cap?"

Melody laughed at his horrified expression. "Don't worry. It won't hurt."

This didn't seem to convince him. "You've done this before, right?" he asked, turning to me with wide eyes.

I offered him a reassuring smile. "Plenty of times." Bald caps were common appliances in SFX. The process was a bit tedious but not painful. I'd learned to put them on by practicing on myself, which was much harder than applying one to a model. The first time I tried, I wasted three caps before I was able to get one on without ripping the thin material.

"His hair is going to be a nuisance," Melody said, tapping her chin as she surveyed Xander. "We'll have to put it back."

Leaning forward, Xander shook out his bangs and combed a hand through the golden-red locks. "Are you saying I need a haircut?"

"That depends. Are you going for a shaggy dog look?"

He shrugged. "What if I am?"

"Then keep doing you, buddy." She passed me a handful of ponytail holders and said, "Can you wrangle the mop?"

Her question made me pause. Melody wanted me to *touch* Xander's hair? That felt intimate somehow, like something only a girlfriend or hairdresser should do. I knew it was stupid, but I suddenly felt awkward. "Can you put your hair back for me?" I asked, pressing the elastic ties into Xander's hand. "It will be easier if you do it."

"Sure thing." Completely oblivious to my discomfort, he separated and tied off his waves into two sections, one at the top of his head that reminded me of Pebbles Flintstone and the second at the nape of his neck.

"That won't work," Melody said, pointing out the top ponytail. And she was right. There would be a huge bump under the cap if his hair wasn't put back properly. She dug around in her case until she located some styling gel and tossed it to me. "Use this instead."

"I guess you have to take that out," I told Xander as I

popped the cap off the bottle. Once he removed the elastic tie, I squeezed a glob of gel onto my palm, sucked in a quick breath, and began working the product into his bangs.

Of course he has great hair, I thought as I smoothed everything into place. It was soft but thick, the kind of hair that was perfect for running your fingers through.

When I finished, I went to wash my hands. Melody had already set the gel with a hairdryer by the time I returned and was cleaning the skin around Xander's hairline with an alcohol wipe. I tore open the package of bald caps, and as soon as she was done, I carefully eased one on. It was too big, and I had to trim the edges so the latex wouldn't cover his eyebrows.

"Do you want to glue or dry?" Melody asked, gesturing between the hairdryer and a bottle of Pros-Aide. I selected the adhesive and a few Q-tips for application, and for the next ten minutes, we worked in silent tandem.

"I feel ridiculous," Xander grumbled once the cap was secured.

"That's because you look ridiculous," Melody answered, offering him a compact mirror. "Hopefully balding isn't a trait that runs in your family, because this is what you'll look like in twenty or so years."

"Thankfully, no," Xander said, turning his head from side to side as he checked out his reflection. When Melody held up her phone with a smirk, he snatched it from her hands with the speed of a lightning strike. "Absolutely no pictures. If JJ saw me, I'd never hear the end of it."

"Fine. Can I have my phone back?"

"Nope. I'm keeping it as a precaution. Indie, I'll need yours too." Turning to me, he held out his hand. "You'll get them back when I'm done being your guinea pig," he added.

The only person who might need to reach me was Violet, so I handed over my cell without a second thought.

Xander nodded in thanks and tucked both devices into his pocket. "Okay. Now that that's sorted, carry on."

Melody rolled her eyes but turned her attention back to our lesson. She picked up a wicked-looking horn that was four inches long and grinned. "Okay, time for step two."

☆♭♪

An hour later, Xander was unrecognizable.

We'd transformed him from heartthrob to alien monster worthy of haunting nightmares. He had scaly skin that faded from purple to black, a Mohawk of deadly spikes, and cheekbones as sharp as razor blades. Melody taught me two different techniques for blending the edges of prosthetics, and it was the most fun I'd had in ages.

"Guys, this is wicked," Xander said as he inspected his reflection. "I could be a character in a sci-fi movie. This looks so real, I'm actually scared of myself."

"This is all Indie's handiwork," Melody replied. "Not mine."

What a truckload of bullshit.

I shot her a pointed look. "You're the one who came up with the alien concept. I just helped you execute it."

She crossed her arms. "Sure, but you did the application."

"And you're the one who made all the prosthetics," I pointed out.

"They're just horns. You could make these in your sleep. Besides, it was your idea to create a Mohawk out of them, and that's what makes this particular look so sick."

When I opened my mouth to disagree, Xander cut me off. "Take the compliment, Indie. She's totally right. This is badass."

I cleared my throat. "Well, thanks."

"You sure you don't want a career in prosthetic makeup?" Melody asked. "I could use some competition."

A blush swept over me from head to toe. "To be honest, I never really considered it as an option."

She shook her head in disappointment. "Well, you should. There's a new school called the Academy of Cinema Makeup opening in LA next year. I'm one of the instructors. We'll be teaching all kinds of things from beauty and editorial makeup to prosthetics. You'd be a perfect candidate, and I'd be more than happy to write you a letter of recommendation."

"Wow, that's incredibly kind of you," I said. "I'll keep that in mind."

Melody held out her hand to Xander. "Give me Indie's phone."

"Why?" he responded.

"Did I ask for lip, E.T.?"

"No, but a please would be nice," he muttered as he grudgingly dug out my cell.

Ignoring him, Melody typed something into my phone before tossing it back to me. "I've added my contact info. Once you realize how much potential you're wasting, give me a call."

I beamed. "Will do."

Xander relinquished Melody's phone. "Now that I look like a badass instead of a balding eighteen-year-old, can you take some pictures for me?"

As Melody took a few close-ups of our creation, I stood off to the side and reflected on today's events. What started off as the world's worst day had turned into a dream come true. Not only had I caught a glimpse of Chelsea Hirano, but I'd met and worked with my makeup hero.

"Indie, come here," Xander said, waving me over. "You should be in this."

"Yeah, okay." I shook out my hair to make sure my waves were in order before stepping into the shot. Xander caught me off guard when he wrapped an arm around my shoulders. When I glanced at him, I actually had to tilt my head back to see his face. It was a pleasant surprise. Most guys were either the same height as me or shorter.

"What?" Xander asked when he noticed me staring at him.

"What, what?"

"You're looking at me funny. Do I have something on my face?" he asked.

I rolled my eyes but couldn't hide my smile.

"Seriously, my forehead is super itchy. Feels like there's something growing out of it." He gestured at one of the spikes. "You sure there's nothing in the general vicinity?"

"Hey, guys, I'm trying to take a picture over here," Melody said. "These candid shots are cute and all, but are you two going to look at the camera or what?"

Snapping my head in Melody's direction, I forced myself to ignore the warmth blooming on my cheeks. Xander's gaze lingered on me for a second longer before he too focused his attention on her. A few pictures later, our photo shoot was finished, and I pulled away from Xander as if my side was on fire.

"So, Melody," Xander said, sinking back onto his chair. He stretched out, draping his long legs over an armrest as he lounged against the opposite. "How does the rest of your day look?"

"I'm meeting up with another YouTuber in thirty minutes. We're doing a collab video. You?"

"I was supposed to do a signing with the *Immortal Nights* cast after their panel, but they didn't need me anymore," he said. "Other than that, there are a few industry parties I was invited to, but I'm not in the mood."

"What happened with your panel by the way?" Melody asked as she started cleaning up her equipment. "You never said."

Because of the makeup, it was impossible to read Xander's expression, but I noticed his hand clench before he tucked it out of view. "Nothing I'm not used to. It's not a big deal."

"You sure?"

His responding smile was small but sunny. "Yup, I'll be fine."

Melody let the subject drop. "Well, what's the plan?" She grabbed a package of alcohol wipes from her makeup case and turned to me. "Should we help him get cleaned up?"

"Actually," I said, "I have a better idea."

CHAPTER 4

"This is crazy. *You're* crazy."

Xander and I were camped outside the exhibit hall next to a food cart. I'd convinced him to walk the convention floor with me since his makeup job was comparable to wearing a mask, but he was still nervous about being recognized.

"That's a bit of an exaggeration, don't you think?" I said, inching away from the food. The freshly baked soft pretzels were making my stomach growl, a reminder that I hadn't eaten since breakfast.

"Indie, you don't understand. If somebody realizes—"

"Nobody will know it's you, I promise." Xander's own mother wouldn't recognize him if she were standing directly in front of us.

"You can't guarantee that."

"Okay, you're right, but when's the next time you'll get an opportunity like this? How often do you get to be just another alien in the crowd?"

Xander hesitated, his eyes cutting toward the doors of the exhibit floor. He considered my question for so long that my smile slipped. Any second now, he'd insist we head back upstairs to the green room. Worst case scenario, I could go without him. I didn't want to, but Violet's career quickly taught me to be okay with doing things on my own.

Luckily for me, Xander caved. His eyes fluttered shut for a brief moment as he released a long sigh. "Oh, what the hell. Let's do this."

"Yes!" Bouncing forward, I clamped my fingers around Xander's wrist in case he had any lingering thoughts of backing out and dragged him across the lobby. Whether he liked it or not, the two of us were going to have a full Comic Con experience.

"I still think this is a bad idea," he said as we wove our way through the crowd.

"I'll take those chances," I replied, casting a smile over my shoulder.

"Easy for you to say," he muttered but let the subject drop.

When we reached the entryway, I freed Xander's wrist and stepped inside. I was immediately barraged with an array of senses. An explosion of color hit me first—rows upon rows of booths that sold all sorts of paraphernalia and stretched in every direction. The one closest to us displayed tubs of plushies ranging from Hello Kitty to No-Face from *Spirited*

Away. Next to it, there was a booth that only carried superhero bathrobes.

People all around us were talking and laughing, but I couldn't hear anything specific. The sounds slipped over my ears, unfiltered and blaring. Overhead, the fluorescent lights seemed to glare directly into my eyes. I froze in the middle of traffic. People streamed past us on either side, like river water rerouted by a boulder.

Xander's fingers flittered against the small of my back, guiding me out of the way. "Hey, you okay?"

His touch jolted me out of the moment. "Yeah, fine," I said, blinking and pushing my bangs from my face. "Just a bit of sensory overload. This…this is *nuts.*"

"Overwhelming, isn't it?"

"Understatement of the year." I scanned our surroundings. We'd entered near the Lucasfilm booth, and directly in front of us were display cases filled with costumes from the *Star Wars* movies. A group of kids had their hands pressed against the glass of the nearest case, gawking over Boba Fett's helmet. "So…what do you want to see first?"

He shoved his hands in his pockets. "This is all you, remember?"

"All right, I have an idea. Follow me." Turning left, I headed to the far end of the hall. With the Saturday crowds, it took a few minutes to actually cross the entirety of the room. Halfway there, a man with a microphone and camera crew cut us off.

"Awesome cosplay," he said, thrusting the microphone in Xander's face. "I'm Gary with Everything Geek, and I was wondering if you can tell our viewers who you're supposed to be?"

I felt Xander go rigid, so I stepped in front of him and shot Gary a look. "He's an Oken warrior from planet Urc Qlevaz, *obviously*. Haven't you seen the *Galaxy Rider* films? How can you work for Everything Geek and not know that?"

Gary snapped his fingers and pointed at me as if I'd reminded him of a long forgotten movie he'd seen as a kid. "Of course! I knew I recognized the look. Okens are so distinct. Anyway, Everything Geek is hosting a cosplay contest later tonight." He shoved an orange flyer into my hands. "You guys should check it out."

A grin slowly stretched across Xander's face as he realized Gary had zero clue who he was. "Yeah, we'll think about it. I'm sure all the G-riders will be impressed," he said, playing along.

"You bet," Gary replied with an enthusiastic nod. A woman dressed as Daenerys Targaryen strolled by us, and when his eyes locked onto her, we were quickly forgotten.

"*All the G-riders will be impressed?*" I mimicked once Gary was out of earshot. "G-riders, seriously?"

Xander shrugged. "What? You try making up a fandom name on the spot."

I crossed my arms. "I created a franchise complete with its own alien race and planet."

"Good point," he said, nodding in agreement. "I wish I could see his face when he realizes *Galaxy Rider* isn't real. I bet they'll cut me from the final edit so they don't look like morons."

"Oh, darn. There goes your five minutes of fame."

We exchanged looks, and a single second of silence passed before we dissolved into a fit of laughter. It took a solid minute, but once our breathing was back under control, we finished our trek across the massive hall, and Artist Alley came into view.

"Good place to start?" I asked when Xander realized where I was taking him.

He nodded. "The perfect place. Let's go find a commission."

"A what?"

"I want an artist to do a commissioned sketch of me. Nothing fancy. Just something to remember all this by," he said, pointing at his face.

We spent the next thirty minutes roaming through the aisles of artists, trying to find someone with a style Xander liked. We'd seen nearly everyone's work when I noticed a girl at an empty table. Her chin was propped in her hands, and she had a long look on her face. The artist at the table next to her had a line of customers snaking around the corner to the next aisle.

"Do you know who that is?" I nodded to the man whose table was getting all the traffic. The banner stand behind him read BLUE HOOD GRAPHICS.

Xander shook his head. "Must be a big deal comic book artist. Most of them rent booths, but sometimes they opt for a table in Artist Alley because there's fewer regulations on what they can sell."

"Whoever he is, his line is blocking the poor girl next to him," I said, pointing her out. "I don't think she's getting any business."

As if he knew what I was thinking, Xander asked, "Should we go change that?"

I smiled. "My thoughts exactly."

The girl, who was probably in her early twenties, held still expectantly when she noticed us approaching. She had black hair that was pulled into a ballerina bun, round glasses, and lips painted bright red. The sign hanging off the front of her table read ASHLEY RIDDLE.

"Hey," Ashley said, sitting up straight when we stopped in front of her. "How's your con going?"

"Pretty good," Xander answered, already paging through her portfolio. "Yours?"

"As good as can be expected. This is my first time." It was impossible to miss the longing in Ashley's eyes when her gaze momentarily flicked over to Blue Hood Graphics. "Cool mask, by the way."

"It's actually prosthetic makeup." Xander jerked his thumb at me. "This one here did it. She's pretty talented."

Her attention shifted to me. "Wow, that's incredible!"

Heat pooled in my cheeks. "I had a lot of help, but thanks. These are fire too," I said, nodding at the prints displayed behind her.

"Thank you!"

"Do you have time for a commission?" Xander asked, even though the sign-up sheet in front of her was empty. "I don't need anything elaborate. Just a quick sketch."

She beamed. "Yes, of course! My prices are listed here."

We both glanced down at the sign she pointed to.

```
Headshot, pencil, 7" x 10":............ $30
Headshot, inked, 7" x 10":............. $50
Headshot, color, 7" x 10":...............$70
Half figure, inked, 9" x 12":.......... $100
Half figure, color, 9" x 12":............$130
```

"How about a half figure, inked?" Xander said after considering the list.

"Awesome choice." Ashley pulled out a drawing board. "Do you have a specific character in mind?"

"He wants a mashup of an Oken warrior from *Galaxy Rider* and the lead guitarist from the Heartbreakers. What's his name again? Xavier something?" I rubbed my chin, pretending to rack my brain. "He's the one with the glasses."

"You mean Xander Jones?" Ashley supplied.

I snapped my fingers and pointed at her. "Yeah, him!"

Her eyebrows squished together. "Um, okay, but I'm not sure what an Oken warrior is. Do you have a reference picture?"

Xander glared at me before turning back to Ashley. "Just ignore her. She's being a smart-ass. I want a sketch of myself."

"Because he's conceited like that," I added.

This time, Xander jabbed an elbow into my ribs to shut me up, and I stifled a giggle.

"Don't worry. Lots of people request sketches of themselves," she said, waving a hand to dismiss my comment. "Will you be paying cash or credit?"

"Cash," Xander replied, presumably because he didn't want her to see the name on his credit card. He extracted a wallet from his jeans and pulled out two crisp fifties.

Once she received the payment, Ashley took a picture of Xander to work from and told us the commission would be done by the end of the day, so we wandered out of Artist Alley and into the Funko toy section. I bought a Jack Skellington key chain, which I promptly attached to my bag, and a Pop! Vinyl Thor for Sofia, since she was obsessed with all things Chris Hemsworth.

Then we worked our way across the exhibit hall. At the LEGO booth, we built a spaceship for the imaginary hero of *Galaxy Rider* to travel the universe in. Xander paid for a picture in a *Star Trek: The Original Series* chair, claiming his parents would disown him if he passed up such a rare opportunity. My mom's favorite author, R. A. Loone, was signing copies of her newest release—the first in a paranormal romance series about a crimefighting succubus—so I tracked down the Acker Publishing booth and picked up a paperback. Finally, we ended at the Xbox station where we played a new first-person shooter game called *The Dread Hunt*.

After I won twice in a row, Xander pulled off the provided headphones and set down his controller. "I yield."

"Aw, come on," I complained, peeling back my own headphones. "Best three out of five?" I puckered my bottom lip in a pout, not ready to give up our spot at the console. We'd waited in line for a solid thirty minutes to play.

"How about some fresh air instead?" he suggested.

"Fresh air?" I scoffed and crossed my arms. "Sounds like an excuse to me. Is someone afraid of getting his ass handed to him?"

A microscopic smirk appeared on Xander's face. "On the contrary, I'm not afraid to admit I'm terrible at video games. Doesn't matter how many times we play—you'll beat me every time."

I glanced over my shoulder, toward the line of con goers eager for a chance to experience the bloodthirsty world of *The Dread Hunt*. "Fine, fine," I said, relinquishing my controller. "I suppose some fresh air would be nice."

☆ ♭ ♪

Fifteen minutes and a taxi ride later, we strolled through the entrance to Central Park off Columbus Circle. Two main footpaths veered in opposite directions, and Xander made an executive decision, pointing toward the path with a better canopy. It was too early in October to witness a full autumn foliage, but some of the trees' leaves were breaking rank with summer and transitioning into a crisp fall yellow.

"So was Comic Con exactly how you remembered?" I asked as we pushed past a blockade of men soliciting tourists for cycle rickshaw rides. A few people—tourists judging by the camera clutched in one woman's hands and the fanny pack clipped around her husband's waist—glanced in our direction when they noticed Xander's makeup, but we ignored them.

He tilted his head, considering. "Yes and no. It's bigger now, more mainstream, but at the same time, I feel like I stepped straight into my childhood. It's amazing how certain details can take you back."

"Like what?"

"Artist Alley for one, and all the badges and lanyards," he replied as we fell into step behind a man walking his golden retriever. "But what really got me was the cosplay. I still remember the first time I saw someone dressed up as Princess Zelda. She was my first crush. My dad had an old Nintendo I played all the time as a kid. There were a bunch of games, but my favorite was *The Adventure of Link*. When I was ten, we went to Emerald City Comic Con in Seattle for my mom's birthday, and there was a girl in a Zelda costume. As soon as I saw her, I told my parents I was going to marry her."

"Any marriageable princesses in the crowd today?" I asked, nudging him in the side.

Xander coughed and cleared his throat. "Might have seen a few," he mumbled.

I threw back my head and laughed. "Well, I'm glad you enjoyed yourself."

"I had a killer time. Although this wasn't exactly how I expected my day to go."

"Is that a good thing or bad?"

"Good, definitely good." He glanced over his shoulder as a woman holding a bunch of balloons jostled by him, two kids in tow. "Don't get me wrong, I was super bummed about the panel, but exploring the exhibit hall more than made up for it. Never would have done that if you didn't push me, so thanks."

The joy in his voice made my chest feel light. "Don't mention it," I told him. "Besides, if you think about it, this was all your doing."

"How do you figure?"

"Well, you introduced me to Melody, who gave me a prosthetics lesson, which resulted in your current disguise," I explained. "And without that, there's no way you could have walked the convention floor."

"So I should be thanking myself?"

"Yup. I suggest sending a thank-you card. It's the polite thing to do."

Xander grinned. "Yeah, okay. I'll get right on that."

As we ambled deeper into the park, continuing our conversation about the convention, the soundtrack of our surroundings played in the background: chatter and laughter from passersby, birds chirping in the trees, the hum of traffic in the distance. Eventually, we reached a large stretch of exposed bedrock overlooking a playground. There were people everywhere: children swarming the swings and slides, parents watching from wooden benches, and groups of friends lounging in the afternoon sun. On the nearest patch of grass, a superhero-themed birthday party was in full swing, and I spotted the woman who'd bumped into Xander collecting presents from a mini Superman, Captain America, and Black Panther.

"Not sure why, but I'm pretty sure this is called Umpire Rock," Xander announced, studying a map he'd pulled up on his phone. "Looks like a cool place to people-watch. Wanna sit down?"

I nodded, and we carefully picked our way across the rock, maneuvering around the other patrons until we found an empty spot. Only then did the name of the outcropping become clear. Through the trees was a scattering of baseball fields, some empty, others in use.

"So," Xander said as I settled onto the smooth, mica-flecked stone. He plopped down beside me, his shoulder accidentally bumping mine as he sprawled out. "Mind if I ask you a personal question?"

"Not at all."

"What's the deal with you and your sister?"

"What do you mean?" I asked as I traced a striation in the rock, my finger fitting perfectly into the groove.

"You and Violet don't get along," he said, but I understood the query behind the statement.

At first, I wasn't sure how to answer. Violet and I rarely fought, but that was because I never saw her. "I think a better way to describe our relationship is lack thereof," I replied. "We were super close as kids, but we don't really know who each other is anymore."

He scratched at one of the horns attached to his temple, his fingernails coming away with a crust of purple paint. "Because she's so busy all the time?"

"That's part of the reason."

"And the other?"

Sighing, I picked at a hole in my jeans. "When Violet was offered the role of Lilliana, she accepted in a heartbeat, and I can't blame her for that. Becoming an actress was her dream. Problem is that decision affected our entire family. It's the reason my parents got divorced, why, even though we live in the same house, I rarely see my dad. Her choice turned my life upside down." I stopped and took a deep breath. Could I really say the next part aloud?

But I didn't have to. Xander said it for me. "Do you resent her for it?"

Absolutely. The response came to me without hesitation, but I knew it was a question better left unanswered. Bitter indignation looked good on no one. Putting on a smile, I gently elbowed Xander. "What is this, an interrogation?"

"Possibly," he said, and there was that sheepish grin of his again, "but you're more than welcome to flip the script. I like to consider myself an open book."

"Okay." If he thought he was so candid, I wanted to hit him with something too embarrassing to answer. "If I looked through your browser history right now, what's the most compromising thing I'd find?"

"Whoa, hold on. Maybe not *that* open," he protested, but a hint of his smile still lingered. "I was thinking more along the lines of what's your favorite color, how many siblings do you have, if you were a pro wrestler, what would your entrance music be?"

"Entrance music?"

"Yeah, the song that plays when an athlete enters the ring or walks onto the playing field? Mine would be 'Save a Horse (Ride a Cowboy)' by Big & Rich, because it's hokey and badass at the same time. What most people don't know about me is that I'm a closet country music fan. Also, who *wouldn't* want to save a horse?"

"I don't know, maybe a glue factory? And I'm pretty sure one of the characters in *Magic Mike* strips to that song."

Xander wiggled his eyebrows at me. "That a favorite movie of yours?"

"No," I retorted. "It's my turn to ask the questions, remember?"

"I'm all yours," he said, waving his hand at me in a take-it-away gesture. "Have at it."

This time, I decided to start with something easy. "Country

music, huh?" I had to admit, his confession caught me off guard. The Heartbreakers were a pop rock band that bordered on punk, and the knowledge that one of its members secretly enjoyed songs about pickup trucks, booze, and achy breaky hearts was more than hard to believe.

He nodded. "I was indoctrinated at an early age. My grandpa was a roadie for Randall Russet, the famous bluegrass star, but he loved all types of country—folk, rockabilly, western swing, honky-tonk, you name it. He had this antique Victrola turntable, and whenever we went over to his house, he let me pick a record to put on. I'd sit on the living room floor for hours playing LEGOs and listening to Jimmie Rodgers, Hank Williams, or Patsy Cline. When he died, he left me all his records."

"That's an amazing memory to have of him," I said, feeling a tinge of jealousy. Both my grandfathers died before I was born.

"It's why I love country music so much. Whenever I hear it, even if it's the cliché, manufactured kind, I feel connected to him, you know? He gave me a piece of himself that's become a part of me. All I have to do is turn on the radio and he's there."

"That's how I feel about classical music. It's all my mom listens to, so I was raised on Bach and Mozart." I paused and then added, "My mom moved out of the house last year. At first, I missed her so much that I curled up in bed and cried to the *Moonlight* Sonata for a solid month."

"That sucks. I'm sorry about your parents."

"Yeah, me too." Feeling the need to take charge of the conversation before Xander bombarded me with another endless string of how comes and whys, I asked, "Are you guys working on any new music?"

The sudden topic change didn't faze him. "Not yet. Our next tour starts in a month. We'll probably write some new tracks while we're on the road, but until then, I intend to revel in all thirty days of my dwindling freedom."

"Oh yeah? What do you have planned?"

"Nothing major. I'll probably go back to Portland for a week or two and spend time with my family," he said. "I also want to swing by the shooting range for some target practice. Who knows? Maybe I'll binge read *Lady Phoenix*."

"Shooting range? Like…with a gun?"

In an attempt to mask a snicker, Xander coughed. "No, like with a bow and arrow."

"*Archery?*" I didn't mean to sound so surprised, but it wasn't the most common of pastimes. The only people I knew who could use a bow were fictional characters like Katniss Everdeen, and I had a feeling that didn't count. "How does one get involved in such an obscure sport?" I paused, then added, "It is a sport, right?"

"Considering it's an event at the Olympics? Yes, definitely," he said, his voice filled with amusement. "I have pretty bad asthma, so I struggled with athletics as a kid. I tried all the asthma-friendly activities like baseball, golf, et cetera, but the truth is I was terrible at everything. Then my doctor recommended archery, which I thought sounded badass, so I gave it a try. Surprisingly enough, I'm a decent shot."

"Do you hunt animals?" I asked. I couldn't help but think about Marshmallow, the French lop rabbit I had growing up.

"No, I only do competitive archery. Basically, you shoot arrows at a target from a set distance. You're judged on accuracy. No killing involved."

As he said this, a new image popped into my head, and I pressed a hand against my mouth to smoother the sound of my laughter.

"What?"

"I may or may not be picturing you as Legolas right now," I admitted.

"Not sure I could pull off the whole flowing blond locks thing he's got going on," Xander said. "Besides, Legolas killed plenty of people."

"Yeah, but only the bad guys. Not adorable, fluffy bunnies."

"Fair enough, but—"

Xander was cut off by a sudden swell of "Happy Birthday

to You," the voices of twenty or so ten-year-olds muffling the background noise of the playground. We both turned toward the party. A picnic blanket had been spread out on the grass, and at its center sat Spider-Man with a large pile of gifts.

As the song came to an end, something—a realization or maybe an idea—lit up in Xander's eyes. He jerked his head in my direction. "Hey, are you free next Saturday?"

His question was simple, but it made me pause. "Um," I said, wetting my lips. "My best friend and I are going thrift shopping for our Halloween costumes." Which was sort of true. Sofia and I had discussed swinging by Deals 'N' Steals, the local resale store, but we never made concrete plans. "Why, what's up?"

"I'm throwing a surprise party for Alec."

"What for? His birthday was in May."

"Yeah, I know. This is to celebrate his new record label. Thought you might be interested."

Letting out a huge breath, I silently laughed at myself. *Jeez, Indie. Assumption, much?* At first, when Xander asked about Saturday, my brain jumped to the ridiculous image of us on a date. But this explanation, an invitation to a party because of my friendship with Alec, made so much more sense.

Xander cleared his throat. "I know this is a bit last minute, but I'd love to hang out with you again."

My entire body stiffened.

It wasn't that I was opposed to spending more time with Xander. He was easy to talk to. Even better, he didn't care that I was related to Violet, whereas most people I met were more interested in talking about her than getting to know me.

But those words—*I'd love to hang out with you again.*

Why did he have to say something like that? One simple statement, and I was analyzing an afternoon's worth of interactions. Was this a you're-cool-but-we're-just-friends hangout or an I-like-you-let's-see-where-this-goes kind of thing? Because here was the fact of the matter: guys like Xander Jones dated supermodels and movie stars. They weren't interested in chubby nobodies like me, so the possibility of something happening between us never crossed my mind.

"I'd like that too, but I shouldn't cancel," I replied, avoiding his gaze. "Sofia's life is pretty much consumed by babysitting her siblings, so she doesn't often get Saturdays off. Thanks for the invite though."

"Yeah, of course," he said, and the kindness in his voice made my chest prickle with shame. Lying to Xander felt awful, but better I feel guilty now than end up with a broken heart down the road. "I totally understand."

To this, I said nothing. Silence settled between us, so I fished my phone out of my backpack and checked my messages to avoid any awkwardness. When I noticed how many notifications I'd racked up—twelve texts, three missed calls, and a voicemail—I groaned.

"What's wrong?"

"It's Violet. She's pissed I bailed," I said, showing him a small portion of her messages. Pissed was the understatement of the year.

Xander flinched as his gaze slid over the texts. "Yikes. That's a lot of expletives. If you need to get back, don't let me keep you."

"You sure?" I asked, even though I had no intention of tracking down my sister. She was, however, the perfect excuse to leave. "I'd feel bad ditching you."

He waved me off. "Nah, don't worry about it. I think I'm going to enjoy the sun for a little while longer before taking one more lap around the exhibit hall. I still need to pick up my commission from Ashley."

"Oh, I forgot about that," I said, my heart sinking. "I really wanted to see how it turned out."

"How about this?" Xander replied. He plucked the cell from my hand and replaced it with his own. "Let's trade numbers. I'll text you a picture of the sketch, but you have to promise to let me know if your plans for Saturday change."

He was probably just being nice, but I allowed myself a small smile. "I think I can manage that." We both entered our information into each other's contacts and traded back phones. "Well, I should get going." I stood and brushed off the back of my jeans.

"Bye, Indie," Xander said as I slung my bag over my shoulder. "Thanks for today. I had a blast."

"Ditto," I called, already picking my way down from Umpire Rock. "See ya around, E.T."

Once I reached solid ground, I hurried past the birthday party and toward the footpath. As I made my way out of the park, I could feel Xander's gaze fixed on me, but I forced myself to keep moving and not look back.

CHAPTER 5

"Let me get this straight. You left him in the park?" Sofia asked as we walked into homeroom on Monday. "What'd you do that for?"

When I arrived at school, Sofia was lying in wait at my locker in order to maximize our conversation time before the bell rang. While I collected my books, I filled her in on my weekend—the fiasco of losing my Comic Con badge, what it was like to meet Melody, and how I'd hung out with Xander Jones.

I shrugged. "I don't know. Things got weird, and I sort of freaked out."

"Define weird," she said, shrugging off her backpack as we took our usual seats at the back of class.

"Well, we were talking and having a good time, and then out of nowhere, he asks me what I'm doing on Saturday and says he'd love to hang out again."

Sofia raised an eyebrow at me. "I don't know what alternate

reality you live in, but in the real world, when a guy says something like that, it's a *good* thing. It means he's interested in you."

"That's exactly why it's weird," I said, digging through my backpack in search of my calculus homework. When I found it, I passed it to Sofia for her to check since she was a math wizard. "Why would he be interested in me?"

"Hmm, I don't know," she replied, voice drenched in sarcasm. "Maybe because you're freaking awesome?"

Grinning, I tossed my hair over my shoulder. "Well, obviously, but I also have to be realistic."

She looked up from my assignment and gave me a hard look. "Realistic about what exactly?"

"Oh, come on," I said and gestured at myself with an eye roll. "I'm so not the type of girl he would date."

Her expression turned incredulous. "Wait a minute. Are you telling me you ditched Xander because you don't think you're skinny enough?"

"Absolutely not!" I said, bristling at her question. I didn't need to lose a single inch of my curves to be worthy of a guy. "This isn't about what I think of my body. It's about what someone like him thinks."

"Someone like him?" she repeated. "What does that even mean?"

"A celebrity," I clarified. "I've spent enough time around

Gabe Grant and Ryan Klein to know guys like them don't go for thick girls."

Instead of responding, Sofia refocused on my homework and made a small correction. Then she handed it back to me, lips pursed.

"What? Just say it."

She crossed her arms. "I think you're being awfully hypocritical."

"How so?"

"You won't give Xander a chance because you assume his fame makes him incapable of seeing through bullshit beauty standards," she said, "but you're the one being judgmental, not him."

Easy for you to say, I thought, clenching my jaw to keep from snapping. Sofia had a bone structure so delicate she looked part pixie. She never had to wonder if a boy would turn her down due to the fat roll below her bra or because her thighs were bigger than his.

"I wasn't trying to imply that Xander is a bad guy. He's the exact opposite, but this isn't something you would understand."

"And why's that?" she asked. "Because I couldn't possibly understand the fear of rejection? News flash: anyone can have their heart broken, Indie. Skinny, fat, pretty, ugly—doesn't matter. If you put yourself out there, there's always a chance those feelings won't be reciprocated. That's just life."

I opened my mouth, ready to snap back, but the PA system crackled to life, signaling the start of morning announcements. Mr. Wilkie looked up from his desk and instructed everyone to quiet down, so I focused on the chalkboard and pretended I hadn't heard a word of what Sofia said.

☆ ♭ ♪

After school, I spent my evening half-heartedly attempting to finalize an audition program, but my mind kept wandering back to my conversation with Sofia in homeroom. Maybe she was right about me being judgmental, but I needed to do what was best for myself. And that included finishing high school and getting into Juilliard, not worrying about boys. Which, apparently, was easier said than done.

I couldn't stop thinking about Xander.

I'd gone to bed hours ago, but our day at Comic Con kept replaying in my head.

With a sigh of frustration, I rolled over to check the time and found that it was nearly three o'clock in the morning. Crap, when had it gotten so late? I considered grabbing an issue of *Lady Phoenix* to read myself to sleep with, but I was too lazy to get out of bed. Maybe I could find something interesting online to read? Xander mentioned there were stories written about the Heartbreakers, so I pulled up Safari.

My finger hesitated over the search bar.

The thought of reading a fan fiction about someone I knew in real life made my cheeks flush, but maybe if I did, I could purge him from my system? Pushing my embarrassment down deep, I googled "Xander Jones fanfic." Once the results popped up, I clicked on the first website and scrolled through its offering of stories until I found one with a description that wasn't typo riddled.

HEARTSTRINGS

FANFICFILES

Discover   Fandoms   Forum   Search

Celebrities & Real People > Heartbreakers

Rhythm of Your Heart X.J. AU by JonesFervor15

Five years after World War III, the New California Federation rules what was once the West Coast of the United States with an iron fist. All forms of art, from painting and poetry to music and dance, have been banned for public safety.

Rachel Hensley knows in her heart that she was born to be a ballerina. Living in a world where she can't express herself is impossible, so she practices in secret. When a soldier catches Rachel dancing in the field behind her home, she is arrested and sentenced to death. Rachel is willing to die for what she believes in, but on the day of her execution, she's rescued by Xander Jones, the mysterious leader of the rebel group fighting to free society from the federation's steel grip. Xander gives Rachel a choice: flee the only

> home she's ever known and never return, or join the revolution and fight.
>
> Rated: Mature Language: English Parts: 84
> Hits: 156M Comments: 765K

The story sounded dystopian, which wasn't really my thing, but what the hell? Reading fan fiction was already out of my comfort zone, so I might as well jump in with both feet. After squeezing my eyes shut for the briefest of moments, I clicked the link and started to read.

☆ ♭ ♫

For the past twelve years of my life, Thursday nights had belonged to me and my mom. It was the only day of the week she didn't teach violin lessons, originally at Vintage Sound, the guitar store near our home in San Bernardino, then at New Wave Academy once we moved. Our evenings consisted of ordering a pizza—half cheese, half veggie supreme—from Pacific Crust and practicing all our favorite violin pieces together, a tradition that started when I was six.

That's how old I was when my parents realized I had a gift. They immediately hired a private instructor to hone my skills, but the hours I played alongside my mom on her night off were my favorite. After all, she was the reason I'd wanted to learn in the first place.

HEARTSTRINGS

Before she knew Dad, Josephine Mitchell was a rising star in the classical music circuit. She played with some of the top orchestras around the world, even performing as a soloist with the San Francisco Symphony. The *Los Angeles Times* wrote a piece about how she was on track to become one of the best violinists of her generation, which Mom kept a clipping of along with other mementos inside an old cigar box on her nightstand.

Things changed when Edward Jamiolkowski came along. They each had their own version of the story, but Mom and Dad met one fated night when he rear-ended her car. A year later, they were engaged with Violet on the way, so she decided to settle down and raise a family instead of chasing a career in a field where very few succeeded.

But she never stopped playing.

My childhood memories were set to the tune of her music. When I was little, she always practiced after putting me and Violet to bed. I loved hearing her play, so I would sneak out and lie in front of her bedroom door just so I could listen. There was something about the intricate melodies I found peaceful and mesmerizing, and more often than not, I drifted off to sleep right there on the floor.

After the divorce, Mom promised our training sessions wouldn't end when she moved out. And for the first few months, she kept that promise. Every Thursday night, she drove from her apartment in Anaheim to Violet's house in Laguna Beach so we could practice together. We both needed to stay sharp—me in order to get into Juilliard and Mom so she could finally chase her dreams. Now that she had a fresh start, she wanted to repursue a career as a concert violinist.

Which was easier said than done.

Mom had been out of the game for over twenty years, and finding full-time symphony work in one of the most competitive fields in the world was virtually impossible. The two of us searched up and down for a position within a day's drive, but there was nothing. Even when I convinced Mom to expand her search to the entire West Coast, we came up empty-handed.

Then, just as Mom was about to give up, an old colleague called. He'd heard she was looking for a job and knew of a second violin opening at a notable symphony. Mom would have to audition against hundreds of incredibly talented musicians for the spot, but I wasn't worried—she was the best.

However, that didn't mean there wasn't a catch.

The Baltimore Symphony Orchestra wasn't exactly within driving distance. I knew the location was a deal-breaker for Mom because of the promise she made me, and if I hadn't been present when she received the call, she probably wouldn't have told me about the offer. I urged her to audition anyway. Mom had already sacrificed her dreams once before. I wouldn't be the reason she gave them up again. Thankfully, she listened, and nobody in our family was surprised when she landed the job.

Two months had passed since Mom moved to Maryland, and although I was over the moon about her newfound happiness, things didn't feel the same without her: playing wasn't as fun, it was hard to focus during my practice sessions, and I couldn't for the life of me settle on a repertoire for my Juilliard application. Maybe I was being melodramatic, but I even felt like my skills were slipping without her guidance.

More than anything, I wanted to hear her voice.

It was already late on the East Coast, however, so I turned on my laptop knowing I'd have to find solace in written word. It didn't matter if it was a call or text, Mom was terrible at answering her phone. She blamed it on her age, saying it was a generational thing, but considering Dad was glued to his cell, her excuse wasn't very convincing. Email though—that was a different story. For whatever reason, Mom loved typing out long rambling messages, sifting through junk mail, and clearing out her inbox. Ever since she moved, it had been our primary form of communication. Once my browser loaded, I clicked on our latest thread and reread today's exchange.

THANK YOU!!
J Mitchell <hotmommamitchell@outlook.com>
Wed, Oct 14, 11:33 AM to Indie

Hello daughter of mine,

Have I told you lately that you're my favorite youngest child?

Just wanted to let you know I received your package. Thank you so much for the book, that was so thoughtful of you. And it's signed too?!?!? I started reading it last night and I'm already on chapter 14. I'll give you a full review when I'm done.

In other news, my refrigerator died this week and it's going to cost me an arm and a leg to repair. On the plus side, it was the perfect excuse to eat ice cream for dinner!

How are things on your end? Is your father making time for you or is he working twenty-four seven? Have you decided what to play for your Juilliard audition? Tell me everything.

Xoxo,
Mom

Re: THANK YOU!!
Indie <phoenixfreak20@gmail.com>
Wed, Oct 14, 4:12 PM to J Mitchell

Mama Llama,

You mean your best child, right?

Glad the book arrived and that you're enjoying it.

I'm sorry to hear about the fridge. For future reference, you don't have to wait for your appliances to break in order to eat ice cream for dinner.

Nothing too exciting on my end. Last weekend Violet bribed me to be her PA for Comic Con (where I got your book) because Lydia broke her leg. I met one of Alec's bandmates when I was there and he was pretty cool. Dad is Dad. I got an A on my Macbeth essay, so thanks for reading it over.

Any idea when you'll be able to visit next?

Love,
Indie

Re: THANK YOU!!
J Mitchell <hotmommamitchell@outlook.com>
Wed, Oct 14, 9:28 PM to Indie

You're right—best youngest child.

Oh no! I'm so sorry to hear about Lydia, but it was nice of you to fill in for her. Which bandmate did you meet? The cute one with the dimples? If your father is spending too much time at work, you need to let me know. I'll have a chat with him. Good job on your paper. Keep up the hard work.

I'll try to come home for Thanksgiving, but if I can't make it, I'll see you at Christmas.

Xoxo,
Mom

P.S. You forgot to give me an update on your repertoire. I need all the details!

Had Mom realized I purposely didn't answer her question about Juilliard? Hopefully not. I didn't know how to tell her I was struggling to pick my pieces. I knew I could always call her and ask for help. But part of me was terrified that if I did, she would decide leaving was a mistake and come home, which was the last thing I wanted. Nancy Goodman, my old private instructor, would be willing to lend a hand, but she'd retired two years ago, and I didn't want to bug her. So that meant I was on my own, and really, how was that any different from every other situation in my life? I just needed to get my shit together, stop panicking, and finalize my audition program.

Abandoning my computer, I wandered over to my violin case and pulled it out.

"You can do this," I whispered to myself as I settled the instrument into the crook of my neck. "Just take a deep breath and play."

Five minutes later, I was working my way through Caprice No. 24, the Paganini piece I was considering, when my bedroom door swung open with so much force that it rattled against the wall. Violet stormed inside.

"We need to talk."

Oh, now she wanted to talk?

Violet hadn't spoken to me since Comic Con. During our flight home on Sunday, she'd given me the silent treatment—not that I minded—and I hadn't seen her since.

"There's this thing called knocking," I said. "It's considered the polite thing to do instead of barging in on someone, especially when you can hear that they're busy." I waved my bow to make a point.

Violet ignored me and held out a piece of paper. "What the hell is this?"

"I thought it was obvious. It's an invoice for the services I provided as your assistant." Violet still hadn't given me the money I was owed, so this morning before I left for school, I'd written up the statement and slipped it under her bedroom door.

She scoffed. "Did you actually expect to get paid after ditching me? That was beyond unprofessional."

Rolling my eyes, I set my violin into the velvet cushion of its case. "And forgetting your promise to me wasn't unprofessional?" I asked. "Don't try to lie to me. I saw the look on your face when I asked to leave for Melody's panel. You completely forgot about it, and despite that, I still ran your stupid errand for you. But what did you do when I needed your help? You left me out in the cold and sent a she-devil to patronize my abilities as a PA, which, by the way, isn't my freaking job!"

"Indie, that was never my intention—"

I cut her off before she could finish whatever bullshit excuse was on the tip of her tongue. "Doesn't matter. We had an agreement, and the way I see it, I'm the only one who made an attempt to follow through. Hindsight, I'm not surprised, but I gave up my free time in order—"

"Oh, get off your high horse," she snapped. "You weren't

helping me out of the kindness of your heart."

"If you acted more like my sister and less like a selfish diva, maybe I would have."

Violet's entire body tensed. Three long seconds passed as my harsh words settled between us. "Is that really what you think of me?"

The hurt in her voice made me pause, but only for a moment. This fight wasn't merely about yesterday. It was a long time coming.

"Does that honestly surprise you?" I countered. "You've been choosing yourself over this family for the past five years."

"Oh, that's right. Sometimes I forget you cast me as the villain of our little family tragedy," she said, her tone so sharp it could have cut glass.

"What the hell is that supposed to mean?"

At first, Violet didn't respond. She surveyed me with an expression that bordered on pity, like I was a dying animal and she couldn't decide whether to put me out of my misery. "That there's always another side to the story," she said at last. "When you decide to stop playing the victim, talk to Dad. Maybe he can enlighten you."

☆ ♭ ♪

The equipment trucks crowding the driveway were my first hint that something strange was going on. The second was a man guarding our front door. As I climbed the porch steps Friday afternoon, he narrowed his eyes at me as if assessing a threat.

"Name?" he asked, looking down at his clipboard.

I glanced around. Was this some sort of joke? "Excuse me?"

"Your name," he repeated, voice flat.

"Uh, Indie Mitchell-Jamiolkowski?"

Clipboard dude clicked his tongue as he scanned a list. With his precisely combed hair and all-business attitude, he reminded me of a male version of Sadie. "Sorry, but I don't see an 'Indie' here. I'll have to ask you to leave the premises." His lips curled into a smirk, as if denying me access to my own home brought him joy.

"But I *live* here," I exclaimed. I stood on my tiptoes and peered over his shoulder, searching for someone I knew. From what I could see, the house was in a state of frenzy. There were people everywhere—grips hauling gear, two PAs arguing, a woman pushing a rack of costumes—but no one who could tell this holier-than-thou asshole to move aside.

"Hilarious," he said, looking down his nose at me, "but you need to leave before I'm forced to call security."

My fist clenched at my side. Little Eddy, Violet's head of security, was the one who let me up the driveway in the first place. I was pretty sure I could take this idiot; he was tall but wiry with no discernible muscle. Not the ideal choice for a doorman.

"Darren, stop being a prick, and let her in," someone said just as I was preparing to shoulder my way through.

We both turned. Standing at the foot of the staircase was Gabriel Grant, arms folded over his very massive, very naked chest. He was dressed in his standard *IN* attire: bare feet, ragged jeans that looked like they'd been worn through an apocalypse, and nothing else. I blinked. What the hell was he doing here?

The smug expression dropped off Darren's face. "Of course," he replied, scrambling to step aside. "Right away, Mr. Grant."

Rolling my eyes, I shoved passed Darren and crossed the foyer. "Saved by a werewolf," I said, taking on the haughty voice Violet used when playing Lilliana. "How very peculiar."

Gabe's eyes sparkled in recognition, and he played along, placing a hand on his heart. "Not peculiar at all, my lady. Since the moment our eyes first met, my heart and soul have been shackled to you. I could not bear to see your light leave this world, even if it meant a most egregious betrayal of my pack," he said, reciting the cheesiest yet most quoted line from book one of *These Immortal Nights*. The scene it came from was iconic, as it spurred the torrid love affair between the series' main characters.

I grinned. Under normal circumstances, I couldn't stand my sister's costar, but he'd helped me get past Darren the

Douche, and apparently, hidden beneath layers of ego, Gabe had a sense of humor. Who would have thought?

"In all seriousness," I said, dropping the awful Lilliana accent, "thanks for the save. I was ready to punch that guy in the face."

He lifted his shoulder in a lazy half shrug. "No big deal. If I saved anyone, it was Darren. He looks like a gust of wind could take him out."

"Gabe?" asked an unnervingly familiar voice, and my amusement quickly faded when I realized it was Sadie. "Sorry to interrupt," she said, "but they need you on set."

"Thanks, I'll be down in a minute."

Sadie nodded and backed away without so much as a glance in my direction. It was like I was invisible, which I suppose was an improvement from our last interaction.

"Okay, what the hell is going on here?" I asked, glancing around at the commotion. I didn't particularly care for the solitude of Violet's house, but this was straight up freaky.

"We're shooting an *IN* promo today."

"*Here?*"

Another shrug. "The original location fell through. There was a backup, but the venue double-booked with a wedding, so your dad suggested we do it here on the beach. Ten bucks they'll have me do a shirtless slow motion run through the surf," he explained, and I got the distinct feeling Gabe was genuinely excited about the prospect.

"Well, you're already halfway there," I said, gesturing at his lack of clothing, "but back to my dad. Have you seen him recently?"

"Last I saw, he was in the kitchen."

"Thanks, and good luck with the whole *Baywatch* thing."

As I made my way to the back of the house, I knew I was wasting my time. With the shoot taking place, Dad would be too busy for me, but I couldn't get Violet's words out of my head: *Talk to Dad. Maybe he can enlighten you.*

What the hell had she meant by that?

I had to know.

Sure enough, I found Dad right where Gabe said he'd be, parked on an island stool where craft service had set up. He was on the phone, talking animatedly in legal terms that went over my head, but when he saw me, he smiled and held up a finger.

While I waited for him to finish his conversation, I grabbed a handful of M&M's from the snack selection and wandered over to the kitchen window. On the beach below, my sister was posing in the sand. The red dress she wore billowed in the air behind her, compliments of a large wind machine positioned beyond the view of the photographer's lens.

"How was school?" Dad asked as soon as his call ended.

"Fine." Twisting my amethyst pendant around a finger, I turned away from the window. "But Violet mentioned something to me yesterday that I'd really like to talk about. I know you're probably busy, but I was hoping you could—"

His ringtone cut me off. "Hold that thought," he said, checking the screen. "I need to take this. Why don't you wait in my office, and when I'm done, we can talk. This will only take a couple of minutes."

"Yeah, sure thing."

In the small den he used as his workspace, I made myself comfortable at my dad's desk. There was no way he'd be done in a few minutes, so I decided to get a head start on my homework. As I opened my European history notebook, I noticed a manila folder haphazardly tucked under a pile of bills. What caught my attention was the white booklet sticking out of it.

My heart skipped a beat.

Glancing through the French doors to make sure my dad wasn't coming, I pushed aside the bills to get a better look. There was nothing written on the folder's tab to indicate what was inside, but somehow, I already knew.

When I flipped open the file, I was met with the crisp white title page of a TV script.

But it wasn't just any TV script.

It was the pilot for a TV adaptation of *Lady Phoenix*.

CHAPTER 6

As I pulled up in front of the familiar Mediterranean-style house, I nearly sobbed in relief. There wasn't a single thing about the Hernandezes' home I didn't adore. From the stucco walls and terra-cotta tile roof to the colorful artwork hanging on every wall in every room and the perpetually cluttered kitchen, each square inch radiated warmth and love and safety. It reminded me of what our house in San Bernardino used to feel like, back before we moved. I raced up the front walk and rang the bell.

Thirty seconds passed before the door flew open. Sofia stood on the other side, her youngest brother, David, perched on her hip and a phone pressed to her ear. Her face lit up when she saw me.

"Hey! What are you doing here?"

I opened my mouth to respond, but a shout from the kitchen cut me off.

"Is that the pizza?!"

"No, it's Indie!" she yelled back. David stretched his chubby arms in my direction, so Sofia pawned him off on me before switching the phone to her other ear and saying, "Yes, of course I'm still listening."

Another shout: "What about the Indy?" It sounded like Javier.

"Not the race, you idiot! My best friend!" Sofia hollered, her gaze flicking upward in annoyance. She must have been on the phone with her mom, because she quickly added, "Lo siento, Mami. It won't happen again." Waving me inside, Sofia continued her conversation. "I have the grocery shopping covered, but that birthday party Emma was invited to is at the same time as Javi's cross-country meet, so I asked Mrs. Holliburger to pick her up."

We headed toward the kitchen. As soon as I crossed the threshold, something barreled into me, nearly knocking David from my arms. Emma, Sofia's seven-year-old sister, wrapped her arms around my waist.

"Indie!" she exclaimed. "It's been so long. I missed you."

"Whoa. Careful, kiddo," I said, returning her hug. "I nearly dropped your little brother."

"That's okay. He's got a hard head. He fell out of his high chair yesterday when Javi was feeding him. Didn't cry at all."

"That wasn't my fault," Javier grumbled. He was perched on an island barstool, his face all but pressed against the small TV positioned alongside the wall. "You're the one who put him in, Emma. How was I supposed to know the buckle wasn't clipped?"

Emma grinned mischievously and pulled me over to the table. Colorful string sat in a pile alongside a pair of scissors and a container filled with plastic beads. "I learned how to make friendship bracelets at Girl Scouts today. Want me to make you one?"

"I'd love that," I told her. David started squirming in my arms, so I transferred him to my other hip.

"What color do you want?" she asked, pushing the selection of string toward me. "You can pick anything but blue or green."

"Why's that?"

"Blue's my favorite, so it's reserved for me." She set aside a tangle of turquoise and navy. "And Javi already claimed green."

"I didn't claim anything. If she wants green, she can have it. I don't care," Javier said, eyes still glued to the TV. Some kind of race was on, and he seemed transfixed by the blur of cars.

"Hmm. How about red?" I suggested.

She nodded in approval. "I can work with that."

By the time Sofia got off the phone, Emma was already in the process of braiding. "I'm sorry. Mom's gone on a business trip, so it's chaos around here," she explained. Mrs. Hernandez was the top management consultant at Berry

Wagner & Company, a local consulting firm. Although most of her work was based in California, she sometimes took jobs that required her to travel around the country. When she wasn't busy advising clients on how to better run their business, she taught a kickboxing class at the YMCA. Basically, she was a badass.

"Where's your dad?" I asked, glancing at the living room couch where Mr. H usually camped out with his laptop. He ran a web design business from home so someone was always around to look after David and Emma, but today he was nowhere to be seen.

"Taking care of his aunt in Phoenix. She came down with smallpox or something."

I frowned. "Pretty sure smallpox was eradicated back in the eighties."

"She has shingles, you dipshit," Javier clarified.

"Oooh! If Mom knew you used a swear word, you'd lose TV privileges for a week," Emma told her brother.

He whirled around on the barstool. "But we both know she won't find out, right, Emma? Because if she does, Abrahamster Lincoln will go poof in the dead of night, and you'll never see him again."

Eyes wide, I leaned toward Sofia and whispered, "Did he just threaten to off your sister's hamster?"

She glanced at her sibling and shrugged. "That's the least

of my problems. My parents left me in charge while they're gone, which means I have to do everything around here."

"Hey, I took care of dinner tonight."

"Congrats, Javi. You picked up the phone and placed an order. David can't speak in full sentences, and he could've done that."

"Fruloo!" David squawked in response. "Fruloo, fruloo, fruloo!"

My brain wasn't hardwired to interpret baby babble, but Sofia understood what he was asking for and pulled a box of Froot Loops from the pantry.

"So what's with the impromptu visit?" she asked, pouring the colorful cereal into a small bowl. "Not that this isn't a totally awesome surprise, but I thought we weren't hanging out until tomorrow?"

Her question slammed me back to reality. For a few precious minutes, I was so blissfully distracted I nearly forgot about my discovery at home. "We were, but...something happened, and I had to get out of the house." After finding the script, I'd packed an overnight bag and slipped out without telling anyone I was leaving. I wondered if my dad, who was still on the phone when I'd glanced into the kitchen, had even noticed I was gone.

Frowning, Sofia took David from my arms and put him in his high chair. "With Violet?"

"Kind of," I said, my gaze darting between Sofia's siblings before returning to her, "but do you mind if we talk somewhere more private?"

"Sure thing. Javi, I'm gonna catch up with Indie. You're in charge of Emma and David while I'm gone. That means you have to pull yourself away from the TV for five seconds to answer the door when the delivery guy arrives. Think you can handle that?"

"Hey!" Emma complained. "I'm almost eight. I don't need a babysitter."

"You're right. Almost eight-year-olds are practically adults. Why don't you keep an eye on Javi for me? We don't want another high chair incident."

Emma grinned and saluted her sister while Javier protested. "That wasn't my fault!"

But Sofia ignored him, grabbed my wrist, and pulled me out of the kitchen.

Upstairs, I pushed a stack of Marvel movies away from the foot of her bed and took a seat, leaning against the old wooden frame. There was nowhere else to sit. Every inch of space was utilized.

The single mattress was buried beneath a tower of tie-dyed pillows and laundry so high that I wondered where Sofia slept at night. A tiny worktable held her most prized possession, a heavy-duty Singer sewing machine, along with a collection of fashion magazines and a garden of tomato pincushions. In the corner, bolts of fabric were stockpiled against the wall next to stackable storage bins filled with lace and zippers and bows and buttons.

My favorite part of Sofia's space stood directly in the middle—a vintage wire dress form that always displayed her current design. Today, pale blue chiffon poured down over the mannequin like liquid sky while the bodice sparkled with hundreds of hand-stitched crystals. It was a modern-day ball gown fit for Cinderella.

"This is gorgeous," I said, eyeing the dress. My mind spun with inspiration, already considering different makeup concepts that would match her creation. Something ethereal and otherworldly, like an ice queen or fairy princess.

Sofia opened her closet, peered inside, and slammed it shut before an avalanche of shoes spilled out. "Thanks," she said, barely acknowledging my compliment. "It's for my cousin's quinceañera."

I cocked my head and watched as she flitted from one end of the room to the other, digging through a basket of scarves and ransacking her collection of stuffed animals on the windowsill. If I wasn't feeling so shitty, I'd have laughed at how ridiculous she looked. "What are you doing?"

"Emma hid the old nanny cam in my room last week and used it to spy on me, so I'm making sure we're totally alone."

She dropped down to her knees and searched under the bed before popping back up. "All right, I think the coast is clear. Tell me what's going on."

"I found this on my dad's desk today," I said, pulling the manila folder from my bag and thrusting it in Sofia's direction.

"Holy crap!" she gasped after scanning the page. "Didn't they just announce this at Comic Con? How'd you get your hands on an actual script?"

A single, humorless laugh escaped me. "How do you think?"

Sofia rubbed her chin as she considered my question. Finally, her eyes lit up. "Wait—is Violet *auditioning*?"

"Looks like it."

"But I thought she was taking a break from acting to focus on her music career?"

"Yeah, I thought so too," I replied, picking a pink sequin out of the carpet. "My dad swore we'd spend time together after all the promotional work for *IN* wrapped up, but I guess that was just another empty promise. If Violet takes a new role, he'll be too busy to hang out with me. My mom lives on the other side of the country, and I talk to her more often than him. It's ridiculous."

"Oh, Indie," Sofia said, her face falling as she tossed the script aside. She sat beside me and wrapped an arm around my shoulder. "I'm so sorry."

"You know what pisses me off the most?" I squished the shiny, fuchsia disk in half, flicked it away, and watched as it disappeared underneath the folds of a lacy bandeau. "That Violet would even consider auditioning when she knows how much *Lady Phoenix* means to me."

Sofia leaned back to get a better look at me, her brows pinched in confusion. "Why is that a bad thing?"

"Because if she's cast, I won't be able to watch the show."

"Sorry, but I'm still not following."

"I don't know what part she's auditioning for, but Violet isn't a good fit for any of the characters. Even if she nailed the role, it wouldn't matter. I'd still just see my sister," I explained as I clenched and unclenched my fists. "Any time she's on-screen, it'll be impossible for me to suspend my disbelief. This is my fandom, my obsession. I've been hoping for an adaptation for years, and she's going to ruin it for me."

"Oh," Sofia said as sudden understanding dawned on her face. "I never thought about it like that."

"And on top of all my family bullshit, I still can't figure out what to play for my audition." Exhaustion suddenly washed over me. I let my head fall back against the bed, and I stared up at the ceiling. At one point, a scattering of glow-in-the-dark stars had lived there. Now all that remained were yellowing dots of the putty meant to keep the plastic night sky in place.

"I take it things aren't going well?"

"Nooo," I replied with a theatrical groan. "I wanted to finalize my repertoire by the end of summer so I'd have plenty of time to practice, but it's like there's a block in my brain preventing me from making any kind of decision. This shouldn't be difficult, but I'm so stressed I'm pretty sure the pimple forming on my chin is going to be the size of Jupiter."

"Why is that surprising?" There was a note of amusement in Sofia's voice, like she thought my issue was self-explanatory. "This audition means everything to you. You're terrified of choosing wrong."

"I get that, but I'm running out of time." I dragged a hand through my hair and released a heavy sigh. "I don't know how to handle this. Normally, I do well under pressure, but the fear is paralyzing me. What if…" I trailed off, unable to say the words out loud.

"What?" she prompted.

"What if I'm not good enough to get in?" I whispered, feeling nauseous at the thought.

"Okay, I'm going to stop you right there, because you're being ridiculous. You're getting in, Indie. You were born to play violin like LeBron was born to play basketball or like—"

My snort cut her off. "First off, did you just compare me to *the* LeBron James? Because that's sacrilege. Also, I don't believe in all the fate crap."

"Fine. If you're so set on being a pessimist, what's your backup plan?"

I shrugged. "There isn't one. It's always just been Juilliard."

"Then we need to come up with one," she said, pushing up her sleeves like she was about to get down to work. "For starters, there's more than one elite conservatory you can apply to. Curtis Institute of Music is a phenomenal school, or there's always Berk—"

"If I'm not good enough for Juilliard," I interrupted, "then I won't make the cut at Curtis either."

Sofia took my hand in hers and gave it a light squeeze. "Then come to UC San Diego with me. Think of how much fun we'd have if we went to the same college."

It wasn't a terrible idea. Besides the added bonus of avoiding winter in New York, I'd get to experience what was supposed to be some of the best years of my life alongside my best friend. Still, something didn't feel right to me, but I couldn't pinpoint what. "I suppose that's an option, but what would I study?" I asked.

"They have a music program, Indie."

"Yeah… I don't know." I picked at a loose thread on the cuff of my flannel and avoided Sofia's gaze. "It wouldn't be the same."

"Okay, well, you don't have to pick your major right now. College is the definition of self-discovery. Take a bunch of different classes. Figure out what else you're interested in."

"The problem is I'm not good at anything besides binge-ing Netflix and playing the violin."

Sofia scoffed. "*So* not true. What about special effects makeup?" As she said this, she sat up straight, eyes sparkling, as if energized by a sudden idea. "Hey, didn't Melody Nguyen tell you about a school she's instructing at? Why don't you apply there?"

Without giving it a proper moment of consideration, I dismissed her suggestion with a wave. "That's just a hobby."

"But it doesn't have to be," she said. "Besides, applying to this school might help you with your audition."

"How?"

"When one of my designs isn't working, I find the best way to figure out what's wrong is to focus on something completely different. Something exciting. You have to get out of your head, find a new way to spark your creativity, and—" Sofia was cut off when, somewhere down the hall, there was a loud crash.

Two seconds of silence passed. Then, "Emma, I'm going to kill you!"

The sound of hysterical laughter quickly transformed into a shrill shriek. "Oww! Stop it, Javi! You're hurting me!"

Closing her eyes, Sofia pinched the bridge of her nose. "Hold that thought." She stormed across the room and into the hall. "What in God's name is going on out here?"

Javier snapped back in response, but I couldn't make out his exact words over Emma's screeching.

"I don't care what she did," Sofia shot back. "You're acting like a child. Let Emma go, and clean up this mess. Am I clear?" With a shake of her head, she slammed the door shut. "Sorry, my siblings are complete morons."

"I'd take them over Violet any day." Maybe Emma and Javier were obnoxious, but at least they were part of Sofia's life.

"That's because you don't know any better," she said with a snort. "Okay, where were we?"

"Vanquishing my all my doubts and fears by way of makeup."

Sofia speared me with a sharp look. "You mock, but I think focusing on something fun will really help you. I'm not saying you actually have to go to this school, but I'd bet my sewing machine there's a portfolio involved in the application process. Creating it could be the spark you need, and if worse comes to worst, it will be a good backup option for you."

I chewed on my bottom lip as I considered. Admittedly, Sofia made some decent points. I wasn't half-bad at the whole makeup thing, and just because I submitted an application to a school other than Juilliard didn't mean I was required to attend.

"Okay," I told Sofia after another minute of thought. "I'll do it. I'll apply."

She blinked, my sudden resolve catching her off guard. "Yeah?"

I shrugged. "It's not like I have a better idea, so what the hell?"

After allowing herself a brief victory smile, Sofia's expression turned serious, and she reached for a notebook. "Okay, tell me what's up with this makeup school. I want to know everything."

"There's not much to tell. I don't even remember the name. All Melody said was that if I was interested in attending, she'd write me a letter of recommendation, but I know how we can find out more." Leaning to the side, I fished my phone out of my back pocket. Once I found Melody's name in my contacts, I hit the Call button.

Five seconds passed.

"Hello?"

"Hey, Melody," I replied as a tendril of excitement rose in my chest. "This is Indie Mitchell-Jamiolkowski. We met at Comic Con? I'm calling because I'd love to hear more about that new cosmetic school you mentioned."

☆ ♭ ♪

An hour later, Melody and I exchanged goodbyes.

Sofia, who had silently listened to our conversation and

scribbled down any and all information, paged through her notes, absentmindedly chewing on the end of her pencil. "Well," she said, glancing up at me. "Thoughts?"

"I think this might actually work," I admitted.

The Academy of Cinema Makeup, ACM for short, had multiple programs I could choose from, such as beauty makeup for film and TV or high fashion and editorial makeup, but I was only interested in the SFX prosthetics route. Melody explained that the program would take a year to complete, and to be accepted, I had to submit a small portfolio demonstrating my skills. The more she spoke about ACM, the more I could picture myself attending school there. This was something shiny, fresh, and not tainted by my family drama or audition stress.

"Told you," Sofia said, a bit smugly.

"Yeah, yeah."

"Any idea what you're going to do for the portfolio?"

I shook my head. "All I know is that I want it to be cohesive. Maybe we can come up with a theme?"

"Hmm… I really loved that tree nymph you did this summer. The one where you had all those leaves sticking out of your hair? What if you create a look that represents a tree during each season of the year?" she suggested. "You could do some kind of play on blossoms for spring, maybe snow-covered branches for winter?"

"That has potential," I said, tapping a finger against my mouth. I liked the concept, but was it too cliché? Before I could fully process the idea, my phone vibrated.

GALAXY RIDER:

> My commissioned artwork as promised. We look pretty badass IMO.

What the hell did Xander mean by we?

I clicked on the picture he sent to enlarge it. Sure enough, it was the sketch he commissioned from Ashley Riddle, although there was more than one figure in the drawing. Standing next to him was a girl with an amethyst pendant and a dazzling smile.

INDIE:

> OMG! Ashley added me?

GALAXY RIDER:

> Yup. Went back after you left and asked her to.

INDIE:

> Wow. That's totally awesome!
>
> Can I ask why?

GALAXY RIDER:

> Because you're an important part of the memory!

Biting my lip, I stared down at his text for a solid minute, trying to compose a good response. I wanted to say something charming and witty, but nothing came to mind.

"Why are you so smiley?" Sofia asked, leaning over to see what I was looking at.

"No reason," I said and clutched the phone close to my chest so she couldn't read over my shoulder. She narrowed her eyes at me in suspicion, but I ignored her and continued to consider my reply. I must have taken too long, because three dots appeared on my screen.

GALAXY RIDER:

> FYI I expect you to hold up your end of the deal.

INDIE:

> What deal?

GALAXY RIDER:

> I promised to send you a picture of my commission in exchange for an update on your plans. Any chance your Saturday freed up?

"You're such a liar," Sofia said, plucking the phone from my hands. "Who are you texting?"

"Hey, give that back!" I lunged after her, but Sofia was too quick. She scrambled out of my reach, eyes already scanning the conversation.

"Galaxy Rider? Who the heck—" She cut off midquestion, and I watched as understanding dawned on her face. "You're talking to Xander!" she exclaimed, her voice full of accusation.

Great, I thought, shoulders slumping. I was never going to hear the end of this. Sofia had been itching to return to the topic of Xander all week. If she wasn't mentioning the Heartbreakers in every conversation possible, then she was playing their music on repeat. She even had the gall to slip the latest edition of *People*, which had the band on its cover, into my backpack. I managed to avoid the subject by feigning obliviousness in spite of her obvious lack of subtly, but there was no way I could ignore this.

I sucked in my cheeks before letting out a noisy breath. "So what if I am?"

"He wants to hang out with you tomorrow," she said, gaping at me.

"Your point?"

The glare she threw in my direction was razor-sharp. "You mean besides the obvious? What happened to focusing on something new and exciting?"

"I don't need to shake up my personal life right now."

"Why not?" she demanded. "I saw the way you smiled when—"

I cut her off with a look. "My life is complicated enough."

"You sure that's what this is about?"

"What are you saying?" I asked, eyes narrowing.

"As soon as Xander showed an interest in you, you ran the opposite direction." She tapped my phone screen. "Him texting you is a sign, one I can't believe you're ignoring."

"Why are you being so pushy about this?" I snapped, finally snatching my cell back from her.

"Because as your best friend, it's my job to let you know when you're being a stubborn idiot." She crossed her arms. "Also, we can't hang out tomorrow. I'm too busy with sibling duty, so you literally have no excuse not to go."

"*Really*?" I let out a sharp laugh. "You're so full of shit."

Sofia didn't reply, instead choosing to return my look of disbelief with a stern gaze. Okay, so maybe she was right about me keeping Xander at arm's length, but could she really blame me? My own family didn't want to spend time with me, so why would he?

Knowing Sofia wouldn't relent, I let out a long sigh. "If I go to the party and nothing comes of it, will you promise to let this go?"

Her lips curled into a smug smile. "Promise."

"Fine. I'll go, but I know you're free tomorrow, so you're coming with me." Not giving Sofia a chance to protest, I texted Xander back.

INDIE:

I might be able to clear my schedule. Can I bring a friend?

GALAXY RIDER:

Absolutely!!!

Party's at 53 Yellowfin Boulevard. Alec is arriving at 5:15, so be here by 5 at the latest. Make sure to park in the back lot.

INDIE:

Awesome, see you then.

GALAXY RIDER:

Can't wait!

CHAPTER 7

Sofia pulled Wanda, her silver Honda CR-V, up in front of a hulking, concrete slab of a building. Wispy palm trees dotted the poor excuse for landscaping, and a neon sign above the door read Zap Zone.

Was this a laser tag arena?

Brows scrunched in confusion, Sofia turned the radio down. "Ah...you sure we're at the right place?"

I had been. Driving from Laguna Beach into the city could take more than an hour depending on traffic, so I triple-checked the address before plugging it into Google Maps. But now I had a sinking feeling something wasn't right. This couldn't possibly be where Xander was hosting Alec's surprise party, could it? Not that I disliked laser tag. It was a blast when you had a good group of people, but this venue didn't evoke a sense of Alec's accomplishment. I'd expected a tasting menu at a trendy LA restaurant, not pizza and arcade games.

I pulled up our conversation from last night and scanned through the texts. "53 Yellowfin Boulevard," I confirmed. "We're supposed to park in the back lot."

"If you say so," Sofia replied, her voice layered with doubt. When she eased around the corner of the building, all doubt that we were in the wrong place vanished.

"Holy crap," I muttered, taking in the collection of luxury cars. My knowledge of the automotive industry was limited, but I knew enough to recognize several different vehicles—the Ferrari was most identifiable, but there was also a Porsche, Lamborghini, and Range Rover among others.

"Double holy crap," she replied, her mouth hanging open. "You know what's funny? I normally have to hit my key fob in parking lots so I don't walk up to the wrong car. Never thought I'd be in a situation where mine stuck out like a sore thumb. You sure there wasn't some weird invite rule that requires guests to arrive in cars that are at least a hundred grand?"

"Shh," I said, gently stroking the dashboard. "Don't hurt Wanda's feelings."

With a snort, Sofia pulled into an empty spot next to a vintage Aston Martin that looked like it had rolled off the set of a James Bond movie. Once we were both standing on the pavement, I hooked my arm around Sofia's and guided us toward the rear entrance of the building.

We stepped into a dimly lit back corridor. Directly in front of us was a drinking fountain flanked by men's and women's restrooms, and to our right was a metal coatrack with a handful of unused hangers. According to a sign on the wall, the lobby was to the left, but before we could find our way to the party, an angry voice cut through the air. I recognized it immediately as Xander's.

"...is a disaster!" he exclaimed.

Sofia and I both froze.

"Dude, relax," came a stranger's response. "I don't know what's been bothering you lately, but whatever it is has you on edge."

"Maybe I'm tense because we're supposed to be celebrating Alec today, not throwing a birthday party for a ten-year-old."

I wanted to peek around the corner to see who Xander was arguing with, but I didn't want to be caught eavesdropping, so I forced myself to hold as still as possible.

The stranger laughed. It was an easy, lackadaisical kind of laugh, like its owner didn't have a care in the world. "You don't have to be ten to enjoy laser tag. Everyone will have a blast. Trust me."

"Seriously, JJ?" Xander snapped. "Can you act like an adult for once in your life?"

JJ as in...the Heartbreakers' drummer? I exchanged a wide-eyed look with Sofia.

"Why don't you try pulling the stick out of your ass, and then we can talk," JJ responded, his tone switching from easygoing to icy in less than a second. "You asked for *my* help, remember?"

Xander let his breath out in a quick huff. "When you said you knew a great place to host this party, I thought you meant a club or something, not Chuck E. freaking Cheese."

"Hey, don't blame me because your venue fell through," JJ shot back.

"Am I psychic now? How was I supposed to know the restaurant would have a fire?"

"Maybe the same way I should've known you'd be a total dick to me for helping you?"

Another heavy sigh. "Okay, fine. I'm sorry. It's just…this isn't how I pictured things going."

"Alec won't care if the party is at McDonald's or some fancy rooftop bar. He'll just be grateful we did something for him, so like I said before, chill out." There was a pause, and then JJ added, "We should head back up front. He's going to be here soon."

"Yeah, you're right," Xander replied, his voice already faint as the pair moved away from where we were hiding.

I waited until their footsteps receded before peeking around the corner. The coast was clear, so we followed the hallway until it opened up into a brightly lit lobby. To our immediate left was a café with a sign advertising the world's cheesiest nachos and, across the room, an arcade filled with flashing games. The space was packed with people. It took me a moment to locate Xander, but once I spotted his lanky frame, I grabbed Sofia's hand and started weaving my way through the crowd.

"Indie!" Xander exclaimed when I reached him. The group he was standing with cast curious glances in our direction. "You made it!"

"Yeah, thanks again for the invite," I said as he pulled me into a side hug. When he released me, I gestured at Sofia. "This is my best friend, Sofia. Sofia, Xander." They exchanged a quick greeting, and then Xander turned toward his friends.

"Guys, this is Indie and Sofia. Indie grew up with Alec."

I did a quick survey of the group as everyone said hello. Standing across from me was JJ Morris. He had dark close-cropped hair, broad shoulders, and peeking out from beneath his shirt sleeve, an armband tattoo. Attractive but in a bad boy, will-break-your-heart sort of way. Next to him was a young couple I didn't recognize—a guy so tall I wondered if he was an NBA star and a girl who looked like a teenage version of Deepika Padukone. The final member of the circle was none other than Oliver Perry, the lead singer of the Heartbreakers. He'd graced the cover of numerous magazines since the band's rise to fame, so his brown waves and deep blue eyes were unmistakable.

Oliver squinted at me. "You're Violet James's sister, right?"

I clenched my jaw to keep from sighing. "The one and only."

"Holy shit." The girl who looked like Deepika waved a hand in front of her face as if she might faint. "You're *Violet's* sister? You don't understand how obsessed I am with *Immortal Nights*. Is she coming today? I'd seriously die if I got to meet her."

Violet, here?

The thought never occurred to me, and I realized how shortsighted I'd been. Why wouldn't she be invited? After all, she was Alec's first recording artist. Hopefully she was too busy to attend. Crossing my fingers behind my back, I turned to Xander for confirmation.

"I sent her an invite," he said with a shrug, "but she had a scheduling conflict."

Thank the Lord for that.

Violet's fangirl looked crushed, but she made a quick recovery. She smiled and introduced herself as Asha. The ridiculously tall guy was Boomer, her boyfriend, but I didn't catch how they knew Alec. Asha spent the next five minutes bombarding me with questions about *IN*. Under normal circumstances, I would have lost my patience, but her enthusiasm was sweet. I could tell she was a true fan, and even though I hated the show, I understood her passion. Who was I to judge when I felt the exact same way about music and makeup and *Lady Phoenix*?

"Excuse me! Can I have everyone's attention, please?" Xander called out, waving his hands over his head. "Felicity just texted me. She and Alec are pulling into the parking lot as we speak. I know this is a surprise party, so we're technically supposed to hide, but since there's so many of us and there's nowhere to do that, I think we can skip the whole jumping-out-and-yelling-surprise bit, okay?"

"Thanks for the update, Dad," JJ said, and the room broke out into a chorus of laughter. "I've been meaning to ask. Did you make an agenda for today? Maybe print out a map of the building? I'd like one of those in case I get lost trying to find the bathroom."

Xander's lips pinched together. "Remind me again why we're friends?" he muttered under his breath.

"Who's Felicity?" I asked.

Asha perked up. "My best friend."

"Alec's girlfriend," JJ said at the exact same moment.

The image of Alec dancing with a petite redhead flashed through my mind. "Was she at Vanessa's wedding?"

Xander nodded.

"Interesting. When did that happen?"

"This summer. Didn't Violet tell you?" he asked, squinting at me. "Figured she'd mention it considering the two of them look scary similar."

"Who, Violet and Felicity?"

The bell above the door chimed, interrupting our conversation, and a guy and a girl stepped inside. I smiled instantly at the sight of Alec who, as always, looked like he'd just stepped off a fashion show runway. His nearly white hair was gelled into submission, and a pair of earbuds hung around his neck. The redhead he was holding hands with had to be Felicity, and I couldn't help but stare. If not for her coloring, she could've been Violet's twin. It was freaky, like looking at an alternate reality version of my sister.

When he noticed the crowded lobby, Alec did a double take. "Whoa, what's everyone doing here?"

"It's a surprise party," Xander explained, throwing his arms up in excitement. "Are you surprised?"

Alec frowned. "Well, yeah. It's not my birthday."

"Oh shit. It's not?" Oliver mock gasped. "Guess we made a mistake. Sorry, people, but it's not Alec's birthday. Everyone can head home now."

Felicity laughed. It was one of those bright, bubbly laughs that made me feel self-conscious of my obnoxious chortle. "We're here to celebrate your record label," she told Alec.

"You worked so hard to get everything up and running. You deserve congratulations."

At first, Alec said nothing. He pressed a hand against his stomach and glanced around, a dazed expression fixed on his face. Slowly, he turned to Felicity. "Did you plan this?"

She shook her head. "It was all Xander."

"Don't forget about me," JJ added. "I came in clutch with this awesome venue."

"Wow." Alec shook his head in an I-can't-believe-this sort of way. "This is amazing. Thank you all so much for being here. I—I'm so overwhelmed, I don't know what to say."

Oliver smirked and crossed his arms. "Instead of saying anything, how about you let me kick your ass in a round of laser tag? JJ and I want payback for that water fight."

"If I remember correctly," said Alec, "you guys are the ones who ambushed me. Just because you lost doesn't mean you deserve retribution."

"Details, schmetails," JJ said, dismissing Alec with a wave. "You're going down."

Alec grinned. "We'll see about that."

☆ ♭ ♫

Everyone who wanted to play gathered around the front counter. The boys decided a schoolyard pick would be the fairest method of divvying up players, with Alec and JJ serving as captains. I ended up on JJ's team, along with

Oliver, Xander, Boomer, and a handful of other guests I didn't know. A few minutes later, we stood in an antechamber off the arena while a Zap Zone employee whose name tag read Roger handed out blasters and explained the rules.

"Okay, Blue Team. Who here has played laser tag before?" he asked. All of us had. "Good, that means I don't have to tell you the number one rule, correct?"

"Kick Alec's ass at all costs?" Oliver suggested.

"Wrong. Laser tag is a noncontact sport. We're not playing rugby, okay, folks? Any player who touches an opponent will be banned from the game." Roger said all this in a flat, my-job-sucks tone of voice.

JJ held up a hand. "But what about an accidental touch? Is that allowed? Because it's going to be dark in the arena, and adrenaline will be pumping. Hypothetically speaking, what if I round a corner and run smack into another player?"

"Also, you said we couldn't touch *opponents*," Oliver added. "Does that mean we're allowed to touch our teammates?" Grinning, he reached out and stroked JJ's arm.

In response, JJ puckered his lips and attempted to kiss Oliver.

"Gentlemen," Roger said with a practiced patience, "keep your hands to yourself, or I'll kick you out of the game, got it?"

"Roger that, Roger!" JJ replied with a mocking salute.

Boomer snorted. "You've been dying to say that, haven't you?"

"Oh, you have no idea how badly."

"Moving on to rule number two," Roger continued, unfazed by JJ's and Oliver's antics. "The sensor on your blaster must be visible at all times. Covering your sensor to prevent yourself from being tagged is poor sportsmanship and will earn your team an immediate disqualification." After going over three more Zap Zone rules, Roger explained the type of match we'd be playing. "There are a handful of different games you can play—immortal arena, civil war, zombie mode, et cetera—but your guest of honor chose capture the flag. I'm sure you're all familiar with the game, but here's a quick rundown of how it's played in our arena. Each team has a home base with an electronic flag. If you get within ten feet of your enemy's base, you can shoot the base to capture its flag. Once this happens, an alarm will go off announcing the flag has been stolen. Your blaster will light up and repeat, 'I have the flag.' To win, you must return to your home base and shoot it. Does that make sense?"

Oliver's expression hardened, like this was a life-or-death situation and not a game. "If a player has the flag, can they shoot other players?"

"No, and if a player is shot when they have the flag, it

disappears and is returned to its home base. Also, each player only gets three lives. Run out, and your weapon will deactivate."

"What's the fire rate on these things?" JJ asked, holding up his blaster.

"Good question. Our rate of fire is set at six hundred RPMs."

"Stun time?"

"Fifteen seconds."

"Match length?"

"Normally twenty-five minutes, but since you guys rented out the building, I'll let you play until someone actually captures the flag."

Putting a hand in front of my mouth, I whispered to Xander. "Are they being serious right now, or are they still messing with him?"

Xander grinned as his friends continued to barrage Roger with questions. "Deadly serious. Oliver and JJ have a habit of turning everything into a competition, and they don't like to lose."

"Any other questions?" Roger said then.

Oliver looked at JJ, who shook his head. "Nope, I think we're good."

"Awesome. I'm going to start the countdown clock. When the timer reaches zero, the door to my left will unlock, and you can enter the arena directly into your base. At that point, all blasters, sensors, and flags will be live. Have fun."

Once Roger was gone, JJ gestured for everyone to gather around. "All right, team, listen up. Oliver and I scoped out the arena yesterday, and we managed to get a good lay of the land."

"Wait a minute," Boomer said, shooting JJ an incredulous look. "The two of you checked this place out ahead of time just so you could beat Alec at a game of laser tag?"

"Damn straight we did. There's a L on my record I need to make up for, so you better get your head in the game. I'm not losing again," JJ told him. "Now, back to the matter at hand. This arena is two stories. Most people stick to the ground floor since it's larger, but they don't realize how difficult it is to capture the flag from there. Like Roger said, you have to be within ten feet of a base to shoot it, but there's no cover surrounding it, so basically you're a sitting duck. However, thanks to my and Oliver's groundwork, we know of a better option. There are balconies overlooking each base, so we can shoot the flag from above and make a clean getaway."

Oliver eyed the countdown and rolled two fingers at JJ. "Hurry up. We only have thirty seconds."

"Okay, okay. Here's the plan. My good buddy Groot"—JJ patted a scowling Boomer on the shoulder—"will guard our base. We don't want him running around since his height makes him an easy target. Oliver and I will take the second floor and attempt to capture the flag. The rest of you will patrol the first floor and keep Team Evil occupied."

Under normal circumstances, I'd be annoyed if a stranger was bossing me around, but I had to admire how dedicated JJ and Oliver were to winning this game. So insignificant in the grand scheme of things, but to them, nothing seemed more important. I could vibe with that.

"Sounds like a good plan to me," I said, shrugging.

Xander beamed at me, almost as if he'd been afraid of what I'd think of his friends. From what I'd gathered, they were weird and intense and immature, but I didn't mind. Better to keep life interesting.

"Then let's do this," JJ said, sticking his hand out. Oliver put his on top of JJ's, followed quickly by the rest of the group. "Blue Team on three. One, two—"

"Hold on," Boomer said, cutting him off. "You of all people can come up with a better team name than that."

JJ paused and then nodded thoughtfully. "You're right. How does Team Deadeye sound? Or maybe the Laser Legends? That has a nice ring to it."

Scoffing, Oliver crossed his arms. "You're joking, right?"

"Okay, not my best material. What do you think of the Power Bolts?"

HEARTSTRINGS

"I'm thinking our team name will have literally zero effect on whether we win or lose," Xander pointed out.

"Oh, I know!" JJ said, ignoring him. "We can be the Master Blasters!"

"I'm partial to Oliver's Super Awesome Sharp Shooters," Oliver said.

Boomer rolled his eyes. "That's kind of a mouthful, don't you think?"

"How about the LED-linquents?" I suggested.

Everyone went silent in consideration.

The countdown buzzer rang.

Grinning, JJ gestured at the door as it swung open to reveal the arena. "Looks like the gods have spoken. LED-linquents it is. Let's go kick some ass."

Oliver and JJ plunged inside with a battle cry. I exchanged a toothy grin with Xander before chasing after them, my blaster raised and ready to shoot. We were immediately transported into a postapocalyptic city, standing in what appeared to be a bombed-out building. Black lights illuminated an array of blue graffiti covering the walls, and an electronic song blared from the arena's sound system.

This might actually be fun, I thought as my pulse picked up.

"Which way should we go?" Xander called over the music.

"You take left," I said, pointing in the direction his friends had disappeared. "I'll go right." Without waiting for his response, I stepped out of our base and into the street.

A labyrinth of broken buildings lay spread out before me. Presumably, the red team's base was positioned on the opposite side of the room, which meant there was six thousand square feet of space for me to cover. I needed to find a hiding spot that had the widest field of view without leaving myself open to ambush. Bringing my pendant to my lips, I kissed the purple crystal for good luck and took off in what I hoped was the right direction.

After several minutes of jogging the twisting roads without encountering any foe, I nearly ran headfirst into Sofia. Before she could see me, I ducked behind a barrel of toxic waste and waited until she disappeared around the corner. When I stood up, I heard a quick burst of laser blasts. My gun vibrated and flashed in my hands before going dark.

"Dammit," I cursed when I realized I'd already lost a life.

Someone chuckled. "Hey, Indie."

I looked up and smiled. "Alec, hi!" There hadn't been an opportunity to say hello in the lobby, so I stepped forward with the intention of pulling him into a hug, but then my blaster lit back up, and I hesitated.

"Truce for two minutes?" he suggested.

With a nod, I threw my arms around him. "It's so good to see you. I feel like it's been forever."

"That's because it *has* been forever," he replied. "I'm sorry we didn't catch up at my sister's wedding."

"Don't worry about it." Vanessa's nuptials had been an extravagant, over-the-top celebration. With over five hundred guests in attendance, it was no wonder the only time I saw Alec was during the ceremony as a groomsman and the Heartbreakers' performance at the reception. "I'm just glad I ran into Xander and he invited me. I haven't had a chance to congratulate you."

"Seriously, congratulations aren't necessary. It's not a big deal."

"Not a big deal? For chrissake, Alec! How many people can say they started their own record label at the age of eighteen?"

"Well, probably not many, but—"

The familiar sound of a laser blast rang out. Alec's weapon flashed and went dark, just like mine had when he shot me.

"Hey!" came a shout from above. "What's your name! Xander's friend! Up here."

I titled my head back and found JJ leaning over the railing of the bridge above us. The scowl on his face was aimed in my direction.

Frowning, I pointed at myself as if to say, "Who, me?"

"Yeah, you," he said, gesturing at me with his blaster. "No fraternizing with the enemy!"

Alec let out a loud laugh. "Later, Indie," he said, dashing off before JJ could shoot him again.

"What's your problem?" I asked JJ. "Rule number one forbid us from touching other players. It didn't say anything about talking with them."

"Too bad. I'm making an amendment," he replied. "Besides, if you think I didn't see that little hug of yours, you're wrong. Pretty sure that constitutes as touching. Get your head in the game, James!"

"That's my sister's name, not mine!" I shouted, but he was already gone.

The next half hour passed in a wild, adrenaline-fueled blur. I exchanged fire with a guy I didn't know multiple times, both of us claiming one of each other's lives. At one point, I was pinned down by Felicity, who was sniping people from a second-story tower, but Oliver took her out before I lost my final life. Just when I was starting to get sick of playing, the alarm at the red team's base began to blare.

"Yes!" I cheered, pumping a fist into the air. It was about time JJ and Oliver's plan worked. I wanted to help protect whoever captured the flag, but I had no clue where they were, so I began making my way back toward our base. I didn't make it far before the alarm cut off.

I paused, not sure what to do. Had we won?

"Indie, there you are!" It was Xander. He doubled over,

placed his hands on his knees, and attempted to catch his breath.

"You okay?"

"Yeah, just a little winded."

"What's going on?" I asked when he finally straightened up, his breathing under control. "Is it over?"

"No," he said, shaking his head. "Asha got Oliver. He and JJ are both out of lives." Despite his bad news, he smiled at me. "Looks like it's up to you and me. I've got one life left. You're still in this, right?"

"Yeah, I have one left too. What's our plan?"

Xander carved a hand through the mess of bangs that had fallen into his eyes. Under the crimson strobe lights, his hair looked red. "To be honest, I don't really have one. I say we wing it."

"Good enough for me."

It took us a minute to cross the massive arena and find the red team's base, another bombed-out building identical to ours with the exception of its red graffiti. Nobody was in sight, but I was willing to bet my last life that a few people were concealed in the surrounding shadows.

"How do you want to do this?" I asked as we crouched behind an abandoned police cruiser. The lights on the top of the car were flashing, bathing me and Xander in a glow of red and blue.

"You go for the flag," he said decisively. "I'll cover you."

"Okay." I licked my dry lips and took a quick breath to ready myself. "On the count of three. One, two, three!"

Exploding upward, I shot out from our hiding spot and sprinted across the floor. Someone, it sounded like Sofia, yelled to her teammates in warning. I kept moving, eyes on the prize. As I neared the base, I raised my blaster and took aim, but nothing happened when I fired.

Damn, not close enough.

I forced my legs to move faster. When I was roughly five feet away from the crumbling walls of the building, I pulled the trigger once more. This time, I didn't miss.

Turning on my heels, I spun around and dashed back toward Xander. Just as I allowed myself to believe I might actually pull this off, Sofia stepped into my path, her blaster pointed straight at me. Without thinking, I dodged to the right and vaulted the cop car at full speed, landing butt first and sliding across the hood to the other side of the vehicle. As soon as my feet were firmly planted on the ground, Xander grabbed my hand, and we raced back through the maze of winding hallways.

"Faster," he urged as we flew down a ramp and into a dark alleyway, the sound of our footsteps echoing off the walls. "She's gaining on us." Two seconds later, we spilled out of the narrow passage and onto a familiar road.

HEARTSTRINGS

"There!" I jabbed a finger toward our base, where Boomer was sitting against the wall. His weapon lay discarded on the floor beside him, its lights extinguished. When he saw us coming, he scrambled to his feet.

"Watch out!" he shouted, pointing at someone behind us. I glanced over my shoulder in time to see Alec targeting me with his blaster, brows furrowed in concentration. Before I could react, Xander shoved me out of the way and took the hit himself. His gun blinked three times and went dead, but his sacrifice gave me precisely enough time to zero in on our graffitied building and let off a final round.

And just like that, the game was over. Team LED-linquents had won.

CHAPTER 8

"That's the saddest-looking dinner I've ever seen," I said, eyeing Xander's food as we claimed a spot at one of the laminated square tops in the café.

Following our win, Oliver immediately tried roping us into another game of capture the flag. Everyone agreed with the exception of me, Xander, and Alec. I wanted a break after playing for nearly an hour, so Xander suggested we grab something to eat, while Alec begged off in order to greet the rest of his guests.

"I don't disagree." He opened the single serving bag of Lay's Classic potato chips, set it on the table, and pulled what looked like a plastic soap case out of his pocket. "Be right back. I have to wash my hands. Can you make sure no one touches these?"

"Sure thing," I said as I arranged my own lunch in front of me. The world's cheesiest nachos turned out to be a bag of stale tortilla chips and fake liquid cheese, but I didn't discriminate against any form of my favorite dairy product, even the processed kind.

When Xander returned a few minutes later, I noticed how careful he was not to touch anything as he sat down. Maybe he was a germaphobe? If so, eating lunch at a laser tag arena probably wreaked havoc on his blood pressure. I wondered if he was grossed out that I'd skipped a trip to the bathroom and opted for the hand sanitizer in my purse?

"I should have packed a lunch," Xander said glumly as he stared into the bag.

"Not a fan of concession stand food?" I asked, rescuing a stray jalapeño from the nacho sauce before it sank to its cheesy depths.

He shook his head. "It's not that. I can't have anything they're serving, and unfortunately, this was the only item in the vending machine I knew would be safe to eat."

"You gluten free or something?"

"Or something." He popped a chip in his mouth as he settled back into his chair. "Remember at Comic Con when I mentioned I have allergies? Well, that was a bit of an understatement. I could write a book on all the foods that would send me into anaphylactic shock, so I have to be super careful."

"Like what?"

"Gluten, soy, shellfish. Any kind of nut. I also try to stay away from dairy and red meat, but that's more of a food intolerance than an actual allergy."

I froze, a nacho halfway to my mouth. "Jesus, what *can* you eat?"

"Salad, baked potatoes, eggs, and green smoothies are my go-to. A bit of rice and lentils. Oh, and chicken. Lots and lots of chicken."

"I wouldn't survive," I said, shaking my head. "Seriously. You'd have to pry the pizza from my cold, dead hands."

"My allergies started developing when I was a toddler, so I don't know what pizza tastes like," he admitted.

My mouth dropped open. This must have made him uncomfortable, because he ducked his head. A tangle of reddish gold bangs spilled forward, but he quickly finger combed them back into place. When he straightened up and his eyes met mine, I realized I was staring.

"That," I said, forcing my gaze back to my food, "is a catastrophic crime."

"Maybe, but it's a life-saving one."

"Death by pizza wouldn't be a terrible way to go."

This coaxed a small smile from him. "I'd rather die peacefully in my sleep at the ripe old age of ninety-five."

"Yeah, me too," I agreed as I turned over this new piece of information about Xander. It had to be scary for him, monitoring everything he ate. Going to a restaurant was probably a nightmare. What if someone messed up his order? "Do you have to carry an EpiPen around with you?"

Xander stood, propped his foot on the chair, and yanked up his pant leg. A black pouch with an EMS emblem was strapped around his calf. "I have a case that attaches to belts as well, but I don't like the way it bulges underneath my shirts, so normally I wear the leg holster. Sexy, huh?"

Hearing this, I nearly choked.

"You okay?"

"Food down the wrong pipe," I coughed out. I took a sip of soda and, once I was able to breathe again, decided to pretend the last five seconds hadn't happened. "Is that thing uncomfortable?" I asked, gesturing at the EpiPen holder. It looked like one of those armbands people used to carry their phone when exercising.

"The holster? Nah," he said, rolling his jeans back down and taking a seat. "I don't even notice it's there. I actually had more difficulty getting used to this when I was a kid because I didn't like wearing jewelry." He slid his arm across the table so I could inspect the medical alert bracelet hanging from his wrist. It was a simple stainless steel chain attached to an engraved plaque that read:

XANDER JONES
ALGY: SOY, GLUTEN,

SHELLFISH, PEANUTS, TREE-NUTS
GIVE EPIPEN CALL 911
ICE 503-555-0127

An alarmed look must have crossed my face, because Xander laughed. "Don't worry about me. I've been dealing with this my entire life, so I know how to handle it. I haven't had an attack in years."

For some annoying reason, a flush crept up my neck. I masked my embarrassment with what I hoped was an air of nonchalance. "Who said anything about being worried?"

Xander smirked. "You didn't have to. Your expression was clearly one of concern."

"Psst, yeah right," I said, dismissing him with a wave. "I don't have the energy to worry about someone who's going to live to the ripe old age of ninety-five."

"Whatever you say."

Rolling my eyes, I said, "Can I ask you one more question?"

"Sure."

"What's with the soap?"

"The soap?" he repeated, his eyes still sparkling with amusement.

"Well, when you went to wash your hands, you took out a box that looked like one of those travel soap thingies."

"Oh, right." Xander fiddled with his shirtsleeve. "I bet you thought that was super weird."

"Maybe a little."

"Well, I promise I'm not some bizarre soap savant, but I always have to bring my own with me. The kinds used in most public restrooms have dairy or nuts in them."

Damn. The poor guy couldn't catch a break. Not only did he need to monitor every morsel he ate but the entire world around him. A peanut or dairy product could be lurking around any corner.

Out of nowhere, some type of electronic buzzer went off, and we turned toward the arcade. A group of people were crowded around one of the games, which was flashing and spitting out tickets. I blinked in surprise. Somehow, over the course of our conversation, I'd managed to forget we weren't alone.

"Guess what?" I asked, making a point to switch gears once we turned back around. Xander was being perfectly polite, but I could tell he wasn't entirely comfortable with the subject. "I decided to apply to that cinema makeup school Melody told me about."

"Really? That's awesome, Indie. You'll be a shoo-in for sure," he said, and I could tell by the way his face lit up that he meant every word.

"Thanks. I'm not sold on a career as a makeup artist, but

I've been in a major funk lately. I have to submit a portfolio as part of my application, and I'm hoping the creative process will snap me out of it. First things first, I need to come up with a theme."

"Sounds fun. Can I help?"

Was he serious? I couldn't wrap my head around why Xander was so willing to lend a hand.

Someone cleared their throat before I could answer, and we both looked up to find Felicity standing in front of our table. "Hey, guys. Do you mind if I join you?"

Her voice was soft and silvery. Part of me had expected to hear Violet's low, husky tones, but everything about Alec's girlfriend was sweet down to her button nose. Which made sense since my sister was the devil incarnate. Wasn't that how doppelgängers worked? One good twin, one evil?

Offering her one of his wide, lopsided smiles, Xander kicked out an empty chair. "Of course not. Did you guys already finish the second round?"

"No, but I'm not very good. As soon as I ran out of lives, I ditched." She grinned sheepishly and sat down beside me. The similarity between her and Violet still startled me, but up close, I was able to pick out more differences between the two. Unlike Violet, Felicity didn't have a cleft chin, her face was peppered with freckles, and her outfit was too girly for my sister's taste—she wore a pink high-waisted skirt paired with a lacy top and a necklace beaded into the shape of a bird. "So what were you guys talking about before I interrupted?"

"Indie was just telling me about the makeup school she's applying to," Xander said. "We're going to brainstorm ideas for her portfolio. Wanna help?"

"Beauty makeup?" She directed the question at me, but since I'd just shoveled another nacho into my mouth, Xander answered first.

"No, prosthetic. You should see what she did at Comic Con. Turned me into this super freaky alien with purple skin." He pulled out his phone and showed her one of the pictures Melody had taken.

"Is that really you?" she asked, glancing between Xander and the photo.

He nodded. "Awesome, right? I walked around the convention floor, and nobody knew who I was."

Felicity shook her head. "Wow. I didn't realize you could do something like that with makeup. You're super talented, Indie."

"Thanks," I replied, trying not to squirm at the attention. It felt weird to be complimented on something other than a violin performance.

"I was thinking," Xander said as he continued to scroll through his camera roll. "There are some really great shots here. Why don't you do an alien theme for your portfolio? That way, you already have some of the work done."

"That would certainly make things easier," I said, "but aliens, fairies, zombies—basically any kind of mythical creature or monster? They're way overdone. Besides, I didn't make the prosthetics I used on you, and Melody helped with the application, so it's not one hundred percent my work."

"I might have something," Felicity said, leaning into the table, her eyes darting to Xander. "But it would require the assistance of a certain band."

"What kind of assistance?" he asked.

"Well, I find it really interesting how Indie used makeup to help you hide in plain sight. What if, instead of creating a portfolio based around a specific theme, she demonstrates her proficiency by transforming the four of you into someone no one will recognize?" Felicity turned her attention to me. "Then you can go somewhere public and photograph the guys interacting with other people to prove you were able to use your skills to disguise some of the most famous faces in the world."

"It's not half-bad," I said, rubbing my chin as I turned the concept over in my head. I was willing to bet that no one else applying to ACM would submit something like what Felicity was proposing.

The only problem was the actual models themselves.

HEARTSTRINGS

What if the Heartbreakers weren't interested in helping me? Xander and I hardly knew each other, and I'd only just met Oliver and JJ. On top of that, they were leaving for tour at the end of the month. Why would any of them want to spend their remaining free time helping some random girl they didn't know?

I turned to Xander hesitantly. "What do you think?" I asked, crossing my fingers underneath the table.

He offered me another one of his endearing grins. "Sounds like a blast. I'm in, and it shouldn't be hard to convince the rest of the guys to help. Only problem is we'd have to get this done before we leave for tour. Will that be enough time for you?"

My heart leapt. "I'll make it work." After all, ACM was just my backup plan. I couldn't spend all of November making prosthetics. I needed time to practice for my audition.

"What about by next weekend?" he asked as I finished off the last of my nachos. "Would that be possible?"

"Depends on how detailed my concepts are," I replied, brushing salt off my hands. "Why?"

"Soul Harvest starts next weekend," he said. "One of Stella's favorite bands is performing, so she's flying in to visit Oliver, and he's taking her to the concert. I planned on third wheeling, but what if we all tagged along?"

I perked up in my seat. "Hey, that might actually work."

Soul Harvest was an LA music festival that took place during the two weeks preceding Halloween. Most attendees dressed up to celebrate the holiday, and while not as popular as Coachella, Soul Harvest pulled in enough big-name headliners to generate crowds. Not only would it be the perfect place to stage a photo shoot—no one would bat an eye at four guys in costume—but the thought of a famous band gallivanting around a music festival unbeknownst to the other patrons made me grin.

"Wait," I said, enthusiasm fading as another thought occurred to me. "Will we even be able to get in next weekend? Tickets sell out fast."

"Normally, no, but you don't have Courtney in your back pocket," Xander said as he unlocked his phone. "That woman can make anything happen. She's a freaking genie."

"Who?"

"Our manager, remember? Trust me, she'll have no problem getting us tickets."

And he was right. Courtney responded to Xander's text in seconds, asking how many tickets he wanted. We needed four in total: two for the other half of the band, one for me, and one for Felicity. Five minutes later, Xander's phone buzzed again.

"We're in," he announced.

Well, shit. Courtney must really be a genie.

"Perfect," Felicity said, rubbing her hands together as she turned to me. "Now you just need to come up with four makeup designs, right?"

"Yeah." But that was easier said than done.

The next half hour was spent debating potential looks for each of the boys. Felicity's idea for my portfolio was brilliant, but I still wanted my work to be cohesive. We took turns throwing out different concepts until Xander suggested one that made me pause.

"What if you paid homage to Halloween by turning us into classic monsters? It wouldn't be hard. There are a ton to choose from. Vampires, werewolves, mummies, zombies, Frankenstein, the devil—"

"Actually," Felicity interrupted, "Frankenstein was the scientist who created the monster, not the monster itself."

He shot her a look. "You know what I mean. The creepy green dude with the flat head and weird bolts sticking out of his neck."

"British lit isn't my thing," she responded, brushing red curls over her shoulder, "but how have you not read *Frankenstein*?"

"How do you know I haven't?" he shot back.

"Oh, please," she said with an exaggerated eye roll. "That wasn't an accurate description of the monster at all."

"Fine, you caught me, I used SparkNotes for that one, but

the point isn't to be accurate," Xander said, which made me laugh, because I too had skimmed an online study guide instead of reading the book. "The point is for Indie to portray the monster in a way that nonliterary folk such as myself will recognize."

"Fair enough, but don't expect any surprises for your birthday," she said, peering inside the bag of Lay's Xander had given her before shaking it up, presumably in search of the best chip. "You'll be receiving a copy of Mary Shelley's classic and nothing else."

Xander opened his mouth but was cut off when the doors to the laser tag arena swung open and rattled against the wall. Oliver and JJ sauntered out preening and singing their own praises for winning a second round in a row.

"Always so extra," Xander muttered under his breath. Then, with a gentle nudge to my side, he said, "What do you think?"

Of Oliver and JJ's performance? My confusion lasted a full second before I realized he was talking about his suggestion for my portfolio, not his friends. "Halloween is my favorite holiday," I told him, "so believe me when I say I love the idea."

"But?"

"Do you know who Jack Pierce is?"

He shook his head. "Not a clue."

"He was a makeup artist who worked for Universal Studios during its classic horror period. People call him the monster maker because he designed some of the most iconic monster makeup looks in film history. Think *Dracula*, *The Mummy*, *The Wolf Man*," I explained. "There's a reason why the image of a hulking guy with a square head and electrodes on either side of his neck comes to mind when people think of Frankenstein's monster—that's how Jack Pierce reimagined him. That was his design."

"So you don't want to do classic monsters because you feel like you'd be copying this Jack Pierce guy?" Xander asked.

"Copying isn't the right word. People have been doing monster makeup for years. It's more like I don't want to tackle something that's such a quintessential part of cinema makeup history. Besides, I've done vampires and werewolves and other scary stuff before. Where's the fun in that?"

Xander nodded as if my rambling made sense, which I wasn't sure it did, but I appreciated the gesture. "All right," he said. "Guess that means we have to go back to the drawing board, huh?"

"Yeah, I'm sorry." I shifted in my seat, and the movement pitched my purse from my lap.

"Don't be," he said. "This is what brainstorming is all about."

Stretching an arm under the table, I fished around for my

bag. When I found it, I pulled it up and ran my finger over the Jack Skellington key chain clipped to the zipper. As a kid, *The Nightmare Before Christmas* was my favorite movie, but I didn't get to watch it often because it scared the living daylights out of Violet. She preferred tamer Disney classics like *Beauty and the Beast* or *The Lion King*. After a moment of reminiscing, a new idea unfolded in my mind, and I straightened in my seat.

"What is it?" Xander asked, eyes narrowed in question.

A grin stretched across my face. "I've thought of something brilliant."

"Why do I have a feeling I'm not going to like what you say next?"

Ignoring his comment, I said to Felicity, "How hilarious would it be if I turned each of the guys into a Disney character?"

"Oh my God, yes! I love it," she replied, her entire face lighting up.

We both turned to Xander with hopeful expressions.

"There's only one way I'll agree to this plan." He crossed his arms as if whatever he said next would be nonnegotiable, but it was obvious from the gleam in his eyes that he was joking. "I want to be Captain Jack Sparrow."

"Jack Sparrow?" Xander's condition was so far out of left field that it took my brain a moment to process what he said. And as I turned the concept over in my head, it occurred to me that Jack would be an easy character to recreate. I wouldn't even need to make a prosthetic. "I can do that. Shouldn't be difficult at all. Also, I was thinking Oliver would make a good Beast?" His hair was long enough that I wouldn't need to buy a wig.

Felicity nodded in agreement.

"So we have Beast from *Beauty and the Beast* and Captain Jack Sparrow from *Pirates of the Caribbean*. Any other suggestions?" I asked. Prince Phillip from *Sleeping Beauty* crossed my mind. I'd had a crush on him as a little girl, but a clean-shaven human prince didn't make for a very good disguise.

"What about Hades from *Hercules*?" Felicity suggested. "He'd be good for Alec."

I tapped my chin in consideration. "Yeah, actually, that would work well."

Figuring out the first three character looks was easy enough, but coming up with a fourth and final concept for JJ proved to be more difficult. Xander pulled out his phone and googled Disney characters, but the result didn't help.

"There's always Simba," he said, but the suggestion was half-hearted.

Finally, it hit me. "JJ can take a joke, right?"

Felicity scoffed. "He better. That boy deals out jokes like presents at Christmas."

Excitement bubbled up inside my chest. "Good, because I have the perfect idea."

CHAPTER 9

The week blinked by as I hurried to prepare everything I needed for Soul Harvest. My mom had called me on Tuesday with some bad news. She wouldn't be able to visit at Thanksgiving, but I was too busy to dwell on my disappointment. If I wasn't at school or sleeping, I spent my time hunched over a workbench in the garage, bringing my portfolio to life one piece at a time. The shelves above my industrial table were filled with all the supplies I needed: boxes of alginate, silicone, and latex; plaster bandages; buckets and mixing sticks; clay; jars filled with brushes, sculpting tools, scissors, and X-Acto knives; a hot glue gun and the clear sticks that accompanied it; and so much more.

My top priority was creating the prosthetics, which wasn't a simple undertaking. The first step typically began with life casting, which was the process of taking a mold of whichever body part you were creating the appliance for—in this particular case, the boys' faces—so it would fit perfectly against the model. The resulting negative mold would be filled with gypsum cement to produce a positive mold, a copy of the body part. Then I could sculpt the prosthetic directly on the mold using clay. But if I were to life cast all four members of the Heartbreakers, it would be a long, tedious operation. They'd already agreed to give up an entire day to be my models, so I wouldn't ask for any more of their time. Instead, I sculpted the shape of the prosthetics onto mannequin heads and hoped for the best.

Once that was finished, I stippled thin layers of latex over the clay using a sponge, careful to leave the edges as thin as possible. After the latex dried, I peeled it off the sculpture, and *voilà!*—a homemade prosthetic. I didn't finish them until Wednesday night, which only left me two days to make all the wigs, teeth, horns, and the other props I needed. By Friday morning, I'd transitioned into a state of full-on panic. How the hell would I get all this done? Better question, what had possessed me to think I *could* get all this done?

Homeroom started in less than an hour. If I came straight home after school and worked until midnight… No, that wouldn't be enough time. Which meant I probably had to pull an all-nighter.

Or, I thought, as Dad passed my room on the way downstairs, already talking on the phone, *I can just stay home…*

Work consumed Dad's life. He wouldn't notice if an alien

invasion was taking place, let alone if I cut one day of classes. I'd never skipped school before, but if there was ever a reason for me to do so, this was it. Rather than packing my book bag, I waited until I heard Dad's office door close before heading down to the garage and getting down to business. I'd just finished constructing the horns for the Beast when my phone buzzed.

GALAXY RIDER:
> Ready for tomorrow?

INDIE:
> Not even close.

GALAXY RIDER:
> Anything I can do?

INDIE:
> Wish me luck? I'm up to my neck in hot glue and spray paint right now.

Three dots appeared on my screen. I waited for Xander's reply, but it never came. The bubble vanished, but I couldn't spare another moment to consider what that meant. I buckled down, forgetting our conversation, and when a car door slammed in the driveway an hour later, I was so engrossed in my work that my ears didn't register the sound.

"Hey," someone shouted over my music.

With a backward jerk and what was most likely an unattractive squawk, I dropped the scissors I'd been using to thin a brunette wig. "Jesus," I exclaimed, clutching a hand to my chest. Xander stood at the edge of the garage door, awash with early afternoon sun. Flashing me a bright smile, he twirled a set of car keys around his finger before disappearing them into his jeans.

"Sorry," he said. He wore a pair of Ray-Ban sunglasses instead of his usual frames, which made it impossible for me to see the look in his eyes, but there was a note of amusement in his voice. "I didn't mean to scare you."

"What are you doing here?" I asked, turning down the music.

Back at Zap Zone, we'd decided it would be easier for me to do the boys' makeup here at the house instead of lugging my supplies to another location, and I'd given Xander the address so he could make travel arrangements with the rest of the band. But he wasn't supposed to be here until tomorrow morning.

"It sounded like you need help, so I, ah…came." Jamming both hands into his pockets, Xander glanced away from me before adding, "Is that okay?"

The gratitude I felt for him in that moment was so overwhelming, I could barely manage a response. "Oh."

His gaze darted back to mine. "Is that a good 'oh' or a bad one?"

"A good one," I reassured him, my composure snapping back into place. "And it's definitely okay. I'm in serious need of a second pair of hands."

Xander visibly relaxed at my answer; the tension in his shoulders melted, and he crossed the garage to join me at my workbench. "Is that all I am to you? A pair of hands?" Grinning, he wiggled his fingers at me. They were long, slender, and dusted with freckles.

For a single, breathless second, I imagined how they would feel against my skin. Then a burning surge of mortification tackled my hormones into submission.

With a cough, I turned away so he couldn't see the blush on my cheeks. "Of course not."

Hell, I thought, running a hand over my hair. *I probably look like the world's hottest mess right now.* My blond mane was piled on top of my head in an arrangement that more closely resembled a bird's nest than a bun, and I was covered from head to toe in spray paint, glitter, and glue. My outfit wasn't much better—an old pair of athletic shorts and an oversize T-shirt my dad received for running a marathon, clothes I didn't care about getting dirty.

"Because I'm also your laser tag shield and favorite model?"

I spun back around and pointed a finger at him. "Hey, I didn't use you as a shield. You jumped in front of me of your own volition, like some kind of obnoxious, self-sacrificing knight in shining armor."

Xander pressed a hand over his heart. "Are you calling me your hero?"

"You wish."

Laughing, he pulled off his sunglasses and hooked them on the collar of an olive-green T-shirt. The color made his eyes pop. "So aren't you supposed to be at school?" he asked as he took in the tornado that was my workspace.

"Technically, yes, but I'm channeling my inner Ferris Bueller today. Skipping is good for the soul."

"Pretty sure Bueller didn't spend his day off working," Xander pointed out, still surveying my mess. He looked like he was about to add something else, but then his gaze landed on the row of finished prosthetics. Frowning, he picked up the one on the end. "What's this for?"

Last Saturday, Xander and Felicity had watched as I sketched out potential appliance designs. At the time, there had only been four. I didn't need a prosthetic to turn Xander into Jack Sparrow, just makeup, facial hair, and a wig. But when I came home and googled reference pictures for each character, a new idea came to me.

"It's for you," I told him.

His frown deepened. "This looks like a skull." I nodded and waited for him to understand. "Ohhh!" he said after another moment, a mixture of realization and excitement spreading across his face. "Cursed Jack Sparrow? From the first movie?"

"Yeah, I hope you don't mind, but I thought it would be more in the spirit of Halloween and a nod to your classic monsters concept. If you don't like the idea, I can stick to the original plan." It would certainly be less work but not as fun.

"No, I *love* it. It's way more badass." He gently set the prosthetic back in place and grinned at me. "So what do you need me to do, boss?"

"I just started on your wig," I said, gesturing to the one in front of me. "Wanna help?"

He hesitated. "I don't need any actual skills for this, do I? I don't want to ruin anything."

"Nope. Just a willingness to get your hands dirty."

"Dirty?" He winked and added, "I think I can handle that."

☆ ♡ ♪

Thanks to Xander's help, I was fully rested Saturday morning when the doorbell rang. We'd finished making every wig and prop I needed for the photo shoot, no all-nighter required. I scarfed down my last bite of toast, slid out of the breakfast nook, and hurried to let the boys inside. Xander warned me that they might be late, but a glance at my phone revealed it was eight o'clock on the dot.

Perfect, I thought as I made my way down the front hall. I would need at least five hours to transform all four of them.

But when I answered the front door, it wasn't Xander or any of the other Heartbreakers. Instead, a girl who looked around my age stood on the front porch with a camera bag slung over her shoulder. She wore beat-up Chucks, a pair of faded jeans, and a tour T-shirt for a band called the Sensible Grenade. A small strip of her brown hair was dyed aqua, and a diamond stud sparkled in her nose.

"Hey," she said, offering me her hand. "You must be Indie. I'm Stella, Oliver's girlfriend."

"Nice to meet you," I said as we shook. Then I peered around her. "So, ah…is it just you or…?"

"Oh, no. The guys are here. They're just being their usual immature selves." She jammed a thumb over her shoulder at something out of view. I stepped onto the porch to see what she was pointing at.

The Heartbreakers were in various stages of exiting a black Range Rover: Oliver looked like he was unbuckling his seat belt; Xander had the driver's side door pushed open, his hand still on the handle; and JJ was in the process of stepping out of the SUV, one leg in and the other out, his left foot planted securely on the driveway. What caught my attention was that none of the boys were moving. It was as if they'd been frozen in motion.

"What's going on?" I asked Stella, narrowing my eyes at the strange scene. Only then did I notice that Oliver, JJ, and Xander *were* moving, although at what appeared to be a snail's pace.

"They're slow racing." Her eyes flicked heavenward, and she added, "Whoever gets out of the car the last wins, but they can't just sit there. They have to be in motion the entire time. And before you ask me why, the answer is I have no clue. They're weirdos. I've given up trying to understand them."

"Sounds like fun," I said, the corners of my lips rising. "Where're Alec and Felicity?"

"Oliver said something about Felicity having an early shift this morning," she explained. "I think she works at a diner? Alec picked her up when she got off. They're only thirty minutes behind us."

At that moment, Xander noticed me standing on the porch. His face lit up, and he instantly dropped out of the race, climbing from the car at a regular speed. He strode up the front walk and joined us.

"Hey," he said, his voice bright. "Long time no see."

I rolled my eyes—we'd seen each other less than eight hours ago—but couldn't deny him a smile. "Hey to you too."

Yesterday, after we finished everything I needed to get done for my portfolio, Xander and I watched the first three

Pirates of the Caribbean movies. I'd wanted to have a *Saw* marathon instead, but Xander argued he needed to get into character. In the end, I didn't care what we watched. I was just glad I didn't have to spend another Friday night by my lonesome. We made burrito bowls for dinner—minus cheese and sour cream for Xander—and he ended up staying well past midnight.

"So I don't know if Xander's told you anything about me," Stella said then, fiddling with her nose piercing, "but I'm studying photography at school. If you'd like, I can take the pictures for your portfolio today. I have all my equipment with me."

Xander snorted. "You say that as if you don't always have your equipment with you."

"I'd love that," I told Stella. My artistic abilities did not extend to photography. I could have the world's best camera, and someone with an old cell phone would take a better photo than me, so I was grateful for and relieved by her offer.

"Awesome," she said, the trace of apprehension melting from her face. "I was thinking I could get a shot of each of the boys pre-makeup, some of you working, and then as many as you'd like at the festival."

"That sounds perfect. Do you guys want to come in? I have breakfast for everyone." I gestured at the open door and then glanced back at the SUV. Oliver and JJ were still locked in their slow race. "Are we leaving them or...?"

Stella laughed as she stepped inside. "Don't bother. They'll be at it for a while."

☆ ♭ ♪

"What in the hell is that?" JJ asked, eyes wide. He sat with his back to a mirror on the salon chair borrowed from my sister's dressing room, knuckles white as he gripped the hem of his shorts. Before the band arrived this morning, I'd set up a small makeup studio in one of the guest bathrooms where I'd have plenty of room to do my work.

"This?" I glanced at the small metal tool in my hand. "It's an eyelash curler. I need to curl your lashes before I apply the false ones."

"Nope." He scrambled out of the seat and shook his head. "There's no way you're coming near my face with that thing. It looks like a medieval torture device."

Stella laughed as she snapped a picture of JJ. "He does have a point. I've always thought they look scary, especially when you hold it right up to your eye." When I shot her a not-helping look, she quickly added, "But don't worry, JJ. I'm sure Indie knows what she's doing. You won't feel a thing."

JJ took a step back. "No offense, but that wasn't very convincing."

Drawing in a deep breath, I willed myself to stay patient.

Five hours. That was how long I'd been laying beards, applying prosthetics, and blending makeup for. Oliver,

Xander, and Alec were already done, but JJ was proving to be a more difficult model to work with. He kept jiggling his knees and running a finger over the brushes in the makeup belt clipped around my waist.

"I promise it won't hurt, but you have to stop fidgeting." I put a hand on his shoulder and pushed him back onto the stool. "Sit down, and hold still. I'm almost done."

He muttered something under his breath but did as he was told.

Two minutes later, I spun him around so he could look at himself in the mirror. "There," I said, exhaustion washing over me. "All finished."

JJ leaned forward, turning his head from side to side. For a split second, I feared he would blow up and demand I undo all my hard work. After all, he'd put up quite a stink when I explained I'd be transforming him into Ursula from *The Little Mermaid*. Instead, the corners of his mouth tugged into a grin. "This is some next-level drag queen magic. You can't even tell it's me!"

A sigh of relief hissed through my lips. "I'm glad you think so." I rinsed the tacky lash glue off my hands and turned off my music. "Let's go downstairs. Everyone is waiting on us, and I need coffee stat."

We found Felicity and the rest of the Heartbreakers in the kitchen. They were gathered around the island, enjoying the spread of fresh fruit, pastries, and cold cuts I'd assembled before their arrival. Considering Xander and his friends were going out of their way to help me with my portfolio, feeding them was the least I could do.

"Hey, Indie. I was wondering if—" Oliver started, swiveling around on a barstool, but he never finished his sentence. As soon as he caught sight of JJ, he doubled over with laughter and nearly fell off the stool. "You're freakin' purple, dude!"

"Be nice," Stella scolded, but she had to bite down on her lip to keep from laughing.

JJ flipped him off. "Laugh it up, Fuzzball."

His comment made me frown. Titling my head to the side, I scrutinized Oliver's makeup, wondering if he looked more Chewbacca than Beast. Without the horns and tusks, he could definitely pass as a Wookiee. *Whatever*, I decided with a shrug. I was too tired to make any adjustments. I suppose they were both Disney characters now anyway.

"I'll be honest," Oliver said when he finally had his laughter under control. "I was a bit disappointed I didn't get to be Jack Sparrow as I feel we share a certain love of debauchery, but seeing you? I'm just glad I don't look like *that*."

"Ignore him, JJ," Felicity said. "Ursula is my favorite Disney villain. In fact, I have a present for you."

"For me?" JJ asked and, channeling his character, sashayed over to her. "What is it?"

Felicity rummaged through her tote bag until she found a small cloth pouch. After loosening the drawstring, she tipped its contents onto her palm and revealed a gold seashell pendant. "I made this last night. It's a replica of Ursula's necklace from the movie." She motioned for him to turn, and then she fastened the black cord around his neck.

JJ brushed his fingers over the shell and smiled. "A sea witch with style? I love it. Thanks, Felicity."

From where I was standing, I could clearly see Alec's expression, and his face split into the happiest of grins at the pair's interaction.

"That necklace doesn't make you look any less ridiculous," Oliver said, unable to wipe the smirk off his face.

"You're one to talk," JJ shot back. "Your face is literally covered in fur."

"At least I'm not wearing lipstick."

"That's rich coming from someone who went through an eyeliner phase!"

Oliver sucked in a sharp breath. Apparently a line had been crossed, because without warning, he snatched a grape off his plate and lobbed it at JJ's face. The kitchen went still for two seconds. Then, as if she knew what was coming, Stella snatched up her camera and ran for cover, followed quickly by Felicity. The moment they were out of the way,

JJ seized the fruit platter from the brunch spread and started pelting Oliver with blueberries.

"Hey!" Xander exclaimed when one of the berries clipped his temple. He grabbed a container of doughnut holes from the countertop and retaliated. The powdered ball accidentally hit Alec, and a tiny plume of sugar mushroomed off his chest. Before I could tell them to stop, that they might wreck the makeup I'd spent all morning applying, all four boys were flinging food at one another.

"What the *hell* is going on in here?"

Food stopped flying, and we all turned toward the source of the question. My sister stood in the threshold of the kitchen, eyes narrowed. For reasons I couldn't explain, my heart stopped at the sight of her.

"Hey, Violet," Alec said with an air of innocence, as if he wasn't currently lobbing spoonfuls of Chobani at his bandmates.

Violet did a double take. "Alec, is that you?"

"I prefer Hades, god of the underworld," he deadpanned as a glob of yogurt dripped from his hand and splattered on the floor, "but I suppose Alec works."

"Why are you dressed like that?" She glanced around the room as if searching for answers.

"We're helping Indie with her portfolio," Oliver said by way of explanation.

A frown line appeared on Violet's forehead, but before she could ask the question I knew would come next, I strode across the room and took her by the elbow. "Can we talk privately?" I asked, tugging her into the hall.

"Ouch! Indie, let go of me," she complained, but I didn't stop until we reached the front door, well out of earshot.

Dropping Violet's arm, I rounded on her. "What are you doing here? You weren't supposed to be back until Monday." The two of us weren't on speaking terms, but I'd overheard her and Dad talking about a promotional event she was attending in Chicago this weekend. Which meant I was supposed to have the house to myself. That she'd come home two days early was unexpected and left me feeling…flustered. The truth was I hadn't planned on telling my family about my decision to apply to ACM. I wasn't embarrassed, and I didn't care if they approved or not, but part of me wanted to keep this project all to myself.

Violet opened her mouth as if to explain but stopped. "Considering this is my house, I think the real question is why are there a bunch of weirdos having a food fight in the kitchen?"

Despite Violet's cross tone, a sense of accomplishment bloomed in my chest, and I unconsciously rose up onto my tiptoes. "You really don't recognize them?"

"Besides Alec, am I supposed to?"

My mouth stretched into a satisfied grin. "Not at all, but I'm still surprised."

She rolled her eyes. "Whatever. Can you just explain what's going on?"

"Nothing you need to worry about, okay? Just a few friends helping me with something."

"Wow, Indie. Can you be any more vague?" she said, her every word heavy with exasperation. "I heard the hairy guy mention something about a portfolio. What the heck was he talking about?"

"It's part of a college application, okay?" I replied, knowing Violet wouldn't let this go until she knew all the details. She was nosey that way. "I promise I'll clean up the kitchen."

Her head tilted to the side as she tried to figure out what I wasn't telling her. "Since when does Juilliard require you to be proficient in face painting?"

I bristled at her remark. "Don't be condescending. You know it's called special effects makeup, and I never said the portfolio was for Juilliard." *Besides*, I very nearly added, *I don't owe you an explanation*. Violet wasn't Mom or the FBI. She didn't get to interrogate me. This might be her house, but I lived here too.

"I don't understand."

"I'm applying to a cinema makeup school."

"But…Juilliard."

Sucking in my cheeks, I silently counted to three in an attempt to keep my cool. "I can't do both?"

"Well, of course you can," she said, a frown tightening the corners of her eyes, "but I haven't heard you practice for your audition lately. Shouldn't that be your top priority instead of spending so much time on makeup? You practically lived in the garage this week."

In preparation for the argument that was sure to follow, I drew myself up to my full height and crossed my arms. "Maybe I'm considering a career in *makeup* instead." And who was she to tell me what my top priority was and how I should be spending my time?

Violet's eyes bulged. "But you've been training for Juilliard since...forever."

My responding smile was thin. "So I've had plenty of practice. Thirteen years to be exact."

She shook her head and took a step back, as if my behavior was so upsetting that she needed space. "This is a mistake."

Narrowing my eyes, I studied my sister and tried to decipher her stake in the situation. What did it matter to her if I practiced or not? "Why do you care about this so much?" I finally asked.

Emotion flashed in her eyes, but she glanced away before I could identify it. "Because I'd hate to see you throw away your dream."

"First of all, I'm not throwing away my dream. I still plan on applying to Juilliard. Do you have so little faith in my abilities that you think I need to spend every waking moment practicing?" I asked sharply. "Second, what's wrong with me wanting to step outside the box I've been inside my entire life and try something new? After all, isn't that what you're doing? You wanted to be an actress, so why would you 'throw away your dream' to pursue a music career?"

"Do Mom and Dad know about this?" she asked, her eyebrows drawing together as she brushed off my question.

"No, they don't, and you're going to keep it that way." I lifted my chin, silently daring her to challenge me.

For a long moment, Violet didn't respond. Her frown deepened. "Mom will be crushed when she finds out," she said at last.

Would she though? Despite setting aside her dream to raise us, Mom never once forced her aspirations on me. I was following in her footsteps because I wanted to. But if what I wanted changed, I had a feeling Mom would support me no matter what. All she wanted for us was to be happy.

"Actually," I replied, "I don't think she will be."

I didn't understand why Violet was so upset about this,

but I didn't care. This was my life, not hers, and she needed to mind her own business.

Without another word, I shoved past my sister and returned to the kitchen.

CHAPTER 10

"I swear to God, Oliver!" Stella exclaimed, her gaze snapping from the camera screen to her boyfriend. "If you ruin the picture one more time…"

He threw a taunting smirk in her direction. "Yeah? What are you going to do about it? Punish me? I'd be okay with that."

Flushing, Stella turned to me for support, and I hid a smile behind my hand.

"Come on, Stella. We've been at this for *hours*," JJ complained. "I wanna have some fun."

"Don't be a baby," she told him. "It's only been thirty minutes."

"Yeah, thirty minutes of *torture*," he grumbled dramatically.

I had to admit, I felt JJ's pain. As soon as we'd pulled into the parking lot at Soul Harvest, Stella marched the boys over to a festival sign surrounded by straw bales and overgrown pumpkins for a photo shoot. Which was our plan all along, but I hadn't expected Stella to be so...thorough. She treated her role as photographer as if I'd hired her for a job, taking shots of the band as a group and each member individually. Then, after our tickets were scanned and we went through security, she made them repeat the process inside the front entrance as a stream of happy concertgoers populated the background.

"Hey, Stella. I bet you have plenty of great material," I said. "Why don't we take a break, enjoy the festival, and if need be, we can take more pictures before we leave?"

Her face fell. "Are you sure?"

"Positive," I replied, and Xander mouthed me a *thank you*.

She lowered her camera. "Well, I suppose." The words were barely out of her mouth before Oliver whooped with joy and the boys broke rank.

"So where to?" JJ asked, rubbing his hands together as he looked around.

"Hold that thought." Felicity strode off in the direction of an information booth. Two minutes later, she returned with a map, and as she unfolded it, everyone crowded around to get a good look. According to the map scale, there were eight stages spread across fifty acres, some big, some small. In between the stages were icons representing beer tents, food vendors, merchandise stalls, and bathrooms.

"Look," Xander said, jamming his finger at the page.

"There's a giant slide! Why don't we check that out?"

"Don't need to ask me twice," Oliver replied, and everyone nodded in agreement.

The slide was on the opposite side of the grounds, so we set off in that direction. While we walked, Xander and I entertained each other by pointing out our favorite costumes in the crowd. There were your boring Halloween standards, like witches, nurses, vampires, and superheroes, but we focused on the more creative outfits like a blood-covered Patrick Bateman, an Edward Scissorhands worthy of winning a cosplay contest, and a couple dressed as Ash Ketchum and Misty. We were halfway across the park when JJ stopped so suddenly I nearly crashed into him.

He cupped his hands around his mouth. "Yo, Ariel!"

Following his gaze, I spotted a group of girls dressed like Disney princesses. There was Belle, Tiana, and Jasmine, but JJ waved at a redhead in a purple seashell bra and a sparkling green mermaid skirt.

"I think we need a picture together," he said, smirking and crooking a finger at her.

Ariel spared him a brief glance before turning back to her friends, but then Tiana whispered something in her ear, and she turned back to JJ. A small smile inched onto her face as she looked him up and down. Sure, JJ's face currently resembled Ursula, but even I understood why someone might appreciate the rest of him; he was wearing a pair of fitted jeans and a sleeveless Nirvana shirt that left his broad shoulders, muscular arms, and tattoo on full display. Minus the makeup, he looked like the kind of guy that protective fathers everywhere had to chase off with a shotgun.

"Hi, I'm Alice," Ariel said, stepping forward.

JJ grinned. "JJ Morris."

My mouth dropped open at his declaration—how could he tell her his name with no thought for the hours I'd spent trying to conceal the boys' identities?—but Alice laughed and rolled her eyes. "No, really. What's your name?"

"Well, I thought it was obvious," JJ said, smoothing a hand over the bangs of his white wig. "I'm Ursula, misunderstood antihero and cunning businesswoman. Not to mention badass sea witch. Not sure what's wrong with your memory, but you're Ariel. Youngest daughter of King Triton? Traded your voice to me for a pair of legs? And can I just say they're looking stunning in that skirt today?"

"Honestly," Stella grumbled under her breath. "We can't take him anywhere. He's such a perv." But her annoyance didn't last long. Alice seemed flattered by JJ's comment, so she agreed to a picture, and the prospect of another photo shoot cheered Stella up. Soon she was beckoning Alice's friends over, declaring that everyone in a Disney costume needed to be in the shot, then barking orders to position everyone. She didn't even care that Belle latched onto her boyfriend as if she planned on stealing him away.

Twenty minutes later, after parting ways with the princess squad, stopping for *another* photo shoot with a group of frat guys in kigurumi, and crossing the rest of the grounds, our destination came into view. The first thing I noticed about the slide was that it looked like a giant wavy rainbow. Riders could pick from six tracks—red, orange, yellow, green, blue, and purple—that plunged into four steep drops on the way to the ground. The second thing I noticed was that despite droves of attendees, there didn't appear to be anyone waiting in line. Which was probably due to the daunting number of steps one would have to climb. Or maybe it was the price? Ten dollars for a single ride seemed pricey to me.

This didn't bother Oliver though. He pulled out his wallet, slapped two one-hundred-dollar bills on the counter of the ticket booth, and told the lady inside to give him his money's worth. She raised a brow but counted out twenty tickets and slid them under the glass. We made our way through a turnstile and toward the base of the steps, where a second person was accepting tickets in exchange for felt mats.

"I'm staying here," Stella said, pointing to the bottom of the slide. "I want to get more pictures."

Oliver rolled his eyes but shrugged. "Whatever. More rides for me."

"Make sure to read the rules," the man announced in a monotone voice as we started our ascent. The rules he'd referred to were listed on separate, equidistant signs along the climb in bright red capitals letters. Things like MUST BE 48 INCHES OR TALLER TO RIDE! and NO SHIRT, NO SHOES, NO SLIDE! For safety reasons, the signs also warned us to ride sitting up with our legs straight, not to hold hands or lock arms with other riders, and to remain on our mats until we came to a complete stop. Everyone was winded when we reached the top, but we were rewarded with a stunning view of Soul Harvest, the festival grounds spread out before us like a jumbo version of Felicity's map.

"Christ," Xander gasped, extracting an inhaler from his back pocket. "How many steps was that?"

"Two hundred and fourteen," said another employee. He appeared to be in charge of manning the top of the slide but had barely glanced up from his phone when we crested the last step. "You guys can pick any track you want and go when you're ready."

Wanting purple, I crossed the length of the platform and laid out my mat on the far track. As I took a seat, Xander claimed the blue one beside me.

"Wow," he said, peering over the edge. "That's a much steeper drop than what it looks like from the ground."

I turned to him in surprise. "Not scared of heights, are you?"

"Petrified," he said, struggling to subdue a smile. "Will you hold my hand on the way down?"

It was only a joke, yet my heart gave a sudden thump against my chest at his question. "Wish I could," I answered in what I hoped was an equally teasing manner. "Honestly, I'm crushed, but it's against the rules. Didn't you read them on the way up?"

"No, actually. I was too busy trying to breathe."

"Ah, well, that's understandable," I said. "Priorities and all that."

"Everyone in position?" Oliver called, taking a quick survey of our line. We were. "All right then. On your marks," he said, rocking back and forth like he was on a luge. "Get set... Go!"

Grabbing both sides of the track, I pushed myself forward. Gravity took hold, and as I plummeted toward the ground at a stomach-dropping speed, I threw my arms in the air and let out a scream of exhilaration. Much to my surprise, I was the first to reach the bottom, followed closely by JJ. Oliver came in third, and he didn't look too pleased about either of us beating him.

"Let's go again," he said, holding up his stash of tickets, a competitive glint in his eyes.

"Pass," Felicity answered, knees wobbling as she stood. "I'm going to keep both feet planted firmly on the ground, but you guys have fun."

"Same," Xander said, tossing both his and Felicity's mats into a return pile. "If I climb those stairs again, my lungs might actually catch fire."

I couldn't help it when my eyebrows drew together. *You okay?* I mouthed to him.

My concern must have been amusing, because Xander smirked. He hooked a long, elegant finger around my belt loop and tugged me forward. Lips against my ear, he whispered, "Totally fine. Ripe old age of ninety-five, remember? Make them eat your dust." Then he gave me a gentle push in the direction of the stairs.

Too stunned to do anything other than move on autopilot, I tackled each step with the efficiency of a robot, my face in flames from Xander's sudden proximity.

Back at the top, everyone arranged their mats and settled into place.

"Whenever you're ready," the employee said, eyes still locked on his phone, and JJ took advantage of his obvious distraction.

Just as Alec told everyone to get set, JJ jumped to his feet. Before anyone realized what he was doing, he threw himself face-first onto his mat at the same time as Alec shouted "Go!"

"Hey!" Oliver shouted, but he quickly decided to follow JJ's example. Out of the corner of my eye, I saw him grab

Alec's shirtsleeve and try to use his friend's weight to propel himself forward. Alec, however, was having none of it, and he yanked Oliver back by the collar. The boys fought each other all the way down the slide, both trying to gain an edge over the other. In the end, they finished dead even. JJ came in first, and as the only noncheater, I brought up the rear.

"Ha!" JJ jumped to his feet when I reached the bottom and shimmied his shoulders at us in a victory dance. "Beat you all."

"Congratulations," said the mat attendant. "Savor the win, because you're now banned from the slide for breaking the rules. Same goes for you two," he told Oliver and Alec. "Hand over your mats."

"But we still have ten tickets," JJ complained.

The guy pointed at the exit. "Not my problem. Get going."

"Well, this blows," Oliver said as the eight of us passed through another turnstile. He'd offered his remaining tickets to me, but I didn't want to ride the slide by myself while everyone waited at the bottom.

"You know the one thing that will make everything better?" JJ asked. He pointed at a sign above one of the many food stalls. "Three words, my friends—chili cheese fries."

Xander didn't feel comfortable eating from any of the vendors, but he promised he wasn't hungry, so JJ led us over to Mac's Heart Attack Shack. We got in line behind a large group of girls, most of whom were sporting tank tops that identified them as the Sun Valley High School cheer squad. They paid us no mind until Oliver noticed one of the girls was wearing a Heartbreakers tour shirt. He tapped her on the shoulder. When she turned around, I was instantly reminded of a young Gabrielle Union from her teen rom-com days.

Gabrielle pressed her lips together to keep from laughing. "Nice getup. Did you lose a bet?"

Oliver offered her what I assumed was meant to be a friendly smile, but the tusks he was wearing made his expression look a little wild. "Actually, I'm helping out a friend. I was just wondering—do you like that band?" He gestured at her shirt.

She shrugged. "Yeah, I suppose they're okay."

I cringed at her response, my cheeks heating up with secondhand embarrassment for the boys.

Oliver, however, didn't seem to mind. There was a sparkle of amusement in his eyes. "In other words, they suck?"

Another shrug. "They were my favorite in junior high, but I'm more into K-pop now. What's it to you?"

"Just curious. My girlfriend is obsessed with that Oliver Perry guy."

"Oh, I love Oliver!" said another one of the cheerleaders. "He's my favorite too."

Stella let out a single bark of laughter that made Gabrielle's gaze flicker over to her, but she was too focused on scrolling through today's pictures to notice. Gabrielle narrowed her eyes as she took in Stella's appearance, from the aqua stripe in her hair to the camera clutched in her hands. I suddenly wondered how recognizable Stella was. She wasn't famous like my sister or the band, but she'd been dating Oliver for a while now. Surely a dedicated Heartbreakers fan would know who she was? Fortunately, JJ butted in before any realizations could be made.

"That curly-haired guy? You're joking, right? He looks like a total douchewaffle," he said. "If you ask me, the drummer is the class act of the group. What's his name?"

This made Gabrielle smile. "That's JJ. He's my favorite."

"Oh, yeah? Why's that?"

"Because he's beyond hilarious."

An ear-to-ear grin stretched across JJ's face, and he puffed out his chest as he turned toward his bandmates. "Hear that guys? JJ is *beyond* hilarious."

Xander sighed and rubbed a finger over his eyebrow. "We're never going to hear the end of this," he whispered to me.

Suddenly, all the girls were discussing their favorite member of the Heartbreakers. Oliver seemed to be the front-runner, but JJ was a close second. Alec's name was tossed around a few times as well, but I didn't hear a single mention of Xander. Which pissed me off. What the hell was wrong with these girls? Couldn't they see how awesome he was?

As the line inched forward, I peeked over at him. He was kicking a nonexistent stone on the ground. We barely knew each other, but Xander struck me as someone who oozed happiness, a glass-half-full type of person. At that moment, he looked anything but, and none of his friends seemed to notice.

"Well," I said in a voice loud enough for everyone to hear. "There must be something wrong with you guys, because you're all forgetting about Xander. He's fan-fucking-tastic."

A few of the Sun Valley cheerleaders piped up in agreement, which was satisfying, but the feeling didn't last long.

Xander cleared his throat. "Hey, uh…looks like all the picnic tables are filling up," he said, kneading the back of his neck and avoiding my gaze. "I'm gonna go save us a place to sit." He hurried away before I could stop him, head hung low as he slipped into the crowd.

Crap. Had I said something wrong?

Or maybe my comment embarrassed him?

It was also possible that I was overthinking things and his reaction was purely in response to the cheerleaders' conversation, but either way, I wanted to make sure he was okay.

"Indie?" I looked up and found Alec staring at me, a frown marring his face. "Everything all right?"

"I'm not sure, but I'll go find out."

Without waiting for Alec's response, I stepped out of line and chased after the pirate hat I could just barely see weaving through the throng of people. When I finally caught up to Xander, it was only because he'd stopped to inspect the menu at a food stall specializing in all things lentil.

"Mushroom lentil burger?" I said, reading off the first item, a healthy dose of skepticism in my tone. "Do people actually eat that?"

Xander jerked at the sound of my voice, but once he realized it was me, he said, "According to the description, it's their number one seller."

"Weird. Are you going to try it?" I asked, shooting him a sideways glance. It sounded absolutely disgusting. Then again, I wasn't exactly an adventurous eater. Violet teased me whenever we ate at restaurants because I always asked for the kids' menu—chicken fingers and grilled cheese were fine by me.

He shook his head, jostling the beads, bones, and coins I'd sewn into his wig. "Nah. What's the point when I can't eat the bun? I was, however, wishing I could have the Mediterranean bowl."

"And you can't because…?" Multiple signs on the stall proclaimed Loving Lentils was a vegan establishment. Surely there was something on the menu he could eat?

"Ordering food at events like this can be tricky. There's always a chance of cross contamination. For example, look at number ten." He pointed to the Thai crunch salad at the bottom of the menu. Underneath the product description was a red asterisk: CONTAINS PEANUTS. "Sure, there are options I'm not allergic to, but what if the cook makes my meal on the same cutting board he chopped peanuts on? For me, it's not worth the risk."

I frowned. "That doesn't seem very fair."

"How so?"

"Nothing here is safe for you to eat, but it's against the rules to bring food in," I exclaimed, shaking my head. "So what? You're just supposed to go hungry?"

My indignation must have been amusing, because Xander finally cracked a smile. "If I really wanted to, I could've brought my own meal, gone to Guest Services when we arrived, and picked up an ADA wristband."

"What's that?"

"A disability bracelet. It allows me to carry in food."

"Oh, I didn't realize that was something you could do," I said, feeling silly. "It still sucks though. That's a lot of extra work for a basic necessity like eating."

"Yeah, I suppose, but that's how it's always been, so I'm used to it." He shrugged. "Seriously, don't worry about me. I'm fine."

"Are you though?"

Xander dropped his gaze. "What do you mean?"

"Well, you bolted out of line," I said carefully. "I wanted to make sure you were okay."

"Of course I'm okay," he responded, waving me off as if I'd overreacted. "I'm used to fending for myself when it comes to food."

Not what I meant, I wanted to say, but I decided not to push the topic. The uncomfortable look in Xander's eyes made it clear he didn't want to discuss what had happened.

"If you're sure…"

"I am." A line of people was forming behind us, so Xander stepped away from the food stall and gestured to the designated picnic area. "Why don't we go find somewhere to sit?"

It took us a few minutes of hovering next to a couple who'd already finished their meal for us to snag a spot, but once they left, we claimed the table and waited for the others to join us with their food.

"So do I get to see you on Tuesday?" Xander asked.

Frowning, I attempted to pull up my mental calendar. "What's on Tuesday?"

Xander gave me a funny look. "The premiere for the final season of *Immortal Nights*?"

Oh, right. Pretty sure Dad mentioned it a few weeks back, but no surprise I didn't remember. I made a point of tuning out my family's *IN* conversations. And with the exception of Comic Con, I never went to the events. Not even one as monumental as the final premiere. "Wasn't planning on it. Why?"

"The band was invited," he answered. "I was hoping you'd be there."

I felt my heart catch in my chest. "Well," I said hesitantly, "I could always change my mind. That is, if that's what you want?"

"Yeah," he said, a brightness finally returning to his expression. "I'd really like that."

☆ ♡ ♪

"Oooh, look at this! Doesn't it scream Sailor Mars?"

I glanced up from the striped shirt I was considering, which could work as the base for several potential costumes—a mime, a bank robber, a pirate—but each idea felt like a total cop-out. Sofia held up a red skirt for me to inspect.

"Actually," I said, eyeing the pleats, "I'm getting a Velma vibe."

The triumphant smile slid off her face. "From *Scooby-Doo*?"

I nodded.

"Yikes." She hung the skirt back up and continued her search through the rack.

Sofia and I had been combing Deals 'N' Steals ever since school let out, but neither of us were having any luck finding a costume. I supposed the only person I could blame was myself. Usually I started thinking about what to wear when October 1 rolled around, but for the past three weeks, I'd been distracted by so many things—Comic Con, my Juilliard audition, creating a portfolio for ACM, Xander. Now my favorite holiday was five days away, and here I was contemplating whether to dress up as a freaking mime. If I didn't come up with something better soon, my reputation as the costume queen would be at serious risk.

The telltale ping of an incoming text interrupted my worrying.

STELLA:

> Just finished editing the shots from this weekend. They look AMAZING!!!! I'll email you everything tonight. Thanks for letting me help with your portfolio.

Smiling, I quickly typed a response.

INDIE:

> No, thank you for offering up your photography skills. Can't wait to see how the pictures turned out!

As I slid my phone back into my pocket, I noticed Sofia watching me over the top of the garment rack. "What?" I asked.

She leaned forward, eyes alight. "Was that him?"

"No, it was Stella. She's done editing the photos for my portfolio. Said she'd email them to me tonight."

Sofia visibly deflated. "That's great."

"Wow," I said, trying not to laugh at her obvious disappointment. "Don't sound so excited."

"Sorry." She flashed me a sheepish grin. "It's just, I can't believe he asked you to go to the premiere with him."

I refrained from rolling my eyes. Ever since I'd filled Sofia in on what happened at Soul Harvest during homeroom this morning, all she wanted to do was talk about Xander. "That's not what happened," I told her. "He assumed I'd be attending with my family and mentioned he was hoping to see me there. That's all."

"And that's bad how?" she asked.

"I didn't say it was bad," I replied, pulling another hanger off the rack. On it was a white blouse with navy polka dots, and I stuffed the shirt back into place between an ugly Christmas sweater and a burnt orange turtleneck. "I just think you're blowing the situation out of proportion."

"Indie, come on. He's hoping to see you?" She shot me a look that indicated I was being dense. "The boy is clearly into you. I'm not blowing things out of proportion. I'm stating obvious facts."

The warmth of a blush crept up my neck. "You think so?"

She nodded. "Definitely. You should invite him to the bonfire on Saturday."

Lizzie Kravitz, a girl in my grade who I knew from orchestra, always hosted the best theme parties. My favorite, by far, was her Halloween one. It always included a bonfire, enough sugar to open a candy shop, and a costume contest, which I'd won the past two years in a row.

"I don't know," I said, thumbing my ear. "He probably has some cool LA event to go to. I doubt he'll want to hang out at a high school party."

"I'm pretty sure Xander wants to be wherever you are."

"What if you're wrong and he says no?"

"Then he'll miss out on the best girl who's ever walked into his life, but trust me—he's not that stupid," she said. "Besides, Saturday will be your last chance to see him before he leaves for tour."

Although the prospect of asking Xander to a party made my hands feel sweaty, the thought of only seeing him one more time was worse. "Oh, all right," I grumbled. "You win. I'll invite him tomorrow at the premiere."

"Good," Sofia said, her responding smile filled with triumph. "Now we just need to find you the perfect costume."

We spent the next hour sifting through the store's remaining clothing racks. Sofia struck gold with a gorgeous red cloak and decided to go as Little Red Riding Hood, but

I had yet to discover anything Halloween worthy. Just as I was about to call it quits, Sofia extracted a tailcoat from the men's section. It was midnight blue and decorated with brass buttons. Very Victorian looking, like something a steampunk cosplayer would wear.

"Wait!" I exclaimed as she moved to put it back. "Let me see that."

Sofia glanced at her latest find with a look of doubt but shrugged and handed it over. The material was thinner than I anticipated, and I gently slid it off the hanger and eased into each sleeve. It fit my shoulders perfectly, but I wanted to see what it looked like on. After locating a full-length mirror, I turned in a circle, inspecting myself from every angle. The jacket had clearly been designed for a man—it was boxy and unflattering on my curves. Sofia's reflection appeared in the mirror behind me.

"Do you think you could take this in at my waist?" I asked, pointing to where I wanted a little definition. "Maybe add some lace on the cuffs?"

She took a moment to inspect the tailcoat. "Sure, but I don't get it. Who are you dressing up as?"

"Can't tell," I said, tossing her a smirk. "It's a surprise."

CHAPTER 11

I'd just finished lacing up my Doc Martens when someone knocked on my bedroom door.

"Come in," I called, covering my shoes with the length of my skirt and straightening up.

Violet stepped inside wearing a blush jumpsuit, strappy nude heels, and a necklace with enough carats that she'd probably topple over if she leaned too far forward. Her pale hair was pulled back into a sleek high ponytail, and her makeup was minimal. She glanced toward my bed as if expecting me to be curled up with a comic, then scanned the entirety of the room. When she spotted me standing beside my vanity, her eyes widened slightly.

"So it's true," she said, her gaze drifting over the outfit I'd chosen for tonight. "Dad said you'd decided to come, but I didn't believe him."

"What gave it away?" I asked, picking an imaginary piece of lint off my sleeve. Any second now, Violet would comment on my black nail polish or the tiny silver pentacles hanging from my ears.

"Your outfit," she answered, not picking up on my sarcasm. "You look really pretty, Indie."

"I—ah, thanks," I replied, her compliment catching me off guard. For the premiere, I'd chosen a black long-sleeved top tucked into a pleated floor-length skirt that swished around my ankles when I walked. The satin material was a brilliant emerald green, which matched the stone set into the choker around my neck.

"So," she said, fiddling with her necklace. "What made you change your mind?"

I sighed. Of course she had to ask the one question I couldn't answer. More likely than not, Violet would be pissed if I admitted the only reason I was coming to the premiere was to support Xander. "Well," I said, a bit uncomfortably. "Should be fun, right?"

She frowned. "Right…"

We both knew I hated these kinds of events, so I tried again. "This is the last one, so I figured I should be there."

"Okay." Uncertainty laced her reply, but she let the subject drop. "I'm heading out in ten. Do you…maybe want to come with me?"

"Sorry, but no." My answer was swift and firm, but I didn't mean any offense by it. Tagging along with Violet meant walking the red carpet. "I'll catch a ride with Dad." Although his life revolved around Violet's career, Dad was never one for the spotlight himself. He avoided the press as best he could, which meant he'd be slipping in through one of the side entrances for noncelebrity folk. "He hasn't left yet, has he?"

"Of course not. He's in his office, like always."

I blinked. For the second time tonight, Violet's words had taken me by surprise. Never before had she acknowledged Dad's workaholic nature. At least not in my presence.

"Well," she said when I didn't respond. "I need to touch up my makeup before leaving, so I guess I'll see you there."

"Yeah, see you," I said, lost in thought as she closed my door.

Later that night, I clambered down from the back seat of a Cadillac Escalade, careful not to step on my skirt. Dad slid out after me. When he hired a private car service to chauffeur us around for the evening, I'd assumed it was so he didn't have to deal with LA traffic or worry about driving home following the after-party. Once we were on the road, however, I realized it was so he could focus his full attention on work. Any attempt I made at conversation was brushed off. As the SUV pulled away from the curb, I hurried up the steps toward the theater without waiting for him.

"Hey, kiddo," he called. "Wait for your old man!"

I didn't stop, but he caught up to me before I reached the entrance.

Oblivious to my irritation, he opened the door with a flourish and a smile. "After you."

"Wow," I said, staring up at him in mock shock. "I'm so flattered you realized I'm here."

Confusion creased Dad's forehead. "What are you talking about?"

"Dad, you spent the entire drive on the phone."

"I'm sorry, Indie." An exasperated sigh followed his apology, and I knew he didn't mean it. These were just words recited to placate me. "I had important work to get out of the way so I can give tonight my full attention."

I cut Dad a cold look. "You mean Violet."

"What?"

"You had important work to get out of the way so you could give *Violet* your full attention," I said, trying to sound neutral and informative, but I was too angry. My accusation shone through, and Dad's features hardened.

"I don't know what's gotten into you," he whispered so the security guard at the door couldn't hear us, "but I don't want your bad attitude ruining tonight for your sister, is that clear?"

His words pressed heavily on my heart, and the sudden urge to laugh bubbled up my throat. It was the wrong reaction given the situation, but I felt like I'd lost control of my emotions. "Five minutes," I said, swallowing back my bizarre, inappropriate laughter. "You couldn't spare five minutes to talk with me."

"Indigo," he said, frowning down at me. "We have all evening together."

But between the actual screening and rubbing elbows with Hollywood's elite, I knew he'd be too busy for me. Like he always was. "Whatever, Dad," I said, throat tight, and I walked away before the stinging in my eyes could turn into tears.

He called after me, but I didn't turn around to answer him. I made my way up a set of stairs covered in tacky movie theater carpet and emerged into one of New Orleans's historic cities of the dead, a hat tip to the show's setting. An ironwork gate guarded the entrance of the lobby, decorative and rusty with age. Sun-bleached tombs, ornate mausoleums, and stone statues lined the edges of the room, while votive candles flickered from atop cocktail tables.

At least fifty people were milling around the cemetery. I knew a lot of them from their involvement with *IN*, but I wasn't in the mood to socialize. Instead, I took advantage of the free snack bar, grabbing a soda and box of Dots before finding a secluded table to hole up at. The next half hour was spent avoiding humans and waiting for Xander to arrive. I was subtly trying to pick gumdrop from my teeth when a sharp voice sounded behind me.

"Indie, there you are."

Somehow, despite choosing a table with a direct view of guests arriving off the red carpet, I'd missed Xander's entrance, and he'd managed to sneak up on me. I let out an involuntary breath at the sight of him—elegant, black tux; shaggy hair slicked back to magazine perfection; green eyes glinting from behind a pair of brow-line glasses. He looked like a cross between James Bond and Q, dashing and nerdy at the same time. A sudden urge to throw myself at him swept through me. Then finally, I registered the twisted expression on his face, and it iced the desire stirring in my stomach.

"Ah, hi." I glanced around for the rest of the Heartbreakers but didn't see them anywhere. "Everything okay?"

Xander's eyes fluttered closed, and he slowly drew in his breath. "Sorry," he said, the edge in his voice softening. "I didn't mean to sound so harsh."

"Okay?" I replied, still unsure what was going on. "Did something happen?"

At first, I thought Xander would paste on a smile and pretend everything was fine, but then he shook his head. "I know tonight is about your sister." His tone was low with a hint of desperation. "But do you maybe want to get out of here?"

Still hurt from the conversation with my dad, I snatched up my clutch and took his hand. "There's nothing I'd like to do more."

☆ ♭ ♪

Outside the theater, Xander extracted his phone from the breast pocket of his jacket and shot off a text. Countless questions danced on the tip of my tongue, but I bit down on them with every ounce of patience I could muster.

"So," I said, searching for a safe subject. Until he was ready to open up, small talk would have to suffice. "How was the rest of your weekend?"

On Saturday, after Xander's friends rejoined us and finished their food, we attended the concert Stella wanted to see. The Sensible Grenade turned out to be a hardcore punk band consisting of three grouchy-looking dudes covered in piercings. There was lots of angry screaming, stomping around the stage, and raging against the establishment. The music wasn't my cup of tea, but watching Stella enjoy herself was entertainment enough. She jumped up and down, head-banged along with the lead singer, and shouted all the lyrics at the top of her lungs.

To each her own, I guessed.

When the show finally ended, I was ready to drop from exhaustion. Oliver had passes for everyone to meet the band backstage, but it had been a long day, and I decided to bow out. After I gave the guys instructions on how to remove their prosthetics and thanked them for their help, Xander walked me to my car.

"Drive safe," he'd told me as I unlocked my door. "If you get sleepy, call me. We can talk until you make it home."

"Don't worry. There's no way I'm going to fall asleep. This ringing will keep me awake the entire way," I said, stuffing a finger in my ear and trying to wiggle away the pain. "But thanks for the offer."

He nodded. "See you on Tuesday?"

"Yup." I slid behind the wheel, keys jingling in my hand. "But you have to promise to sit with me during the premiere so we can laugh at all the corny lines together."

"Even if I'm in the scene?"

I grinned. "Especially then."

Now, I cast a sideways glance at Xander. His hands were jammed into his front pockets, and as I watched, he tipped his head back to stare up at the sky.

"Eh," he said, shrugging in response to my question. "It was boring. We had a never-ending meeting on Sunday to finalize some tour details."

"I'm sorry," I told him. "That sucks." My Sunday hadn't been much better. I'd spent the entire day catching up on a week's worth of homework I'd blown off in order to finish my portfolio.

Xander didn't respond. His gaze was fixed on the nearby intersection. I was about to ask what he was waiting for when a sleek car turned the corner and slowed to a stop in front of us. As a valet hopped out, Xander stepped off the curb and rounded the hood. He said something to the man I couldn't hear, who nodded in response and handed him the keys. Only after slipping into the driver's seat did Xander remember I was still standing on the sidewalk. He rolled down the window and leaned over to look at me, one hand already on the wheel. "You coming?"

Not needing to be asked twice, I yanked on the handle and climbed inside. "Where are we going?"

He paused for a brief moment of consideration. "Any intention of returning to the premiere?"

I shook my head and buckled my seat belt. "Not if you don't want to."

"Okay then, I'll take you home," he replied, putting the car into drive.

Home? My heart shrank slightly. I'd been under the impression we were going to hang out together. "Oh, all right."

My disappointment must have been plain, because Xander glanced at me, eyebrows raised. "I thought we could finish our movie marathon. Is that all right?"

"*Oh*," I said again, this time in a completely different tone. "Yeah, sounds good."

Xander nodded—it was the crisp sort of nod that punctuated a decision made—and reached over to fiddle with the radio, eventually settling on a station that featured country classics. Neither of us spoke as he wove into traffic. Conversation usually flowed naturally between us, so the gathering silence felt loud and abrasive. Every part of me was itching to say something, but Xander was clearly lost in his thoughts, so I clasped my hands in my lap and stared out the window.

The farther we drove, the more Xander relaxed. Whether it was the music or the act of driving itself, every mile he put behind us seemed to draw the tension from his body. By the time we reached Violet's house, he appeared completely at ease. I, on the other hand, was on the verge of chewing through the inside of my cheek. Xander had yet to explain our hasty exit, and as we climbed from the car, I began to wonder if I'd need to resort to questioning him after all.

The sound of waves crashing against the shore filled an otherwise quiet night as we made our way up the front walk. After withdrawing a set of house keys from my clutch, I unlocked the door.

"Can I ask you something?" Xander said as we stepped inside. They were the first words he'd spoken to me since we'd left the theater.

"Sure, what's up?"

"I swear I wasn't trying to eavesdrop or anything, but, um—while I was looking for the bathroom Saturday, I overheard part of your conversation with Violet. She mentioned something about you applying to Juilliard?"

My lips parted in surprise. For a moment, all I could do was blink at him.

"Sorry, never mind." Ducking his head, Xander prodded an invisible spot on the ground with his toe. "I shouldn't have pried."

"No, it's fine. You caught me off guard, that's all. Come on. Let me show you something." I quickly yanked off my boots and led Xander upstairs. "My family hasn't always lived in Laguna Beach. I actually grew up in San Bernardino, but then Violet's career took off. She always wanted to live by the ocean, so when I was sixteen, my parents sold our house, and my sister bought this property," I explained, stopping in front of a door at the end of the hall. "I wasn't happy about leaving, so during the renovation, Violet designed a place for me to practice. I think she was trying to make up for us moving."

"Practice?"

I gestured for him to go first. "See for yourself."

Xander pushed open the door. It took him a moment to realize what he was looking at, but once he did, his entire face lit up. I bit down on my smile as he turned in a slow circle, taking everything in. The room was long, nearly the length of the house, with a herringbone hardwood floor. A row of wide windows bathed the entire space in moonlight. In one corner, two leather sofas were arranged around a glass coffee table, and hanging on the far wall was a collection of Gibsons. But the centerpiece of the room was a grand piano, positioned so whoever was playing had a perfect view of the Pacific. Sometimes, I'd throw open the windows and play until my skin soaked up the salty scent of the ocean.

Finally, his eyes widened in understanding. "You're a musician?"

Nodding, I flipped on the lights.

"What do you play?" he asked, his gaze eagerly cutting to the guitars.

"A little bit of that," I said, gesturing at the piano, "but mainly violin."

"Why didn't you tell me?" There was no accusation in his voice, only curiosity.

I raised my shoulder in a half shrug. "It never came up." Also, I couldn't imagine a conversation where I didn't come off sounding like a wannabe. *Hey, Mr. Multi-Platinum-Selling Rock Star, guess what? I'm a violinist. Let's bond over our love of music.*

"How long have you played for?"

"Thirteen years," I said, making my way over to the sofas and taking a seat.

Xander trailed slowly behind me, distracted by my dad's vinyl collection, which was organized by genre in a large display cabinet. He ran his fingers over the colorful jackets, pausing now and then to extract a record and study the cover art.

When he finished his examination, he plopped down beside me. "Is this why you told Melody that makeup is just a hobby? Because you want a career in music?"

"Uh-oh," I said, gently nudging him with my elbow. "This is starting to sound like another one of your interrogations."

The crooked grin he frequently wore made an appearance, and damn it—why did he look so cute when he was embarrassed? "Sorry, it's just I have a habit of asking lots of questions when I'm excited about something."

"Don't apologize. I was just teasing," I told him. "And the answer is yes. I've dreamed of being a concert violinist since I was a kid."

Xander opened his mouth, presumably to ask something else, then hesitated, his sheepish smile stretching even further.

"Yes?" I prompted.

"Well, how come? A concert violinist seems oddly specific."

"Because of my mom. She used to be a concert violinist, but then she got pregnant with Violet and decided to settle down instead." My gaze subconsciously drifted to the spot on the wall where I'd convinced Mom to hang her old *Los Angeles Times* article. Beside it, I'd framed a handful of black-and-white photographs taken during one of her performances.

Settled back against the cushions, Xander gave the room another sweep, his eyes lingering again on the Gibsons. "I take it you look up to her?"

"I idolized her. Violet had zero interest in taking lessons, but I was obsessed. My mom gave me my first violin when I was six and started teaching me how to play. The rest is history."

Xander peeled his gaze from the instruments and looked at me. "Meaning what?"

"Remember telling me you had to try a few sports before you found archery? It wasn't like that for me. I was good from the start. Like scary good," I said. "Do you know who Tracy Hoop is?"

He nodded. "Yeah, the band's been on *Talks with Tracy* before."

I pointed at the bookshelf where a picture of me with the talk show queen stood. "Me too. She did a segment on prodigy musicians when I was nine. I got to perform for the audience and everything."

"Seriously?" Xander jumped to his feet, walked over to the picture, and picked it up. He smiled as he examined it. "Wow, this is so cool."

"Yeah, I really rocked those pigtails, didn't I?"

"You were cute," he said, putting the frame back in place.

"Were cute? Ouch."

The smile slid off his face. "I didn't mean—"

"Xander, relax," I said, trying not to laugh at his panicked expression. "I'm giving you a hard time."

"Right, of course. Um—back to your story."

"Well, when I was ten, I was accepted at Worthwind Music. It's the world's leading musical preparatory school, and most kids who study there go on to be famous classical musicians or composers. The thing about Worthwind though is that it's kind of like training for the Olympics; you live and breathe music, and my dad didn't want that for me. He insisted I have a normal childhood—go to public school, play an intramural sport, get a part-time job, that sort of thing. My mom, on the other hand, who gave up her career to raise us, thought he was holding me back."

"What happened?"

"They compromised. Mom agreed to forgo Worthwind as long as I kept up with my private lessons and practiced every day. I've been planning on Juilliard ever since."

"So there was never anything else you wanted to do?" Xander asked. "Nothing besides music?"

I shook my head. "Never."

"Wow." He sounded impressed. Then, like a magnet to

metal, his gaze flickered back to the Gibsons.

"You know, those guitars aren't just for decoration," I told him. "You can try one out if you'd like."

"Really?" Xander shot across the room before I could blink. When he didn't go for the vintage Les Paul, I cocked my head in surprise. He pulled down a Hummingbird instead.

"What about you?" I asked as he tested out the guitar with a few soft strums. "What made you want to play?"

"Let's see: I've worn glasses since the age of four, I was raised on *Star Trek* and *Doctor Who*, my sport of choice is archery, and I'm the opposite of athletic," he explained, reclaiming his spot on the sofa. "Basically, I'm the definition of a geek. I wanted to learn because it's cool, and as I've so amply demonstrated, I need major help in that department." Xander said this all very matter-of-factly, as if he couldn't care less, but his clenched jaw said otherwise.

He returned his attention to the instrument in his hands. I watched as he picked his way through an unfamiliar riff with ease, and as his skilled fingers danced over the strings, I couldn't argue with his logic. Maybe he'd gone through an awkward stage in his early teenage years, but there was nothing geeky about Xander now.

What was it about a guy playing guitar that was so sexy?

Forcing myself to look away, I cleared my throat. "I'm

pretty sure being in a world-famous band makes you certified next-level cool."

"You think so?" The amused tone of his voice made me think there was a smirk on his face.

I peeked over at him. Yup, definitely smirking.

Not wanting him to see the color in my cheeks, I glanced down at my hands. "Definitely."

Xander gave a satisfied hum in response, and whatever song he was playing transitioned into something new, another tune I didn't recognize. As I waited for my blush to fade, I listened to the gentle melody and tried to work out the best way to ask him about why we'd ditched the premiere.

"So, ah...are you okay?" Not exactly the subtle lead-in I'd been searching for, but if I let this go, I had a hunch Xander wouldn't give me any sort of explanation.

He flinched but quickly recovered with a car salesman smile. "Why wouldn't I be?" He sounded too cheery, and I could tell from the way his smile tightened that he realized this as well.

This again, really?

"Because," I said, eyeing him skeptically, "you hightailed it out of the theater like the building was on fire. What happened?"

A range of emotions flickered through his eyes, but they passed too quickly for me to make heads or tails of what he was feeling. "It's nothing. I'm fine."

"You know you're a terrible liar, right?"

Xander sighed and rubbed the back of his neck. "Yeah, I know. I never got away with anything as a kid. My mom could spot a lie from a mile away. I thought it was some kind of parental superpower until JJ admitted I have the world's worst poker face. Of course, that was after he spent our childhood cleaning me out at Texas Hold'em."

"Listen, if you want me to drop the subject, I will. Just say the word," I replied. "With that being said, something is clearly on your mind, and in my experience, I always feel better after getting whatever is bothering me off my chest."

"It's stupid."

"Not to me it isn't."

Another heavy sigh. "There were a bunch of entertainment correspondents on the red carpet—*E! News*, *Access Hollywood*, *Extra*, a few others. They wanted to know about our experience working on *Immortal Nights*, our upcoming tour, that sort of thing," he said, and I had a sinking feeling about where this was going. "But when I say *our*, I don't mean the four of us." He left his explanation at that, but it was enough for me to understand.

A hard knot formed in the pit of my stomach. "I know we're not in the same situation, but I understand what it feels like to be overshadowed by someone. It's like, no matter what you do, you'll never compare." I could discover a cure for cancer or become the first female president of the United States, but regardless of what I did, Violet would always be the sun in my father's universe, while I was merely a distant star, millions of light-years away.

Xander's laugh was humorless. "Have I really been that transparent?"

No, he hadn't, but I was too embarrassed to admit the truth: I noticed what his friends didn't because the more time we spent together, the more aware of Xander I became. Like the way one side of his mouth raised a fraction higher than the other when he smiled, how he fiddled with his glasses when he was nervous, or the almost red gleam in his hair when he stood under direct light.

"I hate sounding ungrateful," he said, hanging his head.

"For what?"

"Everything. My career, our success. I've been blessed with so much, but lately all I can think about is how I'm the guy at the back of the band nobody cares about."

"What?" I exclaimed. "Xander, how can you say that!"

"Because the others…they have such big personalities," he said. "Take Oliver, for example. He's effortlessly charming, not to mention he writes all our music. JJ is the fearless, over-the-top comedian who knows exactly how to get a crowd going. And Alec has the whole mysterious, brooding thing going for him as well as an entire freaking record label. Compared to them, I'm the boring, forgettable fringe member. They don't need me."

The dejection in his voice took hold of my heartstrings and gave them a painful tug. Could he really not see how amazing he was? Yes, his bandmates had distinct personalities, but that was exactly what made the Heartbreakers so successful—all four guys were different and unique in their own way. Xander was cheerful and friendly, the type of person who could put anyone at ease. He made you forget his fame, and suddenly you felt like you were catching up with an old friend, not chatting with a chart-topping artist. And then there was his caring nature. The amount of kindness he'd shown me in the short time we'd known each other was unparalleled, from introducing me to Melody to helping with my portfolio.

Was he as smooth as Oliver? No.

As in your face as JJ? Definitely not.

But if being happy and kind was synonymous with being boring, then we needed more boring people in the world.

I wanted to tell Xander all this and more, but would he believe me? How could I show him he was wrong about himself in a way he'd understand? A mortifying idea came to mind, one I instantly rejected, but when another thirty seconds passed and I hadn't come up with something else, I realized it was my best option.

In spite of an overwhelming urge to flee, I cleared my throat. "You'll find more joy in being yourself than someone else's rip-off," I said. The responding look Xander shot me made my face heat up, and I hadn't even gotten to the embarrassing part yet.

"Sounds like a cheesy quote from one of those inspirational saying posters you see in classrooms," he replied. "Who said it?"

Oh God, here we go. "You did, kind of."

Xander's forehead scrunched up. "What are you talking about?"

"Okay, remember at Comic Con when you told me there were fan fictions written about you?"

Three seconds of what felt like never-ending silence ticked by. Xander's grip on the guitar loosened, and he set it down as if preparing to hear bad news.

"Yes?" The hesitation packed into that one syllable almost made me clamp my mouth shut, but then I remembered the hurt flashing across his face at the theater. He needed to hear this, regardless of how uncomfortable confessing it made me feel.

"I was curious, so…I maybe started reading one? I swear it's not one of those smutty stories. It's dystopian, has all the basic tropes—government oppression, loss of individualism, revolution. There's lots of freedom fighting and all around badassery on your part." I reached for the familiar comfort of my pendant, forgetting that I'd replaced it with a choker for the premiere.

"Why are you telling me this?" he asked, the tips of his ears turning a bright red.

"Two reasons. First, I think you should take some advice from your fictional self: being more like your bandmates won't make you happy. And second—"

"I never said I wanted to be more like them."

His defensive tone took me by surprise, and I stopped to analyze our exchange. Okay, those exact words hadn't come out of his mouth, but that didn't mean he hadn't implied them.

"You're right. I apologize," I told him, laying a hand over my heart. "To me, it sounded like you thought you'd be happier in one of their positions."

A scowl darkened his face. "Well, that's not what I meant."

Instead of responding, I raised my brows at him and waited for clarification. We stared at each other for a single strained moment, but in the end, he heaved a sigh.

"Do I get jealous? Sure. Would I change who I am so more people like me? Hell no. I'm happy with me." He paused, the blaze in his eyes dulling, and in a voice so quiet I almost didn't hear, he added, "I just wish everyone else was too."

Emotion tightened around my lungs, and I fought the

urge to reach out and touch his arm in comfort. "Xander, your fans love you, and I can prove it." On my phone, I opened FanficFiles and showed him *Rhythm of Your Heart.* "*This* is the main reason why I admitted to reading a story about you. Look at the read count. This isn't some trending fic. It's one of the most read books on the entire website. Your fans are wild about it, and it's more popular than anything written about Oliver, JJ, or Alec."

He glanced at the screen, his gaze flickering over the story description. When he finished reading, his lips fluttered, hinting at a smile. "I'm the mysterious leader of a rebel group? That doesn't sound like me at all."

"You'd be surprised," I told him, my own lips curving up in relief. "Minus a ragged scar on your back and a talent for martial arts, I think the author has you down to a T. Of course, maybe you really are a secret ninja with a nasty battle wound?"

"Oh yeah, and I teach parkour classes on Tuesdays and Thursdays. You should come sometime so I can dazzle you with my nonexistent abilities."

"How about archery lessons instead?" I said this jokingly, my attempt at keeping the mood light, but Xander took the question as one of paramount importance. His entire demeanor changed, and he leaned forward, his eyes glowing with excitement.

"Do you really want to learn?" he asked. "Because I'm more than willing to teach you."

"I, um—I don't think I'd be any good," I spluttered, startled by his sudden enthusiasm. Or maybe it was his proximity that was overwhelming? We were so close now I could count the freckles splashed across his face. "But yeah, I'd like that."

My attempt to cheer Xander up finally worked, and a smile rearranged his expression. It was the best kind of smile, full-blown and crooked. "It's a date then."

His statement wreaked havoc on my pulse. I knew he didn't mean anything by the word *date*—this would be a social engagement, not a romantic one—but my poor heart was too stupid to know any better and wouldn't stop racing.

"Cool" was all I could manage in response.

Really, Indie? Cool?

I dipped my head, letting my hair form a curtain between us, and stared down at my hands. The black polish I'd applied this morning was already starting to chip, and there was an angry red sore on my thumb where I'd ripped away a hangnail.

"Hey," he said gently.

"Yeah?"

"Thanks for the pep talk. I really needed it."

"At least something good came out of my utter humiliation," I muttered.

"Humiliation? What are you talking about?"

I jerked my head up to look at him. Was he being polite, or did he really not realize how stalker-level creepy I felt after confessing I'd read fan fiction about him? My gaze swept over his face, but I didn't detect a single ounce of dishonesty. He seemed genuinely confused.

"I'm embarrassed because of the story," I clarified, but the deep furrow in his brow refused to lessen. "The fanfic, *Rhythm of Your Heart?*"

"Why? It's not like you wrote it." As soon as the words left his mouth, his posture went rigid, like someone had jammed a metal rod down his spine. "Unless…you did?"

"God, no!" My nose wrinkled at the thought. I sucked at writing. Besides, if JonesFervor15 really was my secret online persona, I'd never have the guts to share any of this with him. "Not that there's anything wrong with writing fan fiction. I think it's awesome your fans love you so much. How many people can say they inspire thousands of others to be creative?"

"I guess that's cool and all," he said, shoulders slumping, "but it's things like this that make me feel ungrateful and guilty in the first place."

Great, we were back to this again? "Why?"

"Because there's a story written about me that has millions of reads, and here I am complaining about not being the most popular guy in the band? How self-absorbed does that make me?"

I almost laughed. "Xander, it makes you completely normal. Everyone has narcissistic moments. Stop beating yourself up over a fleeting feeling that we all experience at least once in our lives."

"But what if it's not fleeting?" he responded. "What if it's turning me into someone I'm not? Nobody has pinpointed the problem quite like you have, but my friends aren't blind. They sense something is off."

All of a sudden, I was back at Zap Zone hearing JJ's voice: *I don't know what's been bothering you lately, but whatever it is has you on edge...*

"Have you tried telling them you're upset?" I asked.

He crossed his arms. "There's no way I'm talking to the guys about this. Either they won't understand, or they'll give me so much shit, my ears will bleed. Besides, what am I supposed to say? 'Hey, guys, can you stop being yourselves so people will notice me?'" He scoffed, dismissing the notion with the wave of his hand. "They shouldn't have to act any differently to make me feel better. That's not fair."

"All right, then maybe *you* need to do something about it. Find a way to prove to yourself that you're not the 'forgettable fringe member,'" I said, air quoting his earlier phrase.

"Like what?"

"To be honest, I'm not sure." I pulled my hair over my shoulder and twisted it into a knot as I considered Xander's dilemma. I racked my brain for a solid minute before an idea came to me. What was it Sofia had said? When one of her designs wasn't working, she found the best way to get past her block was by focusing on something completely different. Xander's problem was vastly different from Sofia's, but that didn't mean her technique couldn't be applied to his situation. To get out of his funk, maybe all Xander needed to do was to focus on something that excited him. "Have you ever tried writing your own music?"

He shrugged. "A few songs here and there, but nothing for the band."

"Country, right?" I asked, and he nodded. "Well, maybe you should release one."

"I don't know, Indie," he said, wringing his hands together. "If I put out a single, people will get the wrong idea. A year ago, there was this major rumor that the band was breaking up. It caused a lot of tension. The last thing I want is for our fans to think I'm quitting and cause drama again."

"But if you have no intention of leaving, then who cares? Why not explain the song as a side project you're passionate about. This could be your chance to show the world what you have to offer as an individual."

His brows knit together in indecision. "I suppose, but—"

Before he could talk himself out of what I thought was a brilliant idea, I interrupted. "I understand how terrifying it can be to take a chance, but you just need to ask yourself if the happiness you stand to gain is worth the risk." As I said this, a new thought popped into my head. "Besides," I added, "we both know someone who could help you."

"Who?" he asked.

I made a face at him. "You're joking, right? One of your best friends runs his own label."

"Alec?"

"No, Santa Claus." I shot him a look. "Yes, Alec."

"Oh." He rubbed his brow with his index finger as if I'd presented him with some challenging riddle he needed to puzzle out.

"If there's one person who has the means and would be willing to help you, it's Alec. Plus, if you put out a single with his label, wouldn't your fans be less worried?"

Xander stared at me as he contemplated my words, and I stared back, transfixed by his soft green gaze. He swallowed, his Adam's apple bobbing in his throat, and my eyes unconsciously lowered to his lips.

"Yeah, I guess you're right."

"I'd love to hear you say that again," I said, smirking up at him, "but this time in more detail."

His mouth twitched in amusement. "If I'm unhappy, I

need to do something about it. Maybe writing a new song will be cathartic for me."

"So you'll ask Alec for help?"

Xander nodded.

"Good, then I just have one question for you."

"What's that?" he asked.

I took a deep breath. "What are your plans for Halloween?"

CHAPTER 12

I spotted Xander as soon as I pulled into a parking lot marked by familiar golden arches. He was leaning against the same Range Rover he'd driven to Soul Harvest, his nose buried in his phone, and my lips curled into a smile at the sight of his costume. He wore a moss-green jerkin with a matching cloak, which was fastened at the neck by a silver brooch in the shape of a leaf. His forearms were covered by black bracers, and on his feet were decorative leather boots. The best part, however, was the long platinum wig. Or the pointed ears. It was hard to choose.

"Oh. My. God," I said, stepping out of my car. "You *didn't*!"

Xander looked up at the sound of my voice and grinned. "I did. You're the one who said you pictured me as Legolas, so I figured, who am I to deny you that particular fantasy?" He pushed away from the SUV and, holding out his hands, turned in a slow circle. "What do you think?"

That you're a dork. A freaking adorable dork.

"You look like you belong on a movie set," I said, moving forward to get a better look. Up close, I could see the intricate vine-like pattern stitched into the garment. The costume was clearly custom-made, not some mass-produced piece of crap anyone could buy off Amazon. "I love it."

When I invited Xander to the Halloween party, I told him he wasn't required to dress up because I didn't want to give him a reason not to come. Most people did, but as long as he was there, I'd be happy. Xander, however, insisted he would find a costume. With that being said, I never expected him to go all out. Not like this. That he had put so much effort in made my chest feel warm and light.

"I'm glad you approve." His mouth quirked as he scanned my outfit. "So…what exactly are you supposed to be?"

I laughed. Besides the tailcoat Sofia had altered for me, I was wearing black leather shorts, knee-high boots, and a pair of chemistry goggles on my head. Around my wrist hung a bracelet made of wine corks and hex nuts. I'd also used a temporary dye to color my hair the same deep blue as my jacket and glitter gel to add some sparkle to my roots. "A character from *Lady Phoenix* called Kelina Stardust. She's a time-traveling alien who has zero understanding of Earth fashion."

"Wow," he said, looking me up and down again. "I need to start reading pronto."

"Why's that?"

He blushed but said, "Because this Kelina character is kinda hot."

Holy. Freaking. Hell. Was Xander hitting on me?

Thank the Lord for the thick layer of foundation I was wearing, because my cheeks went up in flames. "Do you really think this looks okay?" I asked, tugging at the tailcoat, "or are you just being nice? Because I ran into Violet before I left, and she told me I look silly."

"It's Halloween. You're allowed to look silly," Xander said, "but I don't think you do. Quirky, sure, but in an intriguing, let's-take-a-ride-in-your-spaceship kind of way."

"Was that a sexual innuendo involving aliens?"

"Maybe," he said with a grin, and before I could come up with a clever reply, he jabbed a thumb over his shoulder. "Come on. There's something I want to show you." He retrieved a long, flat case from the back of his car and steered me in the direction of the sidewalk.

"What's in there?" I asked, trying to get a better look at the plastic box as I fell into step beside him.

"You'll find out soon enough."

"Ugh, you suck."

Tuesday night when I asked Xander to come to the bonfire with me, he eagerly agreed. His only caveat? We meet up before the party. Much to my frustration, he wouldn't tell me why. All he said was that he had a surprise for me, and despite my endless pestering, he remained tight-lipped. I hadn't even managed to pry a hint from him. The anticipation had been driving me up the wall ever since. When he'd texted me an address this morning, the first thing I'd done was look it up on Google Maps, only to discover our rendezvous point was a McDonald's. And I highly doubted my surprise was a Happy Meal dinner date. Xander probably chose this meeting spot to throw me off whatever his surprise was.

Where in the world were we going?

I received my answer five minutes later. After walking a few blocks, we crossed the street to where a building that looked like a luxury log cabin loomed over us. The architecture felt out of place in southern California until I read the sign on the wall and everything finally made sense: STONE CREEK ARCHERY RANGE.

Xander stopped underneath the entrance overhang, which was held up by two massive river rock pillars, and cleared his throat. "The other night, you mentioned you were interested in learning archery," he said, rubbing the back of his neck. "I leave Monday morning, so I figured today was my only opportunity to squeeze in a lesson. You game?"

"Absolutely," I replied, mainly because Xander looked unsure of himself, like he was suddenly second-guessing his decision to bring me here. What he didn't know was that my insides had instantly twisted up at his question. I was willing to bet that archery wasn't my sport, and the last thing I wanted to do was make a fool of myself in front of him, but I couldn't tell him no. Not when I remembered how nervous I'd been to ask him to the party. What if he was feeling the exact same way?

"Cool." Xander's relief was evident in his smile. "Follow me."

The inside of the archery range looked like a sporting goods store, but Xander blew by the rows of equipment and led me to a back counter where a lady in her midforties was reading a paperback. She glanced up at the sound of our approach.

"Hey, Carol," Xander called.

She squinted at him—he probably looked unfamiliar in a wig and without his glasses—before breaking out into a grin. "Xander, it's so good to see you," she exclaimed, marking her page and closing the book. "It's been ages since you've stopped in. I was starting to think you'd forgotten about me."

"Don't be ridiculous," he told her. "I could never forget about you."

"Oh, stop." She waved him off. "You're always such a sweetheart. You here to get some practice time in before your next big tour?"

"Actually, I'm teaching today. Carol, this is Indie. Indie, Carol. She's the owner of Stone Creek. I've been a member here ever since I moved to LA."

"Teaching, huh?" She turned to me and put her hands on her hips. "So, Indie, have you ever shot a bow before?"

I shook my head. "No, never."

"Then you're in for a treat."

Carol wasted no time getting started. First, she had me do an eye dominance test to see which one I naturally aimed with, because apparently that determined whether I needed a right-handed or left-handed bow. Next, she tested my draw length, a number she used to figure out my bow size. Finally, she measured my arrow size before giving me arm guards and a finger tab to protect my skin from the bowstring.

After Xander paid for my rental equipment, Carol allowed us through the door next to the counter, which led to an indoor range. Black lines painted on the floor created ten shooting lanes, each one ending in a target. The space reminded me a bit of a bowling alley but without ball returns and the sound of crashing pins. Xander set his case down on the table near the closest lane and motioned for me to do the same.

"So where do we start?" I asked, bouncing on my toes. Despite my earlier hesitation, I was itching to draw the string back and let an arrow fly. Something about holding the bow made me feel badass. I doubted I'd even hit the target, but I was no longer afraid of embarrassing myself. Had I been teaching Xander how to play violin, I'd never think less of him for not being perfect at the onset. I was confident he wouldn't judge me either.

"Well," Xander said and scratched his head. "I've never actually taught anyone before, so I'm not sure."

"Maybe with a demonstration?"

"Good idea." Xander unlocked the plastic case on the table and lifted the cover, revealing his bow. He unlatched the straps holding it in place and gently picked it up. I watched as he inspected the weapon and explained that before shooting, he always checked to make sure the string and screws were tight and that there weren't any cracks or splinters in the limbs and risers. Then he moved over to the black line that indicated the start of the lane.

"The first thing you need to think about when it comes to proper shooting technique is your stance," he said, getting into position. "You want to stand with your feet roughly shoulder distance apart. Your hips should be pointed at the target, and your shoulders should be straight over the center of your body, like so. You also want to make sure you're not leaning too far forward or backward."

Xander went on to illustrate hand placement, how to hold the bow, and coming to full draw, but his explanation was lost on me, unfamiliar terms filtering in one ear and out the other. It wasn't that I didn't want to listen, but I was too distracted by the way his body moved in confident, effortless motions. Clearly, something was wrong with me. How was it possible that someone dressed as an elf looked so hot?

A loud thump startled me from my daydream. Xander had finally released an arrow, and at the other end of the room, it was buried in the center of the target.

"Did all that make sense?" he asked with a hopeful expression.

I shook my head slightly to clear the daze. "Ah…I think so?"

"Okay, time for you to try, but just with the bow for now. I want to make sure you have the technique down before you start shooting."

With a nod, I picked up my rental and joined him at the line. I tried to copy the stance he'd demonstrated for me, putting my left foot forward and making sure my shoulders were aligned with the rest of my body. "Like this?" I asked.

"Almost." Xander pointed at my right leg. "Move that foot back a few inches. Your feet are too close together."

"Now what?"

"Draw back. Remember you don't need to have a death grip on the bow. Let your fingers relax."

I followed his instructions and pulled the string back until my index finger reached the corner of my mouth. Xander moved so he was standing directly behind me, and my pulse jumped when his hand brushed against my hip before reaching up and adjusting my arm.

"Elbow up." He spoke softly in my ear. "You want it parallel with the ground."

The feel of his body against mine made it hard to focus. I sucked in a deep breath and stared at the bull's-eye with all the concentration I could muster, attempting to appear unaffected by his presence.

"Perfect," he whispered, and the word sent shivers down my spine. "I think you're ready for an arrow."

☆ ♭ ♫

"I think," I said, throwing open Stone Creek's front doors and striding out into the night, "that I've found my true calling."

It was a little over an hour later, and we'd just returned my rental equipment to Carol and said our goodbyes. A crisp breeze urged us toward the sidewalk, mussing Xander's wig in the process. He shoved the platinum hair away from his eyes with a grunt of irritation before cutting me a look. "You're a prodigy violinist and kick-ass makeup artist," he said as we headed for our cars. "I highly doubt you were born to be a professional archer."

"Whatever. You're just jealous of my mad skills," I replied. In reality, I wasn't a very good shot, but by the end of our lesson, I was able to hit the target more times than not. Once, I'd even struck the outer ring of the bull's-eye.

Xander snorted. "Sure, that's definitely it."

We came to a stop at a busy intersection, and as we waited for the light to change, I glanced over at him. "Hey," I said, in a tone more sincere than before. "Thanks for taking me. I had a blast."

"Yeah?" he responded, his brows popping up in question.

I nodded. "To tell you the truth, I was a bit freaked out when I realized you were taking me shooting."

"Why?"

"Because I didn't want to embarrass myself," I admitted, "but once we were on the range, I stopped caring about how bad I might be. It was a lot of fun. I get why you enjoy it so much."

The traffic signal switched from green to yellow, and a bus barreled past us in an effort to make the light. Xander watched it disappear down the street, a contemplative look in his eyes, before turning back to me. "Would you maybe want to come with me again?" he asked, his words spilling out in a rush. "It won't be anytime soon because of the tour, but I might be able to—"

I cut him off before his ramble could pick up speed. "I'd absolutely love that."

"Really?" He seemed genuinely surprised.

"Really, really," I told him as the light finally turned red. On the other side of the street, the pedestrian signal flipped from Don't Walk to Walk.

"All right, cool." Xander looked both ways before stepping out into the crosswalk. Tossing a smirk over his shoulder at me, he added, "Just so you know, you'll regret telling me that."

"Oh, is that so?"

"Yup. From now on, whenever I want to practice, I'm dragging you along with me." There was a gleam in his eyes as he said this, like he found the prospect of whisking me away thrilling. "I won't take no for an answer."

My heart thumped against my chest, but I ignored it. "We'll see about that," I said, faking a scoff, but the truth was that Xander didn't have to drag me anywhere—I'd happily go wherever he wanted to take me.

When we reached the McDonald's we'd left our cars at, I gave him Lizzie's address in case we got separated in traffic. The driveway was packed by the time we arrived at the party, so I pulled over on the side of the road and parked in the gravel, making sure to leave enough room for Xander to park behind me. As soon as I killed the engine, the steady thump of music from the party filled the silence left by the radio.

After checking my makeup in the mirror and grabbing my backpack from the passenger seat, I climbed out. Xander was already standing on the pavement, staring over at the front porch, which was lined with flickering jack-o'-lanterns. A group of football players were congregated on the steps, red Solo cups in hand, rating costumes as classmates trickled into the party. I rolled my eyes when a girl in a sexy Hermione Granger costume earned ten points for Gryffindor.

"Big turnout," Xander said, twirling his key chain around a finger.

"Yeah, Lizzie always invites the whole school," I replied, and as if to prove my point, a minivan screeched to a stop on the other side of the road, nearly hitting the curb in the process. The back doors flew open, and a group of girls dressed as characters from *The Wizard of Oz* piled out. One of them shouted a thanks to the driver, and then they made their way up the front lawn without a backward glance. I jerked my head after them. "Shall we?"

Xander nodded and adjusted the cloak around his shoulders. He was quiet as we crossed the street, and when I looked over at him, I could tell he was deep in thought about something. Just as I was about to ask him what, he spoke. "Hey, what's the name of your high school?"

"Laguna Beach. Why?"

"I'm working on crafting my cover story," he said, and there was a hint of mischief in his voice. "This is what I have so far: I'm a transfer student named Alex who grew up in

San Diego and am royally pissed at my dad for getting a new job and making me move. Also, I play cello and am thinking about joining orchestra, which is how I met you."

"Okay... Why Alex?"

"Because," he said, grinning like he'd just told a particularly clever joke, "it's what my family calls me."

"Wait." I stopped walking to gape at him. "Seriously?"

His mouth quirked at the edges, and I got the feeling he was happy this information caught me off guard. "Yeah, my full name is Alexander."

Wow, how had I not known this? Obviously, we were still getting to know each other, and there was so much about Xander that was a mystery to me, but not knowing his real name? The name the people closest to him called him? It felt wrong somehow.

"When did you start going by Xander?" I asked and started walking again.

"When we signed our first record deal with Mongo," he replied. "Management thought Alec and Alex sounded too close, so I took one for the team."

My head spun, almost as if it were trying to recalibrate after receiving this new, unexpected detail about Xander. "And that didn't bother you?"

He shrugged, skirting around a cluster of fake headstones stuck in the grass. "Not really. It was actually harder for

Oliver and JJ to get used to since we've known each other for so long. For the first year or so, they kept slipping up, and now there's this hilarious fan theory that there's an invisible fifth member of the band called Alex."

"It's funny, my sister had a similar experience."

"There's a fan theory about an invisible *Immortal Nights* cast member?"

I made a face at him but otherwise ignored his smart-ass comment. "No, the name thing," I clarified. "The show's producers thought our last name was too hard to pronounce, so Violet took James as her stage name."

At this, Xander jerked his head back. "I didn't realize that. What *is* your last name?"

"Mitchell-Jamiolkowski," I said, happy I'd managed to surprise him as well.

We'd reached the front porch, but instead of heading up, Xander stopped at the base of the steps and looked at me, the corners of his eyes crinkling in amusement. "Yeah, that's definitely a mouthful. Kind of sounds like Mike Wazowski. You know, the green monster from—"

"Hey, Xander?" I said, my tone sickly sweet.

"Yeah?"

"If you plan on living to the ripe old age of ninety-five, you shouldn't finish that sentence." I wasn't actually mad at him, but it was fun pretending to be. He must have realized this though, because he let out a soft laugh. "Also," I added, not giving him the chance to respond, "I hope you realize that cover story or not, someone is totally going to recognize you."

"You're probably right," he said with another shrug, "but while it lasts, I'm going to enjoy every second of posing as Alex No Last Name, the cello-playing senior."

"Hey, Indie," one of the football players called.

Glancing up, I spotted Jacob Hernandez, Sofia's cousin. He grinned, tipping a gold-trimmed bicorne hat at me, and I broke out into a smile when I realized the tallest guy at our school was dressed as Napoleon Bonaparte.

"Hi, Jake," I replied as Xander and I scaled the stairs. "My ride or die here yet?"

"Yeah, she came with me and Ronnie. They headed straight for the kitchen as soon as we got here. Said something about drinking their weight in margaritas."

"Whose brilliant idea was that?" I asked, because Sofia was terrible at holding her liquor. Two beers was more than enough to knock her on her petite ass.

He scowled to himself. "My sister's. We played rock paper scissors to see who's DD tonight. I lost, so she's celebrating."

"Tough break," I said with a laugh as I pushed open the front door. "Have fun conquering Europe and such."

Inside, the house was crammed wall-to-wall with people. I led Xander toward the kitchen, weaving my way through the crowd as we went. We found Sofia and her other cousin, Jake's sister Veronica, exactly where he said they'd be, sitting at barstools along the massive granite-top peninsula. When Sofia spotted me, her face lit up, and she half jumped, half stumbled down from her seat.

"Indie!" she exclaimed, sloshing drink down the front of her lace-up bodice. "You made it!"

I clamped my lips together as I tried not to laugh. *Looks like someone is having a good time.*

"You know I'd never miss a costume party," I replied as she pulled me into a slightly soggy hug. Sofia released me after a few seconds and turned to Xander, but I cut in before she could ruin his cover. "Sofia, Ronnie, this is my friend Alex. He just moved here from San Diego."

Sofia must not have been as drunk as I thought, because she wiggled her eyebrows at him and played along. "Nice to meet you, Alex. How are you liking Laguna Beach so far?"

"Oh, you know." He made an airy gesture. "It sucked switching schools my senior year, but I met a few people who've made the move worth it." Xander's gaze flickered to me, and the look in his eyes was so intense, I had to glance away to hide the color blooming on my cheeks.

Of course, Sofia missed none of this. She glanced between the two of us and grinned like a proud parent. "That's *so* good to hear. Nothing like finding your people, am I right?"

Her response was filled with so much enthusiasm, I was surprised she didn't pull confetti out of her pockets and shower us in it. "By the way, can I get you a drink? Lizzie has everything—beer, wine, hard seltzer. If you want something more festive, there's an actual bartender making Halloween-themed cocktails in the other room."

"Ah, how about a water? I have to drive tonight."

"Sure thing." She turned to me. "Indie?"

"I'll have the same," I told her.

"All right, two waters coming up."

Sofia flitted over to the fridge, saying hi to friends as she went. While she was gone, Ronnie took the time to study Xander, her brows dipping down in scrutiny.

"Have we met before?" she asked. "There's something about you that's so familiar."

Uh-oh. That didn't take long.

Xander leaned back against the counter in a slow, unbothered way and crossed his arms. "Don't think so," he answered. "I started at your school less than two weeks ago. Maybe you've seen me in the halls?"

"No, that's not it." She pursed her lips in thought. "Were you the guy in that Icy Quest commercial?"

The urge to burst out laughing was strong, but I managed to keep a straight face. "The stuff for athlete's foot?"

"I can happily confirm that *wasn't* me," Xander said with

a bemused smile. "I'm not much of an actor. Although I thought my performance as a sugarplum in my kindergarten production of *'Twas the Night Before Christmas* was pretty stellar."

Ronnie's face fell. "Oh."

"Here you go," Sofia said, returning with four waters. She handed a bottle to each of us and kept one for herself. "Figured we could all use some hydration."

"Thanks." Xander twisted the cap off, and as he took a sip, Ronnie cocked her head to the side and continued to scrutinize him. Any minute now, she would put two and two together. Which meant it was time to make ourselves scarce.

"Well, I think Alex and I are going to check out the bonfire, so we'll catch you guys later?"

"Why don't we come with you?" Ronnie said, hopping off the barstool. "I haven't been outside yet."

Sofia must have caught the look on my face, because she hooked an arm around her cousin's. "Actually, I have the sudden urge to hit the dance floor. Let's go find us some cute boys."

I mouthed a *thank you* to Sofia as she ushered Ronnie toward the living room. Once they were gone, I pointed at the back door. Xander slid it open, and we walked out onto the deck.

"So was it true?" I asked, glancing around. There were two

couples making out in the hot tub and a few people seated at the patio table playing king's cup, but everyone else was gathered around the firepit in the yard beyond.

"Was what true?" he asked as we started across the deck.

"The whole bit about your kindergarten play."

Xander slanted his head in mock challenge. "Do I look like a liar to you?"

"I don't know, *Alex from San Diego*. Something about your story isn't adding up."

"Fair," he replied, chuckling to himself and trudging down the steps. "That said, everyone knows the secret to lying is telling as much of the truth as possible. I made a very adorable sugarplum."

I couldn't help but laugh. "I'm sure you did."

When we reached the edge of the bonfire, I recognized most of the people congregated around it and immediately changed directions, steering Xander past the ring of Adirondack chairs and toward the ocean.

"Wait, where are we going?" he asked, twisting his head around to look back at the fire.

"Those are my orchestra friends. Your cover story won't work on them." I stopped at the fence separating Lizzie's backyard from the shore. Next to it was an outdoor storage bin, similar to the one Violet kept on our deck at home, and when I lifted the cover, I found exactly what I was looking for—a collection of towels, sand toys, and noodles. I dug through the box until I found a towel that was big enough for both of us to sit on, then straightened up. "Let's go sit by the water."

With a nod, Xander lifted the latch on the gate and pushed it open. He gestured for me to go first. I tugged off my boots and socks, tucked them behind the storage bin, and stepped onto the beach. The sun had long since set, and without its heat, the sand felt cool as it squished between my toes. We made an unspoken decision to put distance between us and the party, walking down the coast until the music faded away before picking a spot on the edge of the surf and unrolling our towel.

I sank to the ground and stretched out, tucking my legs to one side. Once I was settled, Xander sat down beside me, and as he did, his knuckles lightly grazed my thigh. A trail of goose bumps rippled up my leg, and I felt my breath catch in my throat. Besides the rhythmic crashing of waves, the night was quiet. So quiet, in fact, I was positive Xander had heard me gasp.

I peeked over at him, but he wasn't paying attention. He was too busy removing the more cumbersome elements of his costume. First came the cloak, which he unclasped from his neck, folded into a neat square, and set beside him on the towel. Then he tackled the bracers, loosening the cords binding them to his forearms before laying the leather armguards on top of the cloak. Finally, he ripped off his wig, tossed it away, and sighed in relief.

"That thing should be marketed as a torture device," he complained, massaging the tips of his fingers into his scalp. His hair was flat and sweaty after being plastered against his head for hours. Still, just looking at him made my heart jump.

"Itchy?" I guessed as I willed my pulse to slow down.

He nodded. "It felt like I shampooed my hair with poison ivy."

"Yikes." When I was eight, my family went on a camping trip with the Williamses. Alec and I spent the entire weekend exploring the surrounding forest, and although our moms told us to stick to the hiking trails, neither of us listened. We both came home covered in a poison oak rash that itched for weeks, mine so severe it blistered. Just thinking about the experience made me flinch.

"Yikes is an understatement." He was glaring at the hairpiece with such disdain, I was surprised he hadn't chucked it into the ocean. "I don't normally wear wigs, and after today, I plan on never wearing one again."

"Understandable," I said with a nod.

His brows drew together. "Are you okay? You seem…off."

"Totally," I replied, then instantly wanted to kick myself.

If I didn't quit it with these one-word answers, Xander might think I was pissed at him. The problem was my mind kept wandering back to the way his fingers felt against my skin. It was only a brief, accidental touch, but it had been enough to light up every one of my nerve endings.

For a minute, neither of us spoke, and I was starting to fear I *had* given him the wrong idea.

"Guess what?" he said at last.

"What?" I was so glad Xander wasn't upset, I forgot all about making an effort to respond in more than a single word.

"Come on. That's no fun," he replied, nudging me in the side. "You're supposed to guess."

"Okay, fine." Tapping a finger against my chin, I pretended to be deep in thought. "Oh, I got it! You really were in that Icy Quest commercial, weren't you?"

"You're a terrible guesser," he grumbled.

"Are you going to tell me what I'm supposed to be guessing," I asked, relaxing as we slipped into our regular repartee, "or do you plan on keeping me in suspense for the rest of the night?"

He rolled his eyes but was unable to keep the corner of his mouth from jutting up. "I spoke with Alec. He agreed to help me record a single."

"Oh my God! Xander, that's amazing," I exclaimed. "Have you started writing anything yet?"

"I have a few ideas I want to play around with." As he spoke, he lifted up a fistful of sand, then watched as gravity took hold and thousands of fine grains spilled from between the gaps in his fingers. "Touring is exhausting, but I'll find time to work on them during our days off."

Like rain on fire, his response doused the excitement I'd felt mere seconds ago. Over the course of our maybe, sort of date, I'd forgotten the Heartbreakers' tour started in November. I didn't have any idea which part of the world Xander was jetting off to or whether we'd even be in the same time zone. All I knew was that I didn't want him to leave.

"How long will you be gone for?" I asked quietly.

"That depends on what you're talking about. Do you mean when will I be home next, or how long does our entire tour last?"

"Both, I guess."

"Well, the first leg is short. It ends right before Thanksgiving, so we'll be home for the holiday," he explained. "But the whole tour? That won't wrap until August of next year."

My ribs grew tight at his answer. Ten whole months? That was nearly a full year. So much could change in that time. If things went as planned and I got into Juilliard, I would be getting ready to move to New York by the time he returned.

"Wow." I tried to sound neutral, but my voice betrayed the disappointment coursing through me. "That's a long time."

"Yeah, but we get breaks between each leg," he said quickly, "and we can hang out then. Also, there's this magical thing called FaceTime." He sounded so certain, like us spending time together was a no-brainer, but I couldn't bring myself to respond. Violet had made me a similar promise, and I didn't want to get my hopes up.

"Where are you going first?" I asked instead.

"Latin America. We leave for Mexico City on Monday."

Releasing a heavy sigh, I flopped onto the towel and stared up at the sky. "I'm going to miss you." It was the closest I would allow myself to telling him the truth.

The truth that I liked him.

The truth that a small part of me wished he was a regular, cello-playing senior named Alex, not a famous musician who was about to leave for a worldwide tour.

I heard a rustling noise, and then Xander was kneeling over me. His head eclipsed my view of the moon, outlining his figure in a silver glow.

"Do you really mean that?" he asked.

"That I'll miss you?" Despite the renewed hammering of my heart, my gaze remained fixed on him. "One thousand percent."

Xander's breath hitched. His eyes took in every inch of my face, lingering the longest on my lips, and when they finally found their way back to mine, he swallowed. "What have you eaten in the past five hours?"

"Um, I had an apple. Why?"

"Because I want to do this."

When his head dipped down, it took my brain a split second to process what was happening, but then a dose of adrenaline spilled into my veins, and I rose up to meet him.

I miscalculated, or maybe we both did, but whatever the case, Xander's jaw struck my forehead with an audible crack.

"Shit!" He jerked backward—in pain or shock, I wasn't entirely sure—with a hand cupped around his chin. "Indie, I'm *so* sorry."

"Pretty sure that was my fault," I said, gently inspecting the sore spot on my skull. All I wanted to do was bury my head in the sand, fling myself into the chilly Pacific waters, anything to forget the last thirty seconds. Then, out of nowhere, involuntary laughter surged up my throat. Sure, this would undoubtedly go down as one of my top five most embarrassing moments, but at least Xander had wanted to kiss me.

"What's so funny?" he asked, and beneath the sharp tone of his voice, I could hear how embarrassed he was.

"I was just thinking," I said, still giggling a little, "if anyone saw that, they're probably pissing themselves laughing right now. I bet we looked ridiculous."

Xander's tight expression melted. He sat back on his heels and rubbed the base of his neck. "Yeah, that wasn't my smoothest moment."

"Mine either." Taking a deep breath, I shook out my hair and attempted to project a confidence I didn't currently feel. "Maybe we could try again?"

His eyes snapped back to mine. "You sure about that?"

I nodded and went still, this time waiting for him to come to me.

Xander leaned over, his moonlit hair tumbling forward, and as he brought his face down to mine, a tangle of bangs brushed my cheeks. He circled an arm around my waist, and in the next breath, we were kissing. His lips were soft, his kisses even more so, almost like he hoped to erase our earlier blunder by being as gentle as possible.

But I needed more of him.

Maybe it was because, for the first time in ages, I felt wanted, cherished even. Not a hassle or an appointment on a calendar. Xander held me as if no one else in the universe would ever fit between his arms, a precious treasure he spent a lifetime searching for. I wrapped a hand around his neck, pulling him closer, while my other hand slid over the sharp line of his shoulder blade and down to his hip. He responded by deepening the kiss, his mouth firm and hot on mine in a way that made my toes curl.

It didn't take long for my chemistry goggles to become a hindrance, the boxy plastic knocking into Xander's forehead every time we moved. Grinning against his lips, I reached up and took them off. The elastic headband caught in my hair, but with a quick jerk, I yanked the ugly eyewear free and tossed them into the dark. He gripped me tighter then, pressing his body to mine, and when his long, slender fingers stroked the small of my back, a shiver ricocheted down my spine. Without thinking, I gripped his shirt and tugged him backward, our lips never parting as we collapsed against the towel.

I couldn't say how long we stayed like that for—chests pressed together, legs entwined, eager hands roving over hot skin—but when we finally pulled apart, my lips were numb from kissing. The first thing I noticed when I looked at Xander was the stippling of shimmering blue dots across his face, and I burst out laughing.

"What's so funny?" he asked.

"You're *covered* in glitter."

Eyes gleaming, he reached up and brushed a lock of hair—hair that was responsible for his current sparkly state—away from my face. "And whose fault is that?"

Instead of answering, I lifted myself up, just high enough to press my mouth against the underside of his jaw. His eyes fluttered closed at the contact, and as I worked my way down his throat, peppering every inch of skin with gentle kisses, he tilted his head back to give me better access.

"Hey, Indie?" His voice was low, husky.

"Mm-hmm?" I mumbled against him, and beneath my lips, I could feel his pulse fluttering.

"I'm going to miss you too."

CHAPTER 13

My pocket vibrated with an incoming text as I ditched my backpack in the mudroom. Scrambling to pull out my phone, I nearly tripped over a box of plastic bottles that needed to be taken out to the recycling bin.

GALAXY RIDER:
> Made it in one piece. How was school?

I typed a quick response as I headed toward the kitchen for a snack.

INDIE:
> Boring. Mondays are the worst. How was your flight?

On Saturday, Xander and I had lingered on the beach all night, talking and kissing until the blaze of sunrise announced the start of a new day. After parting ways, we spent the rest of the weekend texting each other. Because once the Heartbreakers' tour started, who knew how often Xander would find time to talk? Their flight to Mexico had left this morning, and I'd made him promise to let me know as soon as they landed. I was not ashamed to admit I'd been waiting all afternoon to receive his text.

GALAXY RIDER:
Eh, I took a nap. Major mistake.

INDIE:
What's wrong with napping?

GALAXY RIDER:
My friends are assholes.

INDIE:
...

GALAXY RIDER:
Oliver and JJ pulled out all the oxygen masks, started shaking my seat, and shouted that the plane was going down.

INDIE:
And you believed them?

GALAXY RIDER:
I was groggy and disoriented from sleeping!

INDIE:
Lmao, I take that as a yes?

GALAXY RIDER:

Yeah, but only for like three seconds. Scared the shit out of me.

INDIE:

How did they even get away with that? Didn't the flight attendants stop them?

GALAXY RIDER:

It was a private plane.

INDIE:

Okay, really? Talk about first-world problems. You're not getting any more sympathy from me.

GALAXY RIDER:

Because you were being so sympathetic to begin with?

I was so preoccupied by my conversation with Xander that I didn't realize there was anyone else in the room.

"Indie," said an uncharacteristically stern voice.

I startled, nearly dropping my phone, and glanced around. Dad was seated at the breakfast nook with only a mug of coffee positioned in front of him, no laptop or his usual spread of papers in sight. Even his Bluetooth headset was nowhere to be found. That the table was empty felt wrong somehow, like my father was missing one of his limbs. Why wasn't he working?

"Oh, hey," I said, giving him a puzzled once-over. "What are you doing out here?"

"Waiting for you." His mouth set into a thin, white line, and he pointed to the spot opposite him. "Sit down, please. We need to talk."

"Okay?" I dropped onto the bench even though every muscle in my body was twitching with the urge to flee. We hadn't seen each other since our fight at the theater, and I had a bad feeling this conversation wouldn't go my way.

"I received a call from your guidance counselor this morning." He paused and gave me a hard look. "Why did you skip school last Friday?"

Oh shit.

My mouth opened and closed as I searched for an answer to explain my absence. There was always the classic sick excuse, but I couldn't bring myself to lie. I ran a hand through my hair and sighed. "Does it matter? I was home the entire time."

"Of course it matters, Indigo. This is completely out of character for you."

"I wasn't drinking, doing drugs, or anything else diabolical," I replied, my palms raised in defense. "There was a project I had to get done, that's all."

"If you're struggling to finish your schoolwork, then you need to start budgeting your time more carefully," he told me. "You can't be so careless in college, or you'll fall behind in your classes."

A needle of annoyance pricked at me. Why was he blowing this situation out of proportion? Truancy wasn't a hobby of mine. I'd never received a detention before, and on top of that, I was a straight A student. "Dad," I said as calmly as possible, "I only missed one day."

"This isn't just about Friday. Violet told me you abandoned her at Comic Con, and you did the same thing to me the night of the premiere. That's not a one-time offense, it's a pattern, so I want to make myself very clear: the kind of irresponsible behavior you've been exhibiting lately is unacceptable. You're grounded until Thanksgiving." He said this firmly, his decision already made. "From now on, you go to school, come home, and that's it. No hanging out with Sofia or watching TV. Am I clear?"

I gaped at him, my jaw on the brink of unhinging. This was a joke, right? Mom had always taken a hands-on approach to parenting. She packed my lunches, helped me with homework, and enforced my curfew. But when she moved out, Dad never stepped up to the plate. Living with him was more like having an invisible roommate than a parental figure. And now, after years of being too busy to be present in my life, he was lecturing *me* on irresponsible behavior?

"Indie, am I clear?" he repeated.

Crossing my arms, I slumped against the back of the bench. "Crystal."

Dad's nostrils flared. "Do you think this is funny?"

In an effort not to snap, I sucked my lips between my teeth and silently counted to five. "No, I'm sorry," I told him in what I hoped was a regretful tone.

He studied me for a moment, but my performance must have been believable, because the livid expression disappeared from his face, and he inclined his head. "Thank you, Indie. I appreciate that. Now why don't we talk about something more pleasant?"

Oh, goodie! "Like what?"

"Well, why don't you tell me how your Juilliard application is coming along?"

"It's almost done," I lied through gritted teeth. "Look, Dad, I don't mean to be rude, but I have a lot of homework to get done."

"Right, of course," he said with a nod. "I have work I need to finish as well."

Three hours later, I wrenched a final note from the strings of my violin and exhaled. My entire upper body was drenched in sweat, and I felt as if my arms had turned to lead.

If one good thing had come from my argument with Dad, it was the angry energy searing through my veins. I used it to tackle the only problem in my life I had control over—my Juilliard application. Too amped up to overthink things, I selected four pieces I knew by heart that didn't require any accompaniment. After running through each one a couple of times, I set my laptop up on my desk and filmed myself playing. Not for my prescreening video—I wasn't even close to being ready for that—but so I could listen to the recording and pinpoint where I needed the most practice.

As I was setting my violin back in its case, the floorboards outside my bedroom door creaked. I whipped around and caught Violet standing in the hallway.

"What are you doing? Spying on me for Dad?" I asked through narrowed eyes. Clearly she had no issue being a tattletale, so I wouldn't put it past her.

A hurt look flashed across her face. "No, of course not. I was just—"

"Just what?"

"I was listening to you, okay?" She tucked a pale blond curl behind her ear and heaved a sigh. "Didn't realize that was such a crime."

"Why?" I demanded. Violet was never interested in my music before. If she wanted to hear me play, she could have attended any number of my many orchestra concerts. Why did she suddenly care now?

"Because it's been weeks since I've heard you play

anything." She hesitated for a moment, then added, "I was getting worried."

I narrowed my eyes. "About what exactly?"

"Your Juilliard audition. After the conversation we had about your makeup stuff, I thought maybe you'd decided against applying and—"

"This *again*? I already told you, my college applications are none of your business." I knew I was being unfair, that it was Dad who upset me, not Violet, but it felt good to take my anger out on something other than my violin. Right now, I wanted to be left alone.

My words had their desired effect. Violet's expression turned to stone. "Okay, Indie. Message received."

☆ ♭ ♪

Just checking in
J Mitchell <hotmommamitchell@outlook.com>
Tue, Nov 3, 8:02 AM to Indie

Hi honey,

Is everything okay? Your father informed me that you skipped school and he had to ground you.

Also—any updates on your Juilliard application?

Xoxo,
Your slightly concerned mother

Re: Just checking in
Indie <phoenixfreak20@gmail.com>
Wed, Nov 4, 3:57 PM to J Mitchell

Dear Slightly Concerned Mother,

Everything is fine except for Dad overreacting. Any chance you can put in a good word for me so I'm not stuck at home until Thanksgiving???

My Juilliard application is almost done. I selected all my pieces and am in the process of fine-tuning them. I'll send you the videos once everything is recorded and finalized. There's something I have to tell you though. I've decided I need a backup plan. Please don't freak out, but I'm also applying to a cinema makeup school. You know how much I love that stuff, so I figured why not?

That's why I skipped school. I had a very brief window of time to create a portfolio. It won't happen again.

Love,
Your Slightly Rebellious Daughter

Just checking in
J Mitchell <hotmommamitchell@outlook.com>
Wed, Nov 4, 10:43 PM to Indie

Rebel Child,

Sorry, but I won't go over your father's head on this decision. If you can't do the time, don't commit the crime.

It's so good to hear everything is finally coming together!!! I can't wait to see what you picked out. I know you'll blow me (and Juilliard) away.

Also, why would I freak out about you applying to a different school? I think it's a great idea to keep your options open. As long as you're happy, I'm happy. You'll do great things no matter what you decide.

Love you lots.

   Xoxo,

Mom

SUN, NOV 8, 1:43 P.M.

INDIE:
Hey stranger! How did your first week of touring go?

GALAXY RIDER:
Pretty good. I only fainted onstage once.

INDIE:
WHAT! Are you okay???

GALAXY RIDER:
Lol gotcha!

How have things been on your end?

INDIE:
Hilarious

Things here have been rainbows and sunshine.

GALAXY RIDER:
I'm assuming you're being sarcastic.

HEARTSTRINGS

INDIE:
You assume correct.

GALAXY RIDER:
What happened?

INDIE:
My dad found out I skipped school, so I'm grounded until Thanksgiving.

GALAXY RIDER:
Ouch, that blows. At least you still have phone privileges. Also, I thought we were more than friends.

INDIE:
Sorry, I'm not a friend with benefits kind of person.

GALAXY RIDER:
Good, me either.

TUE, NOV 10, 11:29 A.M.

GALAXY RIDER:
Guess what?

INDIE:
You were offered a spot in an Icy Quest commercial?

GALAXY RIDER:

Wow, you're good. Alas, I had to turn it down because I'm booked for a Gas-X ad the same day.

INDIE:

I fully support this decision. I've always thought Icy Quest was a shady brand. Gas-X is much more reputable.

GALAXY RIDER:

My thoughts exactly.

INDIE:

So what's up? Oliver and JJ pull another prank on you?

GALAXY RIDER:

I'm going to ignore that and cut to the chase. I picked up the first few issues of Lady Phoenix.

INDIE:

OMG! What do you think so far???

GALAXY RIDER:

The artwork is phenomenal and I really like the storyline, but the whole Soul Whispering ability is confusing.

INDIE:

Yeah, I'll be the first to admit the concept wasn't explained well. Basically, because

> she is a phoenix, Hotaru dies and is reborn every one hundred years. In times of need, she can access the memories and knowledge of her past lives to help herself, which is called Soul Whispering. You'll understand it better the more you read.

GALAXY RIDER:
> Guess I'll have to keep reading then

FRI, NOV 13, 3:08 P.M.

INDIE:
> I need your advice.

GALAXY RIDER:
> About what?

INDIE:
> Well, there's this guy I have a crush on...

GALAXY RIDER:
> Wow. I don't even know who he is and I'm jealous.

INDIE:
> I think you'd really like him. His name is Alex. He's from San Diego, he plays the cello, and he's SUPER cute.

GALAXY RIDER:
> Wow, he sounds awesome. I have a feeling I'm no match for a guy like him.

INDIE:

Yeah, sorry. Nobody really compares. That's why I'm nervous to ask him to turnabout.

GALAXY RIDER:

Okay, I lost you. What the heck is turnabout?

INDIE:

It's a winter formal where the girls invite the guys.

GALAXY RIDER:

Ohhhh! In that case, you should just come right out with it and ask him. I have a feeling he'll say yes.

INDIE:

How do you know?

GALAXY RIDER:

Because any guy would have to be an idiot to turn you down.

INDIE:

So is that a yes?

GALAXY RIDER:

I'm already picking out a suit.

MON, NOV 16, 9:51 P.M.

HEARTSTRINGS

GALAXY RIDER:

I finally got to the issue where Kelina is introduced.

INDIE:

!!!!!!!

And?

GALAXY RIDER:

Do you still have your Halloween costume?

INDIE:

Yeah, why?

GALAXY RIDER:

I'd be down for some alien roleplay. You can dress up as Kelina. I'll be an Oken warrior.

INDIE:

You did NOT just say that.

GALAXY RIDER:

Lmao

But seriously. I get why you like her character...

She's outta this world.

INDIE:

You need to stop it with the alien jokes before you hurt yourself.

ALI NOVAK

THU, NOV 19, 12:35 P.M.

GALAXY RIDER:

Hey kitten

From now on I want u to call me daddy

INDIE:

WTF?

GALAXY RIDER:

Indie, I'm so sorry! Please ignore those texts. JJ stole my phone.

INDIE:

Ah, that makes so much more sense. Where are you guys at right now?

GALAXY RIDER:

Brazil but we leave for Peru tonight.

INDIE:

Sounds like so much fun!

GALAXY RIDER:

It is, but I wish you were here with me.

INDIE:

I wish I was there with you too, Daddy

GALAXY RIDER:

You're really gonna go there, huh?

HEARTSTRINGS

INDIE:
Don't blame me. JJ started it.

GALAXY RIDER:
All right. Night, kitten.

SAT, NOV 21, 2:16 P.M.

GALAXY RIDER:
So...how are things going between you and Violet?

INDIE:
Wow, world's most random text ever, but to answer your question...normal, I guess? She's busy all the time and I avoid her when she's home. Why?

GALAXY RIDER:
Sorry, just curious. I know you wish the two of you had a better relationship.

INDIE:
I've slowly come to the realization that it will never happen.

GALAXY RIDER:
You never know. Maybe she wants the same thing you do.

INDIE:
I'm not going to hold my breath.

MON, NOV 23, 10:07 P.M.

GALAXY RIDER:

It's finally finished!!!

Well, mostly. There's still some rough parts to tweak, but the overall concept has been hammered out.

INDIE:

Sweet! What are we talking about again?

GALAXY RIDER:

My song. It took forever to write.

INDIE:

CONGRATULATIONS!

When do I get to hear it?

GALAXY RIDER:

After Thanksgiving? I'll be in Portland with my family until the 30th, but Alec reserved a studio for us the first week of December, so I'm flying back to LA to record the track. It would be cool if you could come.

INDIE:

I wouldn't miss it for the world.

WED, NOV 25, 8:24 A.M.

GALAXY RIDER:

Guess what?

HEARTSTRINGS

INDIE:

Really, Xander? Another Icy Quest commercial? You need to tell your agent you're looking for more respectable work.

GALAXY RIDER:

I'll be back in LA by the end of the day.

INDIE:

I. Can't. Wait.

CHAPTER 14

"Want a piece?"

I glanced over my shoulder, away from the dirty dish I was scrubbing, and looked at my dad. He stood at the island, a pumpkin pie in front of him and a sleepy, food coma smile on his face.

"No, thanks," I replied, my fingers tightening around the sponge clutched in my hand. Our annual Thanksgiving Day football scrimmage would start once we finished cleaning, and I didn't want to puke in the middle of a play because I'd overeaten. "I'll have some after the game."

"Suit yourself," he said, pulling the plastic lid off the pie container as I turned back to the sink.

Three weeks had passed since my grounding, and although my punishment was up, a palpable tension still lingered between us. We tiptoed around each other, only engaging in polite conversation when absolutely necessary. In fact, this was the first time we'd been alone together since our fight, and I could barely get through a simple yes-no question without wanting to hurl the sponge, a plate, anything really, at his face.

But what pissed me off the most?

My dad's swift return to being as uninvolved in my life as possible, like nothing had happened at all. Even though his attempt at discipline was nothing short of infuriating, a tiny, minuscule part of me had hoped it was a sign—one that meant he was trying to change, that he wanted to be my dad.

I resumed scrubbing, taking my anger out on the crusty bits of food baked onto the side of a casserole dish. Two more pots found their way to the drying rack before my cousin stomped into the kitchen carrying a broom and dustpan.

"Does anyone know where Violet is?" Hillary asked. She threw open the pantry door and dumped the contents of the dustpan into the garbage with more force than necessary. "I don't mean to be a crab, but she hasn't helped at all."

I smiled to myself, glad I wasn't the only person who was irritated by my sister's disappearing act. Right at the end of dinner, her phone rang, and she excused herself to take the call. Nobody had seen her since. Now that I thought about it, I wouldn't put it past Violet to have Lydia call her just so she could avoid washing dishes.

Dad shrugged as he polished off his last bite of pie. "No clue."

Sighing, I dried my hands on a dish towel before turning to Hillary. "Leave whatever else is still on the table," I told her. "I'll go find Violet, and she can finish what's left."

Except locating my sister wasn't the easy feat I thought it would be.

The first place I looked was the living room where most of our family was congregated around the TV, but unsurprisingly, Violet wasn't there. Maybe she was still on the phone and had shut herself up in Dad's office for privacy? But a single glance through the French doors let me know the room was deserted. After doing a thorough sweep of the main floor, I went upstairs to check her bedroom. That was empty too.

Where the heck was she?

I was heading back toward the stairs, thoughts focused on bribing Wyatt or Quinn, my two youngest cousins, to help me with my search, when I heard my name.

"I understand, but Indie is an adult. She can handle this."

To my left, the door of an unused guest room stood ajar. Violet's voice was coming from inside, so I paused in confusion. Why was Violet hiding in one of the spare bedrooms? More importantly, why was she talking about me? I leaned in to hear more.

"I've been trying to fix things, but it's not going well," she continued. A pause. Then, "Okay, maybe you should tell her."

No longer able to keep quiet, I pushed the door open. "Who are you talking to?"

Violet, who was standing by the window looking out at the ocean, jumped so high it was a miracle she didn't shoot through the ceiling. Without saying goodbye, she ended her call and spun around to face me. "What do you want?" she demanded, her neck and cheeks flushing red as she shoved the phone into a back pocket.

"I've been looking all over for you," I replied. "We're almost done cleaning up dinner, and you haven't pitched in at all. No need to bite my head off."

"Okay, fine. Give me a few minutes, and I'll meet you downstairs." She turned away as if to dismiss me, but she had yet to answer my question. No way was I letting her off the hook.

"Who were you talking to?" I asked again.

"Someone I work with." Her response was brisk, flippant. "Nothing you'd be interested in."

"But I am interested," I said, putting a hand on my hip as I took another step into the room. "I heard you say my name."

"Weren't you the one who told me to mind my own business the other day?" Violet snapped. "Why don't you do the same and butt out?"

"There's a huge difference between you meddling in my

life choices and me wanting to know why you're talking about me," I told her.

"Despite what you think, the world doesn't revolve around you, Indie."

I gave a humorless laugh. "That's rich coming from you."

Violet's nostrils flared—it looked like she was resisting the urge to explode—and three tense seconds of silence passed. "Oh, really?" she finally said. "I don't suppose you know where my script for *Lady Phoenix* went, do you? Obviously someone as perfect and considerate as you would never snoop through my stuff, but I wanted to ask just in case."

Oh, crap.

I'd been so caught up in the excitement of ACM and creating my portfolio that I'd forgotten all about returning the script to Dad's office. I'd left it in Sofia's room, which in all likelihood meant it had been swallowed up by an endless mountain of laundry. I shifted my weight from one foot to the other and crossed my arms. "I thought you were taking a break from acting."

Pinching the bridge of her nose, Violet said, "I mentioned *wanting* to take a break, but that doesn't mean I can afford to."

"Why not?"

"Because I don't want to be remembered as a vapid vampire princess for the rest of eternity!" she said, throwing up her hands. "I want to be cast in dynamic, meaningful roles that earn me Oscar nominations. I want to have a career that lasts a lifetime and for people to take me seriously."

I snorted. "And you think *Lady Phoenix* will help you accomplish that?" Although I loved the series with all my heart, I wasn't naive. Things teenage girls liked—whether it was the Heartbreakers, *Twilight*, or Taylor Swift—were always mocked by the rest of the world as uncool and less than. This would be no different.

"Maybe not, but it's a step in the right direction." Violet sank down on the end of the bed and briefly closed her eyes before letting go of a frustrated gulp of air. "My screen test is next month, so I need to start practicing. Any idea where my script disappeared to?"

A heaviness settled over my body at her response.

So she really was auditioning. Despite Dad's promise to spend more time with me, Violet's desire to press pause on acting, and her forthcoming album, she was still going to try out. I knew I was being childish, but the realization made my eyes water. Sure, there was always a chance Violet wouldn't get the part, but I knew better than to hope for that. Not only was she good at her job, but after the phenomenon that was *Immortal Nights*, Violet was a hot commodity. What director or producer wouldn't want to tap into her massive fan base?

"Not a clue," I lied through the lump in my throat. I'd deal with returning the script later. Right now, there were more pressing matters at hand. "What role are you auditioning for?"

Please not Kelina. Please not Kelina! Anything but her!

"Some weird alien girl," Violet said, pulling her hair over her shoulder and twisting it into a thick rope. "I think her name is Kelly Stardust. You read the comic, right? Is she a good character?"

"No!" I gasped, the word erupting from my mouth before I could stop myself.

My outburst must have caught Violet off guard, because she accidentally dropped her hair, which sprang free and unraveled. "So…she's not a good character?"

"That's not what—" With the shake of my head, I broke off. Violet's mouth opened, but I held up a hand to ward her off until the bile burning at the back of my throat subsided. "You can't audition for her," I said at last.

She scratched her forehead. "Why not?"

"Because. She's my *favorite* character."

The expression on her face turned stoic. "What does that have to do with anything?" she asked, her voice low and seething.

"Everything!" I breathed hard to keep back a sob. "Look, I know this probably doesn't make sense to you, but I've been waiting for a *Lady Phoenix* adaption for years, and if you're in it, I don't think I'll be able to watch—"

Violet shot to her feet in one swift motion. "You're unbelievable! I'm not allowed to have a conversation with you about your college applications, but you can ban me from an audition? Do you realize how selfish you sound?"

Shaking my head, I willed her to understand. "Violet, I don't care if you audition for every role that comes your way from now until the end of time, but please, I'm begging you," I said, clasping my hands together in a plea, "not this one."

There was a long pause. Finally, "Maybe if you acted more like my sister and less like a bitter bitch, you wouldn't have to beg," she said, using a twisted version of my own words against me. "And for future reference, I don't need your permission to do my job."

Without waiting for my rebuttal, Violet shoved past me and slammed the door shut. All I could do was stand in the spare bedroom, one hand flattened against the wall for support, the other pressed to my chest. My whole body felt shaky, like I'd somehow come down with the flu in a matter of seconds, and I had to count my breaths to fend off a wave of dizziness. Suddenly, the thought of playing football with my entire family—having to interact with other people and pretend to be happy—made my stomach churn.

All I wanted to do was be alone.

I spun on my heels and dashed down the stairs, tears pricking my eyes. I took the back hallway so I wouldn't bump into anyone, grabbed my keys from the mudroom, and hopped into my car. Then I was backing out of the driveway and whipping down the street.

Without any destination in mind, I started driving.

It wasn't until I reached Sofia's subdivision that I realized where I'd taken myself. Maybe it wasn't that I wanted to be alone but that I couldn't stand to spend another minute with Violet, let alone the rest of the day.

The Hernandezes' driveway was a *Tetris* of cars, so I pulled up to the curb and parked on the street. As I climbed out, I could hear music spilling from the backyard, along with the hum of conversation and laughter. Instead of knocking on the front door, I cut across the lawn and followed the stone path that wrapped around the house. When I rounded the corner and spotted the gathering, I stopped in my tracks.

Sofia had a moderately large family, but this wasn't a big holiday get-together—it was a full-on party. At least thirty people were milling around the patio, most of whom I didn't recognize, and I suddenly realized I was intruding. I tried to retreat, but before I could back away, Emma noticed me.

"Indie!" she exclaimed and took off in my direction. When she reached me, she wrapped her arms around my waist and looked up. Something brown was smeared around her mouth. "What are you doing here?"

"I think the better question is what's all over your face?" I asked with a laugh.

Her tongue darted out, and she licked her lips clean. "Chocolate. My abuelita makes the best champurrado. Do you want some?"

"Thanks," I said, ruffling her hair as Sofia approached us, a confused smile on her face. "I need to talk to your sister, but I'll try some later, okay?"

Emma shrugged and dashed away as quickly as she'd appeared, joining a group of kids on the swing set.

"Hey," Sofia said once her sister was gone. "What's up?"

"The usual," I told her. "I couldn't deal with my family for the rest of the day, so I got in my car and ended up here. Sorry for intruding. I wasn't thinking."

"Indigo, what a lovely surprise." Glancing over Sofia's shoulder, I was met with the warm smile of Mrs. Hernandez. She must have caught the tail end of our conversation, because she put a hand on her hip. "I hope I didn't hear you apologizing for stopping by. You know you're always welcome here."

I glanced over at the patio, where rows of string lights gleamed down from the beams of the pergola. Two long tables, which were covered in steaming dishes, had been pushed together at the edge of the stone pavers to create a buffet line. There were more people than chairs, so everyone stood around with paper plates in hand as they socialized. It was the opposite of my family's formal sit-down meal but somehow more intimate and close-knit.

"Are you sure?" I asked.

"The more the merrier," she said, wrapping an arm around me and guiding me toward the party. "We're just started eating. Why don't you grab a plate and join us?"

☆ ♭ ♫

"You can't lie here all night."

I cracked open my eyes. Sofia stood above me, arms crossed as she frowned down at me. "Says who?" I asked.

"Well, I guess you can if you want, but the sprinklers turn on at midnight, so you'll be in for a rude awake—ooh, I *love* this song!" Sofia's head whipped toward the patio, which, at some point during dinner, had turned into a dance floor. "Let's go dance."

"Can't," I said, patting my stomach. "I'm digesting."

Her bottom lip jutted out in a pout. "Please? Moving around will help."

"If I move an inch from this spot, I'm going to explode."

The Hernandezes' Thanksgiving spread had included a few traditional staples, but there was also birria, three different types of tamales, papas con rajas, and countless other dishes I didn't know the names of. But the best part was the homemade desserts—tres leches and a pumpkin flan drizzled with caramel—which were hands down better than any grocery-store pie.

Skipping the turkey and mashed potatoes, I'd packed my plate with all the foods I'd never tried before. Even though I was picky when it came to food, I'd eaten dinner at Sofia's house enough times to know that Mrs. Hernandez could make rocks taste like magic.

Now, after indulging in meal number two, my too-full stomach was paying the price. All I wanted to do was nap, so I'd stretched out on the rope hammock secured between two trees, which was the perfect spot to watch the party from.

"You're such a poop," she said with a huff. "Make some room."

The ropes of the hammock creaked as she climbed in beside me, and the motion sent us rocking.

"Ugh," I groaned. "Do you think your family will judge me if I undo the top button of my jeans?"

Sofia's shoulder shook against mine with laughter. "My mom would take that as a compliment. Also, what kind of noob wears jeans at Thanksgiving? It's all about the yoga pants." She patted her own stomach.

"Mistakes were definitely made," I agreed.

There was a loud crash on the patio, and I lifted my head to see what had happened. By the looks of it, Emma had tripped Javier, and he'd tumbled straight into one of the chaise lounges. Jake and Ronnie, who were sitting around the nearby firepit, burst out laughing. I grinned and lay back down.

"I swear those two can't go five minutes without torturing each other," she said, shaking her head. "So…did you turn in your Juilliard application yet?"

Even though I was practically done, anxiety spiked through me at her question. "No, but the benefit of being grounded for three weeks is that I had plenty of practice time. I think I'm as ready as I'll ever be," I told her. "The plan is to record my audition videos this weekend."

One of Sofia's eyebrows popped up. "Cutting it a bit close, don't you think?"

"Hey, you're the one who sidetracked me with the whole makeup portfolio."

"Oh, that reminds me! You never told me how that went."

"I submitted it and am waiting to hear back, but even if I'm accepted, I'm not going. Juilliard is still the plan."

Sofia rolled her eyes. "You don't say?"

My phone vibrated before I could respond. I'd been waiting for a seething call from my dad for the past hour. No doubt Violet had filled him in on our fight, and now there'd be another grounding in my future. But when I took out my cell and looked at the caller ID, it was Xander, not my dad.

Grinning, I hit Talk. "Hey, you. What's up?"

"Happy Thanksgiving!" he exclaimed. "Right now, my mom and grandma are going through my baby photo albums, and I'm slowly dying of embarrassment. What about you?"

"I'm contemplating whether it's physically possible to eat another piece of tres leches," I replied. "My heart says yes, but my stomach says no."

"There's always room for more tres leches," Sofia said.

"Was that Sofia?" Xander asked, his voice laden with confusion.

"Yeah," I said, switching my phone to my other ear. "Things got a little heated at my place, so I crashed her family gathering."

"What happened?" he asked.

Sofia pointed to the patio where her siblings and cousins were sitting, indicating that she was going to join them, and I nodded my head in understanding.

"Violet and I got in another fight," I said, easing back into the middle of the hammock as she got up.

There was such a long pause that, for a second, I thought our call had disconnected.

"Oh," Xander finally said.

Oh? That was it?

"You okay?" I asked him.

"Yeah, totally fine," he replied, but something about his

voice was off. Before I could press further, he changed the subject. "Are you still meeting me at the recording studio on Tuesday?"

"There's nothing I'm looking forward to more."

We spoke for another twenty minutes, but then I heard someone calling Xander's name on his end of the line, and he had to go.

After hanging up, I eased myself into a sitting position and looked around for Sofia. She was sitting with Ronnie, Jake, and Javier, laughing at whatever story her cousin was telling. Watching them all together made my heart twinge. I loved Sofia, but sometimes it was hard to see her with her family. They reminded me so much of how mine used to be—together, happy—and how we'd never be like that again.

CHAPTER 15

"You have reached your destination," my phone announced as I drove up to a small brick building in West Hollywood. A vine with stunning magenta flowers extended up the front facade, like a column of vibrant coral or pink clouds, only interrupted by a fashionably rusted metal sign that read NEW EDGE RECORDING STUDIO.

It was late Tuesday afternoon, and despite the mountain of homework I'd been assigned today at school, I was feeling on top of the world. Not only was I about to see Xander after a month of getting by on phone calls and texts, but I would also get to watch him bring his song to life.

In addition, I had my own surprise to share with him. I had spent the weekend recording and rerecording the videos for my prescreening until they were flawless. Violet and Dad had been AWOL, which meant I got the whole house to myself with no one to interrupt me. My application was due today, but before I sent it off, I wanted Xander to listen to each piece. Not because I was still searching for flaws but because even though our music was different, it was something we shared.

After the past two months of worrying about my prescreening, I finally felt content. With the repertoire I'd chosen and how well I'd played, there was no way I wouldn't get a live audition.

Juilliard, here I come.

The studio's parking lot was surrounded by a large fence, which was covered in the same blooming flower as the building. The gate was open, so I pulled in and parked near the black Range Rover I recognized as Xander's car. After shouldering my bag and fishing my phone out of the cupholder, I hopped out and started up the sidewalk. I was halfway to the building when the glass door at the front entrance swung open and Xander stepped out, almost as if he'd been waiting for me to arrive.

He smiled—the goofy, lopsided one that first endeared me to him at Comic Con—and covered the remaining distance between us in four long strides. Without any words of greeting, he pulled me against his body.

After a few seconds of standing in each other's arms, he asked, "Eat anything in the past five hours that might kill me?"

"Nope." In fact, I'd purposely avoided eating anything at lunch that I knew he was allergic to.

"Perfect," Xander whispered, then pressed his lips to mine.

The kiss was fierce, filled with an entire month's worth of longing and desire, and for a brief moment, I considered dragging him to my car so we could continue kissing in private. When we finally broke apart, a breathless laugh escaped me.

"Hi," I said, grinning up at him.

"God, it's so good to see you," he mumbled, burying his face in my neck, and the feel of his lips against my collarbone sent a shiver of pleasure down my spine. "I missed hearing that laugh."

Heat pooled in my cheeks. "It's good to see you too. I'm super excited about today."

"Me too," he said, placing both hands on my upper arms and pulling back so he could look at me. "But before we go inside, there's something I want to talk to you about."

The change in his tone made me pause. "Okay?"

He gestured at one of the wrought-iron benches lining either side of the entrance, and for some strange reason, a tiny dose of nerves trickled through my system. I did my best to ignore the feeling as I sat down, stashing my phone and purse in the empty space beside me on the bench. Xander took a spot beside me, but instead of settling back, he leaned forward, resting his elbows on his knees and clasping his hands together.

I slanted my head in question. "Everything okay?" I asked.

"There's something I should have told you earlier, but I didn't know how," he said, staring off into the distance at what seemed like nothing in particular.

My pulse jumped at his words. "Why not?"

"Because I made a decision without thinking it through," he admitted. A breeze swept through the parking lot, lifting his bangs and tossing them into his eyes. He brushed the hair out of his face before adding, "I only considered how it would affect me, not you, and now I'm afraid of how you'll react."

I took my bottom lip between my teeth in an effort not to smile. Xander was the kindest, most caring person I knew. He would never intentionally do something to hurt me; he was too good. Whatever was bothering him was probably so insignificant it wouldn't have occurred to me if he wasn't about to call attention to it. Hoping to reassure him, I placed a hand on his arm and smiled. "Xander, relax. I'm sure whatever you're talking about isn't that bad."

"Don't say that." He straightened up and turned to me, and the look in his eyes made my stomach flip. "Just…hear me out first, okay?"

Taking my hand back, I nodded.

"You know how Alec is helping me produce this single?"

"Yeah…" After all, I was the one who'd suggested he ask him for help.

"Well, he had an idea." Xander hesitated, preparing himself for whatever hard thing he had to say, but before he could continue, the studio door swung open a second time.

"Xander, you out here? Alec is ready for—oh. Hey, Indie."

It took me several seconds to process that Violet was standing in front of me, and for a moment, all I could do was stare. Thank God I was already sitting down, because the sight of her was like a gut punch, and I felt as if all the blood in my veins had stopped flowing. What possible reason did she have to be here? I turned back to Xander, brows furrowed in question.

He flinched, then glanced back at my sister. "Can you give us a minute?"

Violet, realizing she'd interrupted something important, nodded and disappeared inside without another word.

"What," I said slowly, "is *she* doing here?" My fingers curled into fists, and the slight bite of pain as my nails dug into my palms kept me grounded.

Xander swallowed. "Look, I know you two aren't on the best terms, but I'm hoping you'll understand that this decision was purely a business one. Working together is beneficial for both of us."

Working together? What is he talking—

But then it hit me. Violet's upcoming album. Xander's song. Alec producing them both. Why not put it all together?

I didn't need to ask. The guilt-ridden expression on Xander's face was all the confirmation I needed—he was recording his single *with* Violet.

"No," I said, shaking my head. "You wouldn't do that." Not after everything I'd told him about my relationship with her.

"Indie, I swear it was never my intention to hurt you." He took my hands in his and squeezed, as if willing me to understand. "I should have said something that night on the beach, but we were having such a good time, and I was afraid of ruining everything. Then I was gone all month, and it didn't seem like the type of thing to explain over text. When Violet told me you overheard our conversation on Thanksgiving, I called you right away, but you were still upset with her and I…I chickened out."

"Why?"

"Because I didn't want to lose you."

"No." I pulled my hands away from his. "Why would you work with her?"

Xander hesitated again but then said, "Because I don't have the same relationship with her as you do, Indie. The two of us are friends, and I—I don't think she's a bad person. The two of us worked together on *Immortal Nights*, so it will make sense to my fans why we chose to do this project together. Hopefully, that will prevent any band breakup rumors. And that's not to mention how featuring on my song will help generate buzz for her album. It's a win-win for everyone."

Except for me.

I knew Xander never had ill intentions—the guy didn't have a bad bone in his body—but that didn't mean I wasn't hurt. Until now, spending time with him had felt like... like there was one perfect part of my life that wasn't contaminated by the craziness of Violet's world. It didn't escape me that I was being hypocritical, because if I hadn't gone to Comic Con with her, I never would have met Xander. But I couldn't help the way I felt.

I glanced away from Xander, attempting to sort through my emotions, and out of the corner of my eye, I noticed Violet watching us through the glass door. Something inside me snapped. I sprang to my feet and stormed over to her, yanking the door open before she could blink.

"Why do you do it?" I demanded.

Violet blanched at my tone. "What are you talking about?"

"Why do you weasel your way into every part of my life and ruin it? I finally find someone who doesn't have anything to do with your crazy bullshit, so of course you have to get involved, don't you?"

Her breath hitched. "Seriously, Indie? Me and Xander working together is completely unrelated to whatever relationship you two have. I get that you don't like my career, but that doesn't make me the selfish, narcissistic person you seem to think I am."

"You're joking right? Your career *ruined* our family." I was so angry, I could feel heat rolling off me in waves. My shoulders rose and fell several times as I tried to keep myself from exploding. "It's the reason why Mom and Dad aren't together anymore, and I will never forgive you for that."

I didn't know what reaction my accusation would elicit from Violet, but laughter wasn't it. Granted, I doubted the noise coming from her mouth could be considered laughter. Not when it sounded so ugly and cold.

"Because Dad worked so much that Mom got lonely, right?" she practically spat.

"Exactly."

"Wrong."

"What do you mean, wrong?"

"Well, maybe you'd know what I'm talking about if, for once in your life, you focused on something other than yourself. But no, you're too busy playing the victim card and whining about me auditioning for *Lady Phoenix*."

My hands started to tremble. "Excuse me?"

"You heard me," she said, her lips curling into an ugly sneer. "You're so self-absorbed that you blame your problems on everyone but yourself. You treat me like crap because you're too afraid to take responsibility for your own unhappiness."

Her words struck me like a sledgehammer. I lurched back a step as my stomach tightened, forcing the air from my lungs. How was it my fault that Dad never had time for me? Or that I'd lost my best friend when she chose acting over her own sister? If *this* was what our relationship boiled down to, then I couldn't do it anymore.

"I'm done with you," I said flatly, even as my eyes burned with tears.

Without another word, I spun on my heels and marched over to the bench where Xander was sitting. He looked shell-shocked, his eyes wide and mouth parted slightly. I snatched my purse off the bench and darted toward my car, not bothering to say goodbye.

"That's right," Violet yelled. "Run away like you always do!"

The volume of her voice must have jolted Xander out of whatever fog he'd been stuck in, because I suddenly heard his feet slapping against the pavement as he chased after me.

"Indie, wait!" he called, but I ignored him.

After unlocking my car door, I threw my purse onto the passenger seat and whipped out of my parking spot as fast as I could. I glanced in the rearview mirror and saw Xander standing in the middle of the lot, watching me drive away, but I didn't stop.

I couldn't.

I needed to get away.

I cranked the volume up on the radio and drove.

And drove.

And drove.

All over LA. Down to Santa Monica Pier. Then all the way up to Griffith Observatory. Eventually I wound up on the interstate heading out of the city.

At first, I didn't know where I was going. What I did know was that with each mile I put behind me, the quieter the pounding in my ears became. I couldn't control Violet's or Dad's actions, but at least here, in the driver's seat, I was in charge.

It wasn't until I saw the first exit sign for San Bernardino that I realized where my subconscious had led me—home. Not Violet's sleek beach house but the cookie-cutter ranch my parents bought as their starter home. The place where I grew up, where I'd been happy and my family whole.

By the time I arrived, it was nearly dark. The neighborhood looked older than I remembered, the trees fully grown and a few of the properties in need of some TLC. But nothing could prepare me for when I laid eyes on our old house. The cheerful sky-blue exterior was now a boring tan, and someone had redone all the landscaping, replacing the dahlias and marigolds Mom planted every year with sturdy bushes. Even more unsettling was the new addition over the garage. Had I not known the address by heart, not biked these streets so often as a child that the route was forever ingrained in my memory, I would have driven straight past.

But the part that broke my heart the most was when I snuck into the backyard, scanned the forest edging the lot, and noticed a gap in the trees. There was a wrongness to that gap, and it took three full seconds of staring at the empty space before my mind registered that the tree house Violet and I played in as children, back before there was any ill will between us, was gone. The towering oak tree it was built in had been cut down. All that remained was a broad stump, a symbolic gravestone, if you will, marking the end of my childhood.

I ran back to my car. Tears were running down my face in silent streams by the time I reached the door, but I didn't let the floodgates go until I was safely inside. Only then did I allow great heaving sobs to rack my body. Too upset to drive but not wanting anyone to see the blubbering mess I'd become, I leaned my seat all the way back until I was staring out the sunroof. Then I cried and cried, letting my anger and heartbreak pour out of me.

☆ ♭ ♪

I woke with a start, not knowing where I was. It took me several bleary moments of blinking at the steering wheel to realize I was in my car and not my bedroom. My cheeks were tight and gritty with that uncomfortable postcry feel, and there was a painful kink in my neck.

What the hell am I doing in here? I thought as I rubbed my eyes.

But then the events of the day came rushing back to me, and I glanced across the street at the unfamiliar building that had once been my home. I'd come here seeking comfort, some sense of familiarity, but only found a strange coldness. My life had changed drastically when my family moved to Laguna Beach, but I never considered how what we left behind might change too. In my mind, this place had remained the same. I should have known that, given time, everything evolved, for better or worse.

I kneaded my chest, right over my heart, but the pain there wasn't physical.

Not wanting to spend another second here, I righted my seat and pressed the engine start button. As the dashboard flickered to life, I glanced at the digital clock—11:51 p.m.

A sudden sinking feeling pressed against my chest. I paused in thought, then yelped in alarm as it dawned on me. I had less than ten minutes to submit my Juilliard application! The plan had been to submit it once I got home from the recording studio, but now I'd have to do it from my phone. Thank God everything was already uploaded and ready to go.

HEARTSTRINGS

With my heart stampeding inside my rib cage, I snatched up my purse and rummaged through its contents. When my cell didn't turn up, I patted my pockets and checked the cupholder where I usually stashed it while driving. It wasn't there. I even climbed out of the car and looked under all the seats, but…nothing.

My phone was missing.

The last time I'd had it was…at the freaking recording studio.

I must have left it on the bench in my hurry to leave. By the time I drove back to LA and retrieved it, I would miss the deadline. I glanced around in panic, but there was nothing I could do, so I climbed back into the driver's seat and watched the clock hit midnight.

And just like that, my lifelong dream slipped away.

☆ ♭ ♪

An hour later, I pulled into the driveway at Violet's house.

Even though it was nearly one o'clock in the morning, every light on the main floor was on, and I got a sinking feeling I was in major trouble. Dad kept a strict schedule and was always in bed by ten on weeknights, so why else would he be up at such a late hour?

After maneuvering my car into its spot in the garage, I slumped back in my seat and released a long sigh. Today had been the very definition of exhausting, and I needed a minute to prepare myself before facing whatever punishment waited for me inside.

I only got thirty seconds.

Before I could rally the remaining embers of my energy, the mudroom door was yanked open, casting a golden wedge of light through the gloom. Dad stood at the threshold, his lips pressed together in a way that made my stomach twist.

"Inside," he mouthed to me. "Now."

Yikes. This wouldn't go well.

Not bothering with my purse, I climbed out of my car and followed him into the kitchen.

He pointed at the breakfast nook. "Sit down."

There was a scary edge to his voice, so I scrambled onto the bench while Dad slid into place across from me. Two empty mugs were perched on the edge of the table, waiting to be carried over to the dishwasher, and I wondered how long he'd been waiting for me. Hopefully not too long.

Instead of diving right into another tongue-lashing, Dad just stared at me. Like an FBI agent about to interrogate his subject. A heavy, uncomfortable silence filled the space between us, and my heart started to pound against my chest.

"Do you have any idea how worried I've been?" he finally asked.

Despite the seriousness of the situation, I felt myself

bristle. "Why?" It wasn't like I had a curfew. Dad was always too busy to care.

"Because no one has been able to get a hold of you for hours, Indigo! I've spent the entire evening calling all your friends, but nobody knew where you were."

I winced so hard my left eye closed. "Yeah, about that... I maybe sorta lost my phone."

"I know." Dad retrieved something from his pocket.

"I—how did you get that?" I stuttered, staring at the *Lady Phoenix* stickers decorating the back of my phone case. My fingers itched to snatch it away from him, but I didn't dare. Not when Dad was glaring at me like I'd committed a felony.

"You left it at the recording studio after your fight with Violet," he explained. "She found it and brought it home." *And told me what happened*, the look on his face seemed to say.

Good. It was about time I aired my grievances. "Sooo..." I said, nodding to my phone. "Can I have that back?"

"I think the more pressing question that needs to be addressed," he said, his grip on my phone tightening, "is where have you been?"

"Just driving around. I needed to clear my head." No way was I going to tell him I drove out to San Bernardino to visit our old house. Or that I fell asleep in my car. Either confession might put Dad, who looked like he was about to have a coronary, over the edge.

"For nine hours?" he demanded. "Indigo, how could you be so irresponsible, especially after the conversation we had three weeks ago? I was about to call the police."

A brief image of myself in the back of a cop car flickered through my head. *That* would have been mortifying, but at least then I'd know he cared.

"I'm not sure what you want me to say other than I'm sorry," I answered. "I didn't mean to lose my phone. It was an accident. If I hadn't lost it, you'd have known where I was. I'll be more careful next time, I promise." Crossing my fingers underneath the table, I casually glanced at the clock on the stove, yawned, and prayed I could wiggle my way out of this. "Is it okay if I go to bed now? I have to get up in five hours."

Dad's nostrils flared. I got the sense that if I moved a single inch, he'd release a guttural roar. "No, Indie. Apart from being nowhere close to finished with this matter, we still need to talk about how you treated your sister. Your behavior was unacceptable."

"I'm sorry, but how exactly?" Because heaven forbid I tell the goddamn princess the truth about how I felt. We didn't want to hurt her precious feelings.

"You blamed Violet for my and your mother's divorce," Dad said, a combination of anger and disbelief coating his tone, as if the mere thought was implausible. As if he hadn't spent every second of the past five years devoted to her success at the expense of the other members of this family.

I lifted my shoulders in a half-hearted shrug. "And?"

He shook his head, his mouth hanging slack. "How could you accuse her of something like that? Do you know how much that hurt her? She cried all evening."

"Seriously? For once, can we not pretend like her career didn't take over all our lives?"

"That's not true—"

"You're shitting me, right?" I pounded my fist on the table, causing the coffee mugs to rattle together. "You of all people should know better. Your life *revolves* around her!"

Fire flashed in Dad's eyes. "Indie, my job as Violet's manager may have thrown my and your mother's relationship issues into relief, but it was never the cause of our marital problems."

"Then what was?" I exclaimed, fighting to control the waver in my voice. "Because I sure as hell don't understand."

"Sweetie," he replied, his tone suddenly gentle, like he was trying to cushion a blow, "sometimes things don't work out even if we really want them to. After many conversations, your mother and I accepted that we're two very different people who want opposing things out of life."

"No, that's not going to cut it." Twice now, Violet had insinuated that there was more to the story, so it was time for

Dad to enlighten me. "I don't want to hear the nice, let's-all-hold-hands-and-sing-Kumbaya version of what happened. I want the truth."

Dad blinked at me, expressionless. After what felt like an eon, he sighed, removed his glasses, and dragged a hand down his face. "It was my fault," he said, more to himself than to me, like this was the first time in years he'd allowed himself to remember.

"Did you cheat on her?" I asked point-blank.

"What?" Dad jerked back like someone had lassoed him around the shoulders. "Of course not! I would *never* do something like that to her."

His shock—explosive but clearly grief-stricken—was believable. "Okay, then what?"

"I—" Dad shifted in his seat and dropped his gaze.

A chill slid down my spine. What could possibly be worse than him cheating on her?

Three unnerving seconds later, he raised a pleading gaze to mine. "Please understand that if I'd known what I was asking of her, I never would have—"

"Just get to the point," I exclaimed, losing patience.

Dad took a deep breath. Held it in. Exhaled. "I asked your mother to give up her dream of becoming a concert violinist."

What? All these years, I'd never understood why Mom

stopped performing when she'd been so close to making it. Everything she'd ever wanted was right there; all she had to do was reach out and take it. Instead, she walked away.

But maybe that decision wasn't as much of a choice as I thought.

"Explain," I demanded.

"Did your mother ever tell you the only reason we decided to get married was because she got pregnant with Violet?"

"Yeah," I said, my shoulders stiffening, "I knew that." Well…sort of. When Mom told the story, she always made Dad's proposal sound like a grand, romantic gesture.

"The problem was neither of us were making enough money to cover the cost of childcare," he continued. "This was before your grandma moved to the LA area, so we didn't have anyone to help us. Our only option was for someone to stay home. At the time, I'd just been hired as a teller at the bank. Didn't earn much, but my paycheck was steady in comparison to your mother's."

To a stranger, this logic would seem reasonable. Responsible even. But anyone who knew my mom would understand how utterly senseless it was. Josephine and performing went hand in hand, like thunder and lightning or sand and shore.

Bile burned at the back of my throat. "How could you?"

"It was so long ago, sweetie. We were young and still getting to know each other. If I'd known back then what performing meant to her, I never would have asked her to quit."

My dad's confession was a lot to take in.

Looking away from him, I clutched my pendant and stared out the window. The moon was high, illuminating the dark waters of the Pacific, and as I mulled over this new information, I watched waves break against the beach. While I was willing to admit that my dad's story was a contributing factor in my parents' split, I had a hard time believing it was the sole reason.

"Indie?" Dad prompted.

I turned back to him and crossed my arms. "You guys seemed fine before Violet—"

"I know you think your sister's career is to blame for all this," he said, speaking over me, "and that me becoming her manager somehow ruined my relationship with your mom, but our marriage was on the rocks long before that. And by the time I realized how unhappy she was? It was too late." I frowned, still not convinced, so Dad added, "None of this means we don't love you, Indie. We'll always be thankful that you and Violet came into our lives."

For a moment, I let his words wash over me, but they didn't soothe my anger.

They fed it.

Dad could say he loved me all he wanted, but when was the last time he'd actually acted like a father?

HEARTSTRINGS

"You know what, Dad?" I asked. Rage swept through me like fire chasing gasoline. "That's pretty damn hard to believe coming from you."

"Indie," Dad exclaimed, recoiling from me as if my words were a physical blow. "How can you say something like that?"

"You say Violet's career hasn't affected our lives, but when was the last time you spent any time with me? Or had a conversation with me that wasn't interrupted by a business call? You're always busy working on stuff for her, but I'm your daughter too. And when I try to talk to you about it, you brush me off. I feel like my existence is just a huge inconvenience to you."

His throat bobbed as he stared at me. "Oh, sweetie, I hate that you feel that way. I wish I'd known."

"But you did know, Dad. We've had this conversation before. In October when you bailed on the horror marathon at Cinépolis, when we arrived at the *Immortal Nights* premiere," I said, counting the examples off on my fingers. "But trying to get you to listen to me is like talking to an empty room—it doesn't matter if I'm shouting at the top of my lungs, because there's no one there to hear me." I paused for a moment, then added, "Subconscious or not, you've chosen work over me every single time."

Dad sank his fingers into his graying hair. He looked gutted.

"Indie," he said, his voice cracking. "I never meant—" He broke off, too overcome to finish his sentence.

"Do you know how lonely it's been for me? Mom's gone, every second of Violet's life is scheduled, and I'm lucky if you bother to have a five-minute conversation with me. All I want is to spend time with you. Is that really too much to ask?"

When Dad finally looked up at me, there was a watery glisten to his eyes. "I'm so unbelievably sorry, Indie. You and your sister have always been so independent. I never realized you needed anything from me."

"I do need you," I replied, my own eyes watering. "And not just when I've been missing for nine hours."

Reaching across the table, Dad took my hand in his. "Kiddo, I promise I'll cut back on my hours and make an effort to be more present. Things are going to change around here for the better, okay?" He gave my fingers a sight squeeze. "I never want you to feel like this again."

"Okay," I said squeezing back. I wasn't sure I believed him, but maybe this time would be different. There was, after all, a first time for everything.

"Now, can you do something for me in return?" he asked.

I nodded. "I suppose that's fair."

"Never disappear like that again."

"Done." Scaring him had never been my intention in the first place.

"Also, can you please make up with your sister? It's not fair to blame her for my mistake, and I'd hate to think that I'm the reason you two aren't close like you used to be."

This time, I shook my head. "Sorry, but I don't think I can do that." Perhaps I was wrong for blaming the divorce on her, but there were so many other issues that contributed to our lack of relationship. The bad blood between us ran too deep.

"Fine." He sighed. "At the very least, you need to apologize to her for what you said this afternoon. Also, I hope you realize that despite this conversation, you're not off the hook. You are very, very grounded."

I guessed that meant I'd have lots of time to figure out what I was going to do with my life now that I wouldn't be attending Juilliard. I knew I should tell him, but after everything that had happened today, I couldn't do it. I was too emotionally drained.

"Yeah, I figured." I ran my fingers through my bangs. They were tangled and greasy and in desperate need of a brush. "How long?"

"We'll discuss that later. Why don't you go to bed? You look like you're going to pass out right here at the table."

CHAPTER 16

I didn't leave the confines of my bed for the majority of Wednesday, instead choosing to hole up under the covers like an injured animal licking its wounds.

Thursday wasn't any different.

Whether it was from emotional stress and heartbreak or because I'd actually come down with something, I'd been experiencing flu-like symptoms for the past two days. Dad, who so far was taking his promise to be more involved in my life seriously, had called me in sick after my temperature registered over one hundred.

To keep my mind off Juilliard and the loss of my childhood dream, I picked a mindless TV show on Netflix to binge. By the time I reached season four, my eyes hurt from staring at the glow of my laptop screen for days on end. As illogical as it sounded, my brain was fried from doing absolutely nothing.

I needed a break.

HEARTSTRINGS

And a shower, I realized as I pushed stringy bangs off my forehead. But I lacked the energy needed for my usual bathroom routine, so I opted for dry shampoo and deodorant.

Once I felt moderately less greasy, I went down to the kitchen for a snack. I wasn't hungry, hadn't been since my fight with Violet, but eating was something to do. After pouring myself a bowl of Frosted Flakes, I took a spot at the breakfast nook and scrolled through the texts I'd been ignoring since Tuesday.

TUE, DEC 1, 6:38 P.M.

GALAXY RIDER:

Indie, I'm so sorry.

I know I should've told you about Violet earlier, but can we talk? I want to explain myself.

Hello?

WED, DEC 2, 1:51 P.M.

GALAXY RIDER:

So...I may have left you the world's longest voicemail where all I do is ramble. Feel free to save me the embarrassment by deleting it. I just wanted to let you know that I spoke with Violet and Alec. The three of us decided to push off recording the single until Friday so you and I could

> have time to talk. If you could give me a call before then, I'd really appreciate it.

THU, DEC 3, 7:13 P.M.

GALAXY RIDER:

> Sofia said you haven't shown up for school the past two days. Is everything okay? I'm worried about you.

> Indie, I want you there tomorrow. I wouldn't be doing this if it wasn't for you and it would feel wrong recording this song without you.

FRI, DEC 4, 6:46 A.M.

GALAXY RIDER:

> Okay, I get it. You want to be left alone. I'll stop bothering you.

I couldn't bring myself to respond to any of his texts.

I knew he hadn't meant to hurt me. And I wasn't mad at him, not really. It was just really hard to ignore the ache in my chest whenever I thought about him working with Violet.

Sighing, I picked up my empty bowl and brought it over to the sink before sorting through yesterday's mail, which was sitting in a pile on the island. A large envelope with my name and ACM's logo printed on the front caught my attention. I ripped the letter open, unfolded the paper, and—

Accepted. I was accepted to ACM.

I should have been happy, grateful that Sofia had pushed me to apply somewhere other than Juilliard so I had a school to attend next fall, but I didn't feel anything. No excitement, no relief. Despite my love of SFX makeup, I was too gutted over my loss to feel anything other than heartbreak. There were other good music schools I could apply to—I was pretty sure Curtis's application wasn't due until December 15—but my heart just wasn't in it.

A knock on the front door startled me out of my thoughts.

"Hello? Anyone home?"

"In here," I called, stuffing the acceptance letter into my back pocket.

Five seconds later, a girl with cat's-eye glasses and French braids strode into the kitchen—Lydia, Violet's personal assistant; between creating my portfolio for ACM, practicing for my Juilliard audition, and trying my best to avoid Violet, I hadn't seen her since early October.

"Hey, Indie! How are you?" she said in her usual bubbly voice. I had to give her props; how someone could work for my sister and still be so cheerful was beyond me.

"I'm all right. You?"

"Good, just delivering some work stuff for your dad," she said, holding up a thick folder before setting it next to the pile of mail. "Now I'm off to pick up lunch for Violet and some other people at the studio. Did you hear she's recording a song with Xander Jones from the Heartbreakers? How exciting is that?"

Just hearing his name was enough to make me flinch. "Oh yeah. Super exciting."

Lydia must not have picked up on my tone, because she offered me one of her sunny smiles. "Do you want to come with me? I could use a hand with all the food orders, and I'm sure Violet would love to see you."

That was highly doubtful.

"Thanks, but I can't," I replied. "I've been home sick for the past few days, so I have a lot of homework to catch up on." Sofia had stopped by this morning with my assignments and promised to return after school with today's workload.

"Ugh, that sounds like the worst."

"Yeah, pretty much."

A pair of car keys jingled as Lydia pulled them out of her purse. "Well, I hope you feel better soon. It was good running into you."

"You too," I replied as she headed back toward the foyer. "And I'm glad to see your leg is better."

Lydia turned back around, her eyebrows squished together. "My leg?"

"You broke it right before Comic Con, right?"

Her frown deepened. "What are you talking about?"

I gave her a weird look. "Violet asked me to be her personal assistant for the weekend because you broke your leg."

"No," Lydia said, shaking her head. "She gave me off that weekend."

"What?" I asked. "Why?"

She shrugged. "Not sure, but it definitely wasn't because I hurt myself. Anyway, I've got to get going. See you around, Indie."

☆ ♭ ♪

Sitting on the piano bench in the music room, I stared down at the keys as if they were pieces to the puzzle I was trying to put together. After Lydia left, I'd come back upstairs with the intention of crawling under my covers again but had somehow wound up in here.

I hadn't played a single note since lifting the fallboard. I was too lost in my own confusion to make room for something as simple as a song. It made absolutely no sense that Violet had given Lydia time off for such a huge promotional event, yet she'd asked me to come to Comic Con instead.

Why?

I closed my eyes and pored over my memories of the trip for any clues. The only thing that made me pause was the conversation we'd had on the flight to New York when Violet had mentioned dinner reservations and mani-pedis. Had she...wanted to hang out with me? She'd said as much, but I'd figured she was just being nice. The thought was laughable, absurd even, but also the only explanation that came to mind.

Things just weren't adding up.

If my ridiculous theory was true and she actually had wanted to spend time with me that weekend, I couldn't help but wonder what had changed. And why now? Because for the past five years, Violet had been too busy being Lilliana LaCroix to be my big sister.

Then again, if I was being truly honest with myself, I hadn't been a very good sister either. I'd spent so much energy resenting the way her career had changed my life, then blaming her for causing Mom and Dad's divorce. I was hurt she'd never come to any of my orchestra concerts, but when was the last time I'd shown up to support Violet for one of her events? She literally had to pay me to go to Comic Con, and the only reason I'd attended the *IN* premiere was because Xander had asked me to. On top of that, I'd congratulated Alec on his record label but hadn't said a word to Violet about recording her first album. And all the while, she'd constantly checked in with me about my Juilliard application, which was way more than Dad had ever done. I'd thought Violet was being nosey and overbearing, but what if she genuinely wanted to make sure I did well?

It was hard for me to admit, but maybe Violet was… different.

At some point, she'd changed for the better, but I had no way of knowing when because I'd been too angry with her to notice. Yes, she was just as busy as she'd always been, but when she was home, she made a point of seeing how I was doing. The two of us had spoken more in the past two months than we had in years.

Whatever her motive for inviting me to Comic Con, I realized I owed her an apology. Violet was right—I needed to stop blaming her for my own unhappiness. If I wasn't pleased with the way my life was going, then *I* needed to do something about it. I was an adult. It wasn't Violet's, my parents', or anyone else's job to make sure I was content. Happiness didn't just exist inside people like blood or bones or DNA—it had to be created.

Violet spent October and November trying to fix the rift between us. But I'd ignored her and spat those efforts back in her face.

It was time for that to change.

With a newfound sense of understanding, I slid off the piano bench and went to my dad's office. He was on the phone, but as soon as he saw me standing in the doorway, he ended his call. There was a look of concern etched into the lines of his face.

"Indie, are you okay?" he asked, the wheels of his computer chair whirling against the floor as he pushed away from his desk. "Your fever isn't worse, is it?"

"Actually," I said, scraping a hand through my bangs, "I'm feeling much better, and I was hoping to talk to you about something?"

"Sure," he said, relaxing into a smile. He wheeled back toward his desk, then pointed to the armchair on the opposite side, indicating that I should take a seat. "What about?"

I pulled it out and sank into the cushion. "Well, I thought a lot about Violet today, and I came to the realization that I haven't been very fair to her. I was wondering if you'd let me go to the recording studio so I could apologize to her."

He frowned. "I don't know, Indie."

"I know I'm grounded," I replied in a rush, "but I'd just be going there and back. I promise I won't stop anywhere else."

"Kiddo, it's not that…"

"Oh." I paused, taken aback. "Then what is it?"

"Your sister isn't very happy with you," he said, giving me a confused look. "After talking with her this morning, I think it's going to take more than one conversation to fix things between you two, and since today is her birthday, I don't want her—"

Dad kept talking, but his words didn't register. My mind was stuck on repeat: *Today is her birthday, her birthday, her birthday.* I tried to swallow, but my throat was thick and tight. How had I forgotten? If I hadn't already felt like the world's shittiest sister, I certainly did now.

"Indie?" Dad was staring at me as if I'd just announced my plans to join the circus. "You sure you're okay?"

"I'm fine," I said, shaking my head to clear the remaining fog. "Look, I don't want to ruin Violet's birthday. I just want to apologize. If she doesn't want to talk to me, I'll leave her alone, I swear."

Dad steepled his fingers, pressing them against his lips as he considered.

"You're the one who asked me to make things right with her, remember?" I added.

"Fine," he said, releasing a sigh. "But you should text her first. If she doesn't want to talk with you, then there's no point in driving all the way out to Hollywood."

"Yes, of course," I said, shooting to my feet with a grin. "Thank you, thank you, thank you!"

☆ ♭ ♪

Violet still hadn't responded to my text by the time I reached New Edge. When I didn't hear back from her after a quick shower, I'd decided that no response wasn't the same thing as a flat-out refusal to speak to me and hopped in my car, fingers crossed her phone died or she was too busy working on the song to answer me. But as I pulled into the parking lot,

Alec stepped outside. He looked like he was leaving—there was a messenger bag slung over one of his shoulders and car keys in his hand. I swung my car into the nearest spot, not caring if I was parked between the lines, and jumped out.

"Alec, hold up a sec!" I called, rushing across the blacktop.

He paused at the edge of the sidewalk to wait for me.

"Is my sister still here?" I asked when I reached him.

Alec ran a hand over his perfectly styled bangs. "Sorry, Indie. She left as soon as we wrapped everything up. That was about fifteen minutes ago."

The uncomfortable look on his face was enough to tell me he knew exactly what was going on between me and Violet. And that she must have received my text and chosen to ignore it. After everything, I couldn't blame her.

"Okay, thanks," I said, my shoulders slumping. "I take it you guys finished the song?"

He shook his head. "Almost. There's something missing I can't put my finger on, but it will have to wait until we get back."

"Back from what?"

"The next leg of our tour. We leave for Dubai Sunday night," he explained. "I wish we could get more studio time in tomorrow, but I made brunch plans with Felicity, and Violet's busy all afternoon with her party."

"Oh, right," I said, even though I had no knowledge of

said party. Was she hosting it at our house? Even if she was, I bet I wasn't invited. "I take it Xander's left as well?"

Another shake of the head. "No, he's still here. Should be right behind me. I think he had to run to the bathroom."

Frowning, I glanced around the parking lot but didn't spot his SUV. Besides mine, the only other car was a black Cadillac.

As if he knew what I was thinking, Alec added, "We drove together."

"Gotcha," I said. "Is there any chance you wouldn't mind waiting around for a bit? I need to talk to Xander about something, and while I have no problem offering him a ride, I don't know if he'll accept one from me right now."

Alec waved me off, already pulling a pair of earbuds from his pocket. "No worries. Tell him I'll be in my car. Good luck."

"Thanks," I said, turning toward the front entrance and squaring my shoulders. "I'm definitely going to need it."

Inside, the studio was dark and cool. A ten-foot aquarium ran the length of the reception area, casting the room in a blue glow. Tropical fish flickered through the water like a moving rainbow, and I smiled when I noticed the pineapple house ornament positioned at the bottom of the tank. The building was larger than it looked from the outside, and before I could figure out which way to go, Xander rounded a corner to my left.

The sight of him made me suck in a breath. He was wearing a green Triforce T-shirt, dark-wash jeans, and a pair of worn sneakers—nerdy, but in a hot, boy-next-door sort of way—and his golden-red hair was a tousled mess. When his eyes locked on mine, he stopped short.

"Indie." There was no trace of his usual smile as he adjusted his glasses. "What are you doing here?"

"Looking for you. I was hoping we could talk."

Xander shoved both hands in his pockets, his gaze darting toward the exit before flickering back to me. "I don't know. Alec is supposed to give me a ride, and I don't want to keep him waiting."

My chest twinged at his response, but I wasn't surprised. Not after I'd ignored him for several days straight. "I ran into Alec on his way out. He said he'd wait for you."

"Oh." Xander glanced around as if searching for a way out of his current situation, then sighed in resignation. "All right then."

"Cool," I said, even though I felt anything but. "Should we sit down?"

His responding nod was stiff. "Sure."

We both turned toward the small sitting area composed of a love seat, two armchairs, and a coffee table with a colorful box placed at its center. At first, I thought it was a board game, but upon closer inspection, I realized the box was a thousand-piece jigsaw puzzle that, when completed, depicted a teeming coral reef. I sat down first, leaving plenty of room for Xander on the opposite side of the small couch. My heart shrank slightly when he chose to perch on the armrest of one of the chairs instead. After settling himself, he crossed his arms and fixed his spring-green eyes on me. They were blank and unreadable.

Unable to meet his stare, I dropped my gaze to my feet. "So," I said, focusing on the scuff mark marring the shiny toe of my boot. "There's a lot I want to say to you, but I'm not sure where to start."

"You're nervous." The surprise in his voice made me look up.

"I—well, yeah. Is it that obvious?"

He jerked his chin at my chest. "You're clutching your pendant as if your life depends on it."

I glanced down and was surprised to find my fingers wrapped around the purple stone in a death grip. "Oh." I let go and folded my hands in my lap. "I didn't realize."

His brows furrowed. "You're never nervous."

"Definitely not true," I told him. *Especially around you.*

"Well, I guess you're usually better at hiding it," he said, lifting his shoulder in a half shrug. "What's going on?"

Besides the fact that I missed my application deadline for Juilliard, was grounded for the next millennium, and had been a raging bitch to my sister for years? Nothing at all. "I shouldn't have freaked out the way I did when you told me you're working with Violet."

"Wait." He unfolded his arms and sat up straighter, an incredulous look spreading across his face. "You're not pissed at me?"

I shook my head. "I was angry with Violet, not you."

"But you've ignored me for the past three days."

"I know," I said, cringing slightly. "That was really shitty of me, and I'm sorry. I just…needed space to figure some stuff out."

"Like what?"

"For starters, you were right."

His eyes widened as if my answer was the opposite of what he'd been expecting. Three unbearably long seconds passed, and then the corner of his mouth twitched, the smallest hint of a smile. "I'm right about a lot of things. What are you talking about specifically?"

A kernel of hope bloomed in my chest at his playful response. I latched on to that feeling and dove into my explanation, fingers crossed I could fix whatever damage I'd caused. "Violet," I replied. "She—she's not the person I've accused her of being. I think deep down I knew that, but it's a lot easier to blame other people for our own problems, isn't it?" Xander didn't respond, only cocked his head, so I quickly added, "I encouraged you to write a song, but when things didn't go the way I envisioned them, I didn't react well, and that wasn't fair of me. I'm so sorry, Xander. This whole thing was supposed to be about you, and I made it about me and Violet. I understand if you want nothing to do with me after this conversation."

"Want nothing to do with you?" Xander repeated slowly, his voice barely more than a whisper. "How could you possibly think that?"

My leg was bouncing, channeling all the nervous energy inside me, and I had to cap a hand over my knee to make it stop. "Well, you didn't exactly give me the warmest of welcomes."

"Indie." His throat bobbed. "I thought you were here to break up with me."

I opened my mouth to respond, but then his words sank in, and I felt my eyebrows shoot up. "I didn't realize we were dating." The thought had crossed my mind that night on the beach—what were we to each other? But the Heartbreakers' tour loomed over the possibility of a relationship, so I never voiced my question.

"Crap, that came out all wrong. I know we're not *dating* dating. What I meant was I thought you were going to put an end to whatever this is between us," he said, his cheeks flushing a deep red, "because there *is* something between us, at least there is to me. We haven't known each other very long, but you feel like home, Indie. I don't want to lose that feeling." Taking a deep breath, he moved over to the couch, his knee knocking against mine as he sat down. "I should have asked you this before I left for tour, but I'm hoping better late than never? Indigo Josephine Mitchell-Jamiolkowski, would you be—"

"Wait a minute. Since when do you know my full name?" I said, startled to hear it come out of his mouth. I never so much as gave him my middle initial, let alone told him that Indie was short for Indigo.

"Really? That's what you're focused on right now?" he asked, his entire face scrunching up in an are-you-for-real look. "I'm trying to ask you to be my girlfriend here."

"Yeah, I get that, but how do you have such top secret information about me?"

"Top secret?" He snorted. "How do you think I know?"

"Violet?" I guessed.

"Yes, Violet," he replied, his response dripping with exasperation. "Now will you shut up and let me ask you out?"

Tapping a finger against my chin, I pretended to consider his question for a moment. "Hmm, I suppose that can be allowed."

Xander let out a breath of relief. "Indie, from the moment I met you—"

"Whoa, hold on," I said, cutting him off again, because

pushing Xander's buttons when he was flustered was too fun to resist. "This is starting to sound like a marriage proposal."

"Oh my God," he exclaimed, throwing his hands up in the air. "You're infuriating!"

A wicked grin curled on my lips. "Yes, but you still *like* me. You want me to be your *girlfriend*."

"Yes, I do," he said, catching my wrists and not letting go. "So will you?"

My smile softened. "On one condition."

Eyes glittering, he heaved a theatrical sigh. "Indie, I've already told you—no alien role-playing, okay? I'm just not into that kinky stuff."

I scoffed. "No, E.T. I want you to kiss me."

Xander released my wrists and leaned over, taking my face in his hands. "Now that," he said, his calloused fingers caressing my cheeks with gentle strokes, "is something I can do."

As my eyes fluttered closed, our lips met in a desperate clash, and then we were kissing like never before. There was an urgency to the way Xander's mouth moved on mine, like he was trying to kiss away any lingering doubts I had about his feelings for me, but I had none, not after the speech he'd given me. My hands slid up his chest, over the soft cotton of his shirt, until they reached his lean, lightly muscled shoulders. I dragged him closer, wanting to feel his body against mine. He responded hungrily, letting go of my face and bearing down on me until I was pinned between him and the backrest of the couch. When his teeth grazed my bottom lip, I let out a shuddering gasp. This was the kind of once-in-a-lifetime kiss that stories were written about—a kiss that could set your heart ablaze and devoured you whole. I never wanted it to end.

After another minute of kissing each other senseless, Xander broke away from me. "Are you sure?" he asked, gasping for breath.

"About kissing you?" Considering what we'd just been doing, I thought my answer was pretty obvious. "Obviously."

"No, about being my girlfriend."

Ohhh. "Well, now that you mention it, I have one more condition."

"Mm-hmm?" he replied, nudging his nose against mine.

"I want to hear your song."

CHAPTER 17

Alec withdrew a ring of keys from his pocket, sifted through the collection of clinking silver and gold until he found the correct one, then unlocked the door. He flipped on the light to the control room, and we filed inside.

The space was long and rectangular, with a couch and coffee table to my left and a massive analog mixing board on the right. The board was positioned in front of a glass window overlooking a live room, the performance area for instrumentalists and singers alike. It was outfitted with microphones and mic stands, along with a plethora of instruments including a rack of guitars, a drum set, and a grand piano.

"Give me a moment to start up my laptop," Alec said, lifting the flap of his messenger bag and drawing it out. After making my request to hear his song, Xander had gone out to the parking lot to retrieve him, and he'd brought us here.

"Does he have to turn on all that for me to hear the song?"

I whispered, nodding at the expensive-looking equipment. There were all manner of buttons and dials and screens, none of which I knew the purpose of.

Xander stuck his hands in his pockets. "Nope. It's on his computer."

"Then why are we in here?" I asked, still taking in the control room. It was a fascinating place, a combination of my imagination—fueled by the glamorous portrayals of recording studios I'd seen in movies and TV shows—and reality, which had more of a cozy home vibe; the furniture was worn, multiple water rings stained the wooden coffee table, and an oversize Persian rug covered the majority of the floor.

"Since you didn't get to watch us record the song, I thought you might want to hear it where you could get a sense of the process." He rubbed the back of his neck. "Is that stupid?"

"Of course not." I felt a slight pang of guilt knowing I'd missed such an important moment. I should have been here for Xander, especially after he'd opened up to me about feeling like the odd one out among his bandmates. Leaning over, I pressed a kiss to his cheek. "Thank you. This was such a sweet gesture."

When I pulled away, Alec was standing in front of us.

He passed his laptop to Xander. "You can hit Play whenever you're ready. I missed a call from Felicity, so I'm going to call her back." Whether it was the truth or an excuse to give us privacy, I was grateful as Alec slipped out of the room, the door clicking shut behind him.

"Shall we?" Xander asked, nodding at the couch. There was a note of nervousness in his voice, so I offered him an encouraging smile.

"I've wanted to hear this song ever since you agreed to write it," I told him, plopping down onto one of the threadbare cushions and folding my legs beneath me. "I can't wait."

"Well," Xander said, sitting down next to me, "I hope it doesn't disappoint."

It didn't.

When he hit Play, I expected to hear an upbeat country song, not a slow-tempo acoustic ballad. When his voice spilled from the computer, I closed my eyes and listened.

> *That first summer I was bathed in light*
> *And it felt like walking on water*
> *But the rush is gone, I stand all alone*
> *Eclipsed by others, greater*
>
> *Now the season's changed, I'm in the dark*
> *And I think I'm taking on water*
> *Screaming, "I'm still here," but no one hears*
> *Am I just a passing phase? I wonder*

But then your voice
So strong and sweet
Echoes back to me
You take my hand
And by your side
I finally feel seen

Just a California girl
With gold in her eyes
And a hopeful boy
Under indigo skies

That cold fall night we lay in the sand
Do you know how that moment changed me?
Talking, laughing, kissing until dawn
Your conviction helped me break free

And now your voice
So strong and sweet
Resonates inside me
With your hand in mine
I'm flying high
Don't need to feel seen

HEARTSTRINGS

Just a California girl
With gold in her eyes
And a hopeful boy
Under indigo skies

You're a California girl
With gold in your eyes
I'm a boy in love
Under indigo skies

By the time the music faded, there were tears in my eyes.

Even with Violet singing the chorus of the song, the lyrics clearly belonged to Xander. They told his story, *our* story, and I was at a loss for words. After several silent seconds ticked by, Xander lifted his gaze to meet mine. His eyes went wide when he saw me.

"Oh my God. Indie, why are you crying?"

"Because that was beautiful," I said, wiping my tear-stained cheeks with the back of my hand. It was taking every ounce of my control to keep myself from sobbing and turning into a blubbering mess.

"You really think so?"

"No, I'm crying because it sucked so bad that I'll probably be traumatized for life," I said, shooting him a look. "Of course I think so, you big dork."

He grinned, lifting his shoulder in a half shrug. "Hey, you never know. Maybe you hated it and didn't want to hurt my feelings. It was a bit personal after all."

"No one has *ever* written a song for me before." Or done anything remotely romantic for me. Just thinking about the lyrics was enough to make my heart race. "I could never hate it."

Xander visibly relaxed. "You don't know how much of a relief that is."

"What's it called?" I asked, even though I had an inkling.

"'Indigo Skies.'"

I opened my mouth, wanting to explain to him how much this meant to me, how proud I was of him for writing it, but Alec had returned.

"I'm back," he announced, slipping his cell into his pocket as he stepped into the room. He immediately focused on me. "What do you think?"

"I love it," I told him truthfully. "It's seriously amazing."

He crossed his arms, his mouth scrunching up on one side as if he didn't like my answer. "Okay, sure, overall, it's fine, but don't you think there's something missing?"

"I don't know," I said. "I've only heard it once."

So Alec made me listen to the song again. And again.

"Now what do you think?" he asked after the third listen.

"It's beautiful, but…"

Alec leaned forward, eyes eager. "Yes?"

"I don't know. The melody is a bit—calm? Almost like it's too subtle," I replied, struggling to come up with the right words to explain what I was thinking. Producing music was outside my area of expertise. "Maybe it needs more intensity. Can you edge it up a bit?"

"*Yes*," Alec said, snapping his fingers and pointing at me in agreement. "That's what I thought too. I tried to amp things up with an electric guitar, but it didn't sound right."

"Hmm." Tugging on my bottom lip, I glanced around the room in thought. When my gaze landed on a rack of instruments in the live room, an idea began unfolding in my mind, but it didn't present itself to me in words. I could hear the notes of a new melody playing inside my head, and my fingers itched to bring it to life. "Can I grab something out of there?" I asked Alec, pointing at the glass window.

Without a word, he extracted his key ring. After flipping through it and singling out a key with red nail polish painted on the head, he passed it over to me. "First door on your left."

"Thanks," I said, striding out of the room. I came back two minutes later with a violin clutched in my hands. "Suppose an electric guitar wasn't the right instrument?"

"Okay," Alec asked, his eyes sparkling. "What are you thinking?"

Taking a deep breath, I settled the violin between my shoulder and chin, raised my bow, and started to play. The new tune flourishing inside my head flowed out of me, filling the room with a wild, haunting sound. When I finished, I lowered the instrument and peeked over at the boys, nervous about their reaction. "Something like that? We could add it to the pre-chorus."

Xander gaped at me. "Did you come up with that just now?"

I nodded. "I—yeah. Was that bad? If you don't like it, you can ignore me. It was just an idea."

"Indie," Xander said, his mouth still hanging open. "That was amazing."

Alec rubbed his chin. "I like it, but can you go higher on that last note?"

"Sure." I started over, this time making a small change to the ending. "How was that?"

"Good," Alec answered, but he wasn't looking at me. He'd thrown himself onto the rolling chair in front of the mixing board and was busy booting up a computer. "I need you to play it again, exactly how you did just now."

"Um, okay. Why?"

He glanced back at me, his brow pinched together as if I'd asked the most obvious question in the world. "For the song."

"Wait a minute." My breath caught in my throat. "You want to record *me* and add it to Xander's song?" I'd never created new music before, only performed existing pieces, but something about this was exhilarating—I felt jittery and ecstatic all at once.

"Yes, Indie. Your idea, your melody, your playing—it's all perfect."

☆ ♡ ♪

"How'd it go?" Dad asked, appearing at the door as soon as I stepped into the mudroom.

After recording the new instrumental part for Xander's song, I wished him and Alec good luck on the next leg of their tour and drove home. Although I wanted to spend as much time with Xander as possible, I'd been at the studio for over an hour and didn't want to push my luck. Not when Dad was trying his best to be as present as possible. Surely he'd notice if I was out all afternoon.

"It didn't." With a sigh, I dropped my bag and car keys into my designated cubby, then bent over to yank off my Docs. "Violet was already gone by the time I got there. Is she home?"

"No," he said, crossing his arms as my first boot thunked against the floor. It was quickly followed by its mate. "I thought I told you to text her before you left?"

"I did, but she didn't answer," I said, straightening up. "I figured she was busy working and hadn't seen it, but I guess not." My heart fluttered uncomfortably around the half-truth, and I quickly looked away.

"Oh, sweetie," Dad said sympathetically. He must have misinterpreted my guilt as disappointment, because he stepped forward and wrapped his arms around me. "I know you feel bad, but Violet will come around. Just give her time, okay?"

Nodding against his chest, I closed my eyes and gave myself a moment to enjoy the comfort of his hug before pulling away. "I ran into Alec at the recording studio. He mentioned something about a birthday party for Violet. Are we throwing one here tomorrow?"

Dad shook his head. "A few of her costars are hosting it at their place, and before you ask, the answer is no—you're not allowed to go. You're still grounded. We're celebrating with your grandma next weekend at Vine & Dine."

"Don't worry. I wasn't planning on it." Heaving a sigh, I gestured toward the back staircase. "Well, I'll be upstairs. I need to get some homework done."

"Okay. I'm ordering Pacific Crust for dinner tonight. What do you want on your pizza?"

"Just cheese, but can you get some of those garlic knots too?"

"Sure thing." Dad turned to go, then paused in the

doorway. When he glanced back at me, I could see the uncertainty in his eyes. "I was also wondering… Would you maybe want to watch a movie tonight?"

"With you?" I asked, not bothering to keep the surprise from my voice.

He nodded. "Since I missed the Halloween marathon, I thought we could watch something scary."

My heart leapt at the suggestion, and I broke out into a grin. "Yeah, Dad. I'd really like that."

"Good," he said, returning my smile, and as if to signal the end of our conversation, his phone rang. "Duty calls, but I'll see you later tonight, okay? You pick the movie, I'll bring the popcorn." Then he was off, punching Talk on his headset and heading down the hall to his office.

I watched him go, pleasantly surprised by our exchange. This was still the same Edward Jamiolkowski who reveled in working twelve-hour days, but now he was finding time to fit me in, even if it was only a movie or a quick chat.

Still grinning to myself, I retreated to my bedroom and closed the door. Dad was probably right, I needed to be patient with Violet, but just in case I was wrong about her ignoring me, I sent one last text.

INDIE:

> Hey, Vi. I know you're mad at me, but can we talk? I really want to apologize.

Once my jeans were swapped for a pair of sweatpants, I brought my backpack over to my desk and took out my physics textbook. I'd missed a lab on Wednesday and had to solve an entire packet of practice problems to make up for it. Before digging in, I checked my phone to see if Violet had responded. There were no new notifications, but I clicked on our conversation anyway. When I spotted the tiny gray message below my text, I did a double take.

INDIE:

> Hey, Vi. I know you're mad at me, but can we talk? I really want to apologize.

READ 4:12 PM

At some point between texting Violet about coming to New Edge and now, she'd turned on her read receipts...so I'd *know* she was ignoring me.

Greeeat.

Unlike me, Violet wasn't normally one to hold grudges, which meant she must be beyond pissed. I had a sinking feeling that a mere conversation wouldn't be enough to get rid of the wedge I'd driven between us.

But what could I do? I was stuck at home while Violet was clearly avoiding me at all costs.

I slouched against my computer chair and let my head fall back as I mulled over how I could show my sister how sorry I was. Ten minutes of staring at the ceiling later, an idea came to me. It wasn't a very good idea, and I'd most likely wind up serving more time on house arrest if I was caught, but it was all I had. I scooped up my phone, scrolled through my contacts, and selected Galaxy Rider.

Xander picked up right away, and my ears were immediately assaulted by whatever loud music was playing in the background. "Hey, what's up?"

"I have a major crisis on my hands, so I figured I'd call the most reliable person I know to help me problem solve," I told him.

He laughed, and despite my situation with Violet, the sound of his amusement was enough to make me smile. "I've never thought of myself as a problem solver, but all right. What's this crisis of yours?"

"Well, I want to apologize to Violet for being a crappy sister," I said, and either Xander moved closer to the music or someone cranked up the volume, because it was suddenly blaring. "The issue is, not only am I being ignored, but—"

"Sorry, Indie, I can't hear you. Hold on a sec." He must have put his hand over the receiver, because everything suddenly sounded muffled. It wasn't muted, however. "JJ, stop being an asshole! I'm on the phone."

A moment passed, but then the music cut off, and Xander's side of the line went crystal clear.

"Sorry about that," he said. "What were you saying?"

"That Violet is ignoring *and* avoiding me."

"Okay. Is there something specific I can do about it?"

"Actually, there is," I told him. "Were you invited to her birthday party tomorrow?" I crossed my fingers and prayed he was. If not, my plan wouldn't work.

"Well, it's more of a backyard cookout than a party, but yeah. The whole band was," he replied. "We're going to play a quick set."

I grinned. "That's even better. I'm going to need your guys' help."

CHAPTER 18

"Sorry I'm late," I called, scrambling out of my car. "I hope you guys haven't been here for too long."

It was Saturday night, and I'd just pulled up to a fancy house in the hills. The Heartbreakers were spread out around a now familiar Range Rover, which was parked on the side of the street—JJ and Oliver were lounging in the grass, while Alec perched on the rear bumper, headphones in. Xander was nowhere to be seen. After our phone conversation yesterday, he'd texted me the address for Violet's party and promised to wait for me out front so we could go in together. What I hadn't expected was for the rest of the band to wait as well, but I was starting to realize the four of them came as a package deal. We'd agreed to meet at four—well after the party would be in full swing, so Violet wouldn't notice me until it was time—but I hadn't anticipated my dad being so strict.

"Absolutely not," he'd said when I told him I was leaving for Sofia's and would be home in a few hours. "I understand this is a relatively new concept for you, Indie, but being grounded means you're not allowed to engage in social or recreational activities."

I blinked at him. *Engage in social or recreational activities?* Who the hell was this man?

"Yes, but this is an *academic* activity." Unzipping the main pocket, I showed him the inside of my backpack, which was loaded with textbooks. "I missed a really difficult lab in physics, and I'm struggling with the practice packet. Sofia offered to help me."

"Why don't you have her come over here?" he asked. "I'm sure she'd understand."

"I did, but she's babysitting her siblings. Please, Dad? We have a test on Monday, and if I don't figure these concepts out, I'm going to fail big time." Which wasn't exactly a lie—Sofia *was* babysitting, we *did* have a test, and I most definitely *would* fail if I didn't get help—but I also had no intention of going to Sofia's.

Twisting the truth churned my stomach, but it was the only way I could get out of the house and explain my absence at the same time. My only consolation was that I didn't have to feel guilty about roping Sofia into my scheme. She was on board with any plan that involved me spending more time with Xander, because what were best friends for?

"No worries," JJ said, slowly smiling at me. "Gave me time

to work on my tan." He was wearing another one of those sleeveless muscle shirts he seemed to love so much, and I rolled my eyes when he flexed his biceps at me.

"Indie?" Xander said, poking his head out the driver's side window. His cell was pressed to his ear. When I waved at him, he said something to whoever he was talking with and ended the call. Then he was out of the car, his long legs covering the distance between us in three quick strides, and pulling me into a hug. "Everything all right?" he asked after pressing his lips against my brow. I loved that he was the perfect height to give me forehead kisses. "I was worried about you. I called Sofia to see if she knew where you were, but she had no clue."

"Yeah, I'm fine," I said, waving off his concern. "Ran into some trouble with my dad, but I managed to talk my way out of it. Who were you talking to?"

"My brother," he said, frowning slightly. "What kind of trouble?"

"Technically speaking? I'm grounded."

"Still?"

I grimaced. "Ah, no…again."

"Ooooh! Looks like we have a rebel on our hands, folks," JJ announced as if he was giving a play-by-play.

Oliver, whose hands were tucked behind his head as he soaked up the dwindling sunlight, snorted.

Xander and I both turned to shoot his bandmates a flat, unimpressed stare.

Heaving a sigh, JJ flopped back against the lawn. "Fine, I'll just be over here, not listening to the conversation taking place five feet away from me, minding my own business, and being bored out of my mind."

Neither of us bothered responding.

"What happened?" Xander said, returning his gaze to me.

"You know the day I blew up on Violet?" I asked, my voice a whisper. It was more of a rhetorical question than a serious one, because despite the fact that we'd made up, I would always harbor a small amount of guilt for how I'd treated Xander. I doubted he'd forget that day anytime soon either. "Let's just say it went downhill from there. I'll give you the details later, but right now, all I want to do is apologize to my sister and get home before my dad realizes I'm not at Sofia's."

"Okay," he said with a decisive nod. "We can do that."

My heart soared at the word *we*, like this was our problem, not just mine, and the two of us would tackle it together. I took Xander's hand and turned toward the house, a boxy, contemporary home with clean lines and a sleek facade made of steel and gray stone. As if sensing our departure, Alec pulled out his headphones and carefully tucked them into his pocket, while Oliver and JJ picked themselves off the ground, brushing grass from their pants as they stood. Xander clicked the lock button on his key fob, the SUV beeped, and then the five of us started our climb up the long driveway.

When we reached the top of the hill and I spotted the front door, I groaned inwardly. Darren, the wannabe security guard from the *Immortal Nights* promotional shoot, was manning the entrance, another clipboard in hand. I slowed my pace, letting the guys go first so he couldn't see me. Maybe if I hid behind Xander and JJ, I could slip inside unnoticed?

"Names?" Darren asked. As each of the Heartbreakers answered, he flipped through the pages clipped to his board, nodding when he found them on the list. "All right, you can head in."

Crouching down, I tried to make myself as small as possible, but Xander, polite as ever, stepped aside and gestured for me to go first. When Darren met my gaze, his eyes gleamed with recognition, and I instantly knew he was going to make this as difficult as possible for me. I heaved a sigh and straightened up.

"So," Darren said, looking down his nose at me as if I'd crawled out of the sewers, "we meet again."

"*So we meet again?*" JJ repeated, glancing from me to Darren without bothering to mask his snicker. "What is she, your adversary? You sound like a second-rate villain in a bad James Bond movie."

Oliver scowled. "There's no such thing as a bad James Bond movie," he muttered indignantly, but everyone's attention was focused on Darren.

"*She*," he said, pointing his finger at me in accusation, "crashed the set of a very important promotional shoot. I tried to stop her." He sounded like the foiled bad guy at the end of every *Scooby-Doo* episode: *And I would have gotten away with it if it weren't for Gabe Grant!*

"The shoot was for *Immortal Nights*, so I'd hardly call that important," I clarified when Xander turned to me, his head cocked in amused confusion. "Plus it was at my house. Pretty sure it doesn't count as crashing if I live there."

Darren shrugged. "Your name wasn't on the list. I was merely doing my job."

Leaning over to JJ, Oliver put a hand in front of his mouth as if he was trying to be discreet but said in a rather loud whisper, "Something tells me this guy gets his rocks off on being an asshole."

This didn't seem to bother Darren. He didn't even deny what Oliver said. Instead, he aimed a smug smile at me. "Rules are rules. Thankfully, that same rule applies today, and since this isn't your house, you can't use that as an excuse to get yourself in the door again."

My teeth clenched together painfully as I tried not to snap. "It's my sister's birthday."

"Yes, but we both know you weren't invited to this party, so I suggest you leave before I call the police and report a trespasser."

JJ crossed his arms, a gesture that was intimidating by itself, but then he stepped forward and leaned into Darren's personal space. When he wasn't smiling and cracking jokes, JJ could be menacing. "She's our plus-one," he said, his voice cold.

To Darren's credit, he didn't back down. "There are no plus-ones."

"So if I showed up with my girlfriend, you wouldn't let her in?" Oliver scoffed. "How rude."

"But Miss James isn't your girlfriend," Darren pointed out.

"Of course she's not his girlfriend," Xander snapped. "She's mine." His eyes were narrowed at Darren, and I'd never seen him look so angry before. "By the way, James is a stage name. Indie's last name is Mitchell-Jamiolkowski. Get it right."

Despite the four guys who were now glaring at him, Darren rolled his eyes. "My apologies, Miss Mitchell-Jamiolkowski, but it doesn't matter who you're dating. You're not on the list."

"For God's sake, Darren. Give it up already and let them in," said a familiar voice.

Glancing over Darren's shoulder, I met the smoldering blue eyes of Gabriel Grant. He stood just inside the entryway, hands casually stuffed in his pockets, and there was a wide grin on his face, as if watching the scene play out had been the most entertaining part of his day.

"Hey, dude," JJ said, sauntering forward and slapping his hand into Gabe's. "How've you been?"

Darren's lips flattened into a tight line, but he did as Gabe instructed and stepped aside. Not bothering to glance in his direction, Alec and Oliver followed JJ, while Xander draped an arm over my shoulder and guided me in after them. Even though it was childish, I stuck my tongue out at Darren as we passed by.

Ha, I wanted to say, *thwarted again!*

"So, Indie," Gabe said once all the guys had clapped each other on the back in greeting. "What are you doing here? Not that it's a problem, but these parties aren't usually your thing."

"I have a surprise planned for Violet," I explained. "It's an apology slash birthday gift."

"Cool, cool," he said, bobbing his head. "Anything I can do to help?"

"That depends." I looked up at Xander. "What time are you guys playing your set?"

Oliver answered for him. "Sixish?" he said, glancing at his

phone. "We should probably say hi to people and wish your sister a happy birthday first."

"Any chance you can find me somewhere to hide until then?" I asked Gabe.

"Yeah, for sure." He turned toward a hallway on our left and gestured for me to follow. "This way."

Xander gave my hand a quick squeeze. "I'll text you when we're ready, okay?"

I nodded, then tagged along behind Gabe, who led me away from the noise of the party and over to a set of stairs. He started up them without a moment's hesitation.

"Um," I said, pausing at the bottom step and glancing around. "You sure it's okay for us to go up? I don't want to intrude on whoever lives here."

He tossed a smile over his shoulder. "This is my and Ryan's place."

"Oh!" Grabbing the banister, I hurried after him. "Well, thanks. I really appreciate it."

"It's the least I can do to make up for Darren. He can be a bit overzealous at times."

You think? I wanted to say. "Who is he anyway?"

"Ryan's PA."

Of course he was. He and Sadie were a match made in hell.

Part of me was curious to know what had convinced Gabe

and Ryan to hire equally evil PAs. Black magic? Mind control? Or maybe they received a two-for-one deal because nobody else wanted to hire Demon One and Demon Two?

Before I could ask, we reached the second floor, and Gabe pointed to the landing's spacious seating area. A large entertainment cabinet took up one wall, a flat-screen TV its centerpiece, and positioned in front of it was a couch with deep, suck-you-in cushions. The best part, however, was that the space overlooked the packed living room below. From up here, I could watch the party without being noticed.

"You need anything else?" Gabe asked as I peered over the ledge. It took me less than two seconds to spot Xander's familiar frame among the crowd. The Heartbreakers were talking to a woman with long, platinum-blond hair, and I instantly recognized Vanessa Williams, Alec's older sister and one of Violet's best friends. "I can have someone bring you a drink."

"I'm good," I said, turning back to him with a grateful smile. "Thank you though."

"No problem," he said. "If you need anything, just ask one of the waitstaff. I'll see you later."

Once Gabe was gone, I leaned against the railing and scanned the gathering for my sister. The entire back wall of Gabe and Ryan's house was made of glass, displaying a jaw-dropping view of their pool and, beyond that, LA. After searching the living room, I turned my attention outside and finally found Violet curled up on one of the wicker patio sectionals with Tara Thomas, another *IN* costar who played the high priestess of a witch coven.

Not long after spotting her, Oliver and JJ approached, and I watched as Violet jumped up to hug them both. They spoke for a minute, smiling and laughing, and then Oliver said something that made Violet turn and point toward a small platform erected near the far end of the pool. On it were multiple mic stands, a drum set, and speakers, along with other equipment the Heartbreakers would need to perform.

A pit formed in my stomach as the reality of what Xander and I were about to do hit me.

I wasn't nervous about performing in front of a crowd. I'd been doing that since I was young. But giving an apology speech with all Violet's friends watching? That was more than nerve-racking. What if I got up onstage, poured my heart out, and Violet still didn't forgive me? For a split second, I considered texting Xander to call off the plan, but I needed to stop running away from my problems.

On my drive over, I'd tried to brainstorm what I wanted to say, because a simple *I'm sorry* wasn't going to cut it. There was no excuse for the way I'd treated her. Was it even possible to apologize for years of blame and anger?

It didn't seem likely.

At this point, all I could do was speak from the heart and hope that Violet would understand.

More to keep my nerves at bay than out of actual interest, I went over to the entertainment cabinet and selected a book at random off the shelf. As I sank down onto the couch, I studied the cover. It was one of those heavy, coffee table books, this particular one about a domesticated squirrel named S'more. A quick flip through showed me that S'more's parents enjoyed dressing him up as celebrities and famous pop culture characters. It felt like a strange book for two bachelors to own, but then I found the page where the poor critter was dressed as Luca. Since I had nothing better to do, I browsed through the pictures until my pocket vibrated.

GALAXY RIDER:

> We're starting. Meet Gabe downstairs.

I slid *Sundays with S'more* back into its spot on the shelf, then hurried down to the first floor.

Gabe was waiting for me at the base of the steps. "You ready?" he asked just as the music pumping through the house's speaker system cut off. "The guys are about to kick things off, so pretty much everyone is outside."

As if prompted by Gabe's statement, Oliver's voice—magnified but also muffled by a wall or two—interrupted the buzz of the party. He introduced the band with his usual charming bravado and wished Violet a happy birthday.

"As I'll ever be," I replied, wringing my hands. "Xander said there'd be a violin for me?" I'd wanted to bring my own, but Dad would have been suspicious if I'd taken my case to Sofia's house to study.

"Oh, right. I almost forgot." Gabe waved me after him. "Come on."

We made our way to the back of the house, and by the time we reached the living room, the Heartbreakers were playing their first song. With the exception of a couple talking quietly on the couch and a few cater waiters, everyone had moved outside to listen. The patio was packed, making it impossible to spot my sister, but I could see Xander onstage, guitar in hand. The sight of him simultaneously calmed my nerves and made my heart skip a beat.

"Earth to Indie?"

Tearing my eyes away from Xander, I turned back to Gabe. Apparently I'd been staring for longer than I realized, because his brows arched up in amusement.

"Here," he said, offering me a violin case.

I blinked, surprised by its sudden appearance. I'd been so preoccupied, I hadn't seen where the instrument had come from, but I was grateful nonetheless.

"Thanks," I said, taking the case from him. After lifting

the latches, I peeked inside to make sure everything was in working order, and Gabe watched as I trailed my fingers over the neck, all the way down to the lower bout.

"Will that work?" he asked, pushing his jet-black bangs out of his eyes.

I nodded. "It's perfect."

His responding smile was so warm, it occurred to me just how wrong I'd been about him. Sure, Gabe knew how ridiculously good-looking he was, but that didn't make him a bad guy. He was considerate and funny and sweet. It seemed I'd misjudged quite a few people recently.

"Good, let's go," he said and led me over to the patio doors.

As soon as we stepped outside, the volume of the music tripled. The Heartbreakers were in the middle of playing their hit single "Astrophil," and as Gabe and I worked our way around the outskirts of the crowd, slowly making our way toward the stage, I hummed along to the song. We reached the small platform just as it finished, and Gabe waved at Oliver to get his attention. He nodded at us in acknowledgment, then whispered something to Alec and JJ.

"All right, everyone, I hope you're having a great time so far!" Oliver called into the microphone, his attention back on the crowd. "Tonight we have a surprise for the birthday girl, so please put your hands together for our special guest performer, Indie Mitchell-Jamiolkowski."

There was a surprisingly loud cheer even though nobody knew who I was, but I felt myself freeze up all the same. Suddenly, the three steps leading up to the stage looked like a mountain, one I was petrified to climb. If it hadn't been for Xander, who turned toward me with his lopsided smile, I probably would have fled. Instead, I swallowed hard and forced myself to take a deep breath.

This was it. My chance to make things right with my sister.

"Good luck," Gabe said, patting me on the shoulder.

"Thanks," I whispered. My palms were a clammy mess, and I hastily wiped my free one on the back of my jeans as I scaled the stairs, violin case clutched against my side. Xander held out his hand and guided me up the final step. My nerves must have been visible, because he gave my fingers a comforting squeeze.

"You've got this," he told me as JJ and Alec filed offstage. Oliver winked in my direction as he followed after them. Then, hands still clasped together, Xander and I walked to the front of the platform. I took a moment to scan the sea of faces until I spotted Violet, who was standing with Tara and Vanessa near the front. When our gazes met, I offered her a hesitant smile, but she stared back at me with a blank expression.

Okay, not the most encouraging reaction ever, but it was better than an all-out scowl. I'd take what I could get.

Giving my amethyst a quick squeeze for luck, I stepped up to the mic stand. "Hi, everyone. Thank you so much for being here to celebrate Violet's birthday. I want to give a big shout out to our hosts Gabe and Ryan for throwing an awesome party and to the Heartbreakers for allowing me to crash their performance," I said, my voice an octave too high. I took another deep breath and willed myself to calm down. "For those of you who don't know me, I'm Violet's younger sister, Indie, and like most babies of a family, I'm a massive pain in the ass." This got a laugh from the audience. "Things haven't always been smooth sailing between us, but of course, like most older siblings, Violet is a role model, and I've come to realize just how lucky I am to call her my sister.

"When we were growing up, our entire family knew Violet was going to be a star years before she decided to pursue a career in acting. She was always putting on plays with her stuffed animals and singing at the top of her lungs into whatever microphone-shaped object she could get her hands on. She also had the distinct ability to walk into a room and steal the spotlight, because people *wanted* to be around her. But Violet isn't just talented. She's ambitious and disciplined and hardworking, which resulted in her landing her very first record deal! Violet's debut album will be out later this year, but tonight I want to share a song she's featuring on, which was written by the equally talented Xander Jones. This is 'Indigo Skies,' and I hope you enjoy."

With the scary part over, I slid the microphone back into the clip and moved out of the way so Xander could take my place. At some point during my speech, he'd swapped his electric guitar for an acoustic. As he plucked out a few notes to make sure it was in tune, I pulled the violin from its case and settled the instrument between my shoulder and chin. When he glanced over his shoulder to see if I was ready, I gave him a nod.

Then he started to play.

CHAPTER 19

A hush fell over the crowd as the opening notes of the song poured from Xander's guitar.

He bowed his head as if he was solely focused on his fingers moving over the strings, but from where I was standing, I could see his eyes were closed. Almost like he was savoring this moment, his first time standing center stage. When it was time for the first verse to begin, his eyes fluttered open, and he raised his gaze to the audience.

There was no way to describe what happened next as anything other than magical. Xander's voice on the recording had been beautiful—deep and silvery, a tone that melted perfectly with Violet's sweet, high range. But live? He sounded raw, filled with emotion, moving. I was left nearly breathless by the sound of it.

In fact, I was so caught up in his performance, I nearly forgot that I was part of it too. But just before the bridge began, Xander turned toward me and nodded, like he was welcoming me into the song. I hastily raised my bow and joined him.

The next three minutes passed in an adrenaline-pumping blur.

"Indie, Xander—that was amazing!" Oliver exclaimed as we stepped offstage to loud applause. He flashed me a dimpled grin before punching his bandmate on the arm in congratulations. "Dude, did you really write that?"

Xander nodded as he lifted the guitar strap over his head and set the instrument down.

Oliver's mouth curled into a smile as he shook his head. "Are you shitting me? What's wrong with you, man?"

"What do you mean?"

"Why the hell haven't you written anything for us before?"

"I don't know," Xander muttered, looking both surprised and pleased by his friend's response. "I guess it always felt like your thing."

This made Oliver frown. "Well, that's stupid. It's clearly your thing too."

"You think so?" The expression on Xander's face was filled with doubt.

"You really have to ask?" Oliver shot back. "Dude, I don't understand why you'd keep a talent like that hidden. I hope you realize we're writing our next album together whether you like it or not."

"Honestly, I don't know what to say." Xander dropped his gaze so his friends couldn't see the look in his eyes, but the emotion was clear in his voice.

"Say you'll do it," JJ replied, slinging an arm over Xander's shoulder and grinning wide. "If you don't, the entire track list will just be mushy love songs about Stella."

"We should also add this song to our tour set list," Alec added. "Everyone tonight loved it."

At this, Xander's eyes practically bulged out of his skull. "Oh no," he said, holding his hands up. "We don't have to—"

"That's an excellent idea." Oliver whipped out his phone. "I'll text Courtney and see what she says, but I think it would fit great between 'All These Stars' and 'Tough Love.' I can't play the violin, but maybe I can do Indie's part on the piano?"

"Ooh! And I can do an interpretive dance in the background. Think we can make time for a costume change?"

"Shut up, JJ."

"Hey, I'm being serious here!"

As the boys continued to discuss the different ways they could work Xander's song into their show, I carefully placed my borrowed violin back in its case and secured the latches. When I straightened up, Violet was standing in front of me.

"Jesus!" I gasped, clutching a hand to my heart. "You scared the living daylights out of me."

"Sorry, I didn't mean to." Her face was a mask as she tucked a curl behind her ear. "Can we talk?"

"Yeah, of course."

Violet and I walked around the side of the house and found a quiet spot on a garden bench where we could have a private conversation.

"Wow, how did you know this was here?" I asked as we sat down. The hedges were tall enough that nobody would be able to see us from the patio.

"Gabe and I have read lines here before," she explained, not meeting my gaze. Her attention was focused on the delicate gold bracelet circling her wrist. As she fiddled with a charm, I recognized it immediately as the gift Dad gave her when she won her first Saturn Award for best actress.

Nodding, I waited for Violet to continue. After all, she was the one who'd asked to talk, and I wanted to give her that opportunity since I'd already said my piece onstage. But Violet seemed content with staring at her hands, and as the hum and chatter of the party drifted in our direction, an uncomfortable silence spiraled between us.

"Look, Vi," I said when I couldn't stand it anymore. "I didn't mean to ruin your party, but I really needed to tell you how sorry I am. I spoke with Dad a few nights ago, and he told me what happened between him and Mom. I never should have blamed you for—"

"Please stop," she said, still not looking at me. "I'm the one who should be apologizing."

Wait, what?

"No," I said, shaking my head. "I'm the one who went all mega bitch on you at the recording studio. You have nothing to be sorry for."

She let out a long sigh and looked up at me. To my complete shock, her eyes were glossy. "That's not true. I've said some pretty horrible things to you the past few months, and even though Mom and Dad's divorce wasn't my fault, I understand why you thought it was. I'm so sorry, Indie. I want to make things up to you, so I'm going to withdraw from my *Lady Phoenix* audition."

Holy. Freaking. Shit.

When I came up with the plan to crash her birthday, I figured the most likely outcome would be that Violet kicked me out. My hope, however, was that she'd forgive me. Even a begrudged form of forgiveness would have been okay in my book.

But an actual, bona fide apology?

That was so unexpectedly mind-boggling that it took me a moment to process the words she'd spoken. My sister was apologizing. To *me*.

What strange new world was this?

"I really appreciate that, Vi, but everything you said? How

I blame others for my problems and run away when things get too hard?" I replied. "That was all the truth."

Shoulders hunching, Violet pinned her arms against her stomach. "Just because what I said was true doesn't mean the way I said it wasn't cruel. I was pissed and frustrated, so I lashed out at you, and that's not fair."

I shrugged, still completely baffled by the direction our conversation was going. "Then I guess I got what I deserved, considering I've been lashing out at you for years."

"Oh, Indie," she said, her voice smaller than I'd ever heard it. "You can't put this all on yourself. A relationship isn't a one-way street. It takes two people. You had every right to be angry with me. I've spent the past five years focusing on my career at the expense of being a good sister. It's no wonder you blamed me for Mom and Dad."

I blinked at Violet. Replayed her confession in my head. For years, I'd been waiting to hear those words. I thought I'd feel a sense of relief or vindication. Instead, an empty, hollow feeling rattled around inside my chest.

"So," I said after a minute, "what changed?"

"Well, I had a very long conversation with Mom after Vanessa's wedding. You'd already gone to bed, but we sat at the hotel bar talking until it closed," she explained. "Mom had just accepted her position with the Baltimore orchestra, and she was really worried about leaving you."

"Why?"

Violet looked at me like I was being dumb. "Oh, come on. If anyone knows how dedicated Dad is to his job, it's the woman who divorced him. She was concerned about you being lonely, so she reminded me of how close we used to be before...well, you know."

"Okay?" I said, still not understanding.

"It hit me that you'll be off to college soon and the next few months might be my last opportunity to fix things. I didn't want you to leave when there was so much animosity between us, so that's why I've been hanging out more often. It's why I invited you to Comic Con."

For a moment, I just stared at Violet as I sifted through the new information she'd given me. "So let me get this straight—you being on my case about Juilliard...that was you trying to fix things?" I asked skeptically. "No offense, but that was pretty much the worst way to go about it."

A flush colored Violet's cheeks. "No, not exactly."

"Then...why?"

"It's just—I've always been a little bit jealous of you with the violin. You're so talented, and I didn't want to see that go to waste."

"Violet," I said with slow disbelief, "don't be ridiculous. You're a famous actress. Why would you ever be jealous of *me*?" And before she had a chance to answer, I added,

"Besides, you could've learned how to play, but you gave up after a handful of lessons."

"I quit because I didn't want to slow you down," Violet told me. "I wasn't terrible by any stretch, but I also wasn't a child prodigy. Mom was always patient with me, but she was different when she taught you. Her eyes would light up, and I could tell how thrilled she was that you had a knack for it. Everyone who heard you play knew it was something special. I think that's the reason why I started putting on plays and trying to entertain people—I wanted them to see me too."

"But—" I broke off and shook my head. "I don't even know how to respond to that."

"You don't have to say anything." She reached out and took my hand in hers. "I wasn't trying to make you feel guilty. I just want you to understand why I pushed so hard. A gift like yours shouldn't be wasted."

I shifted uncomfortably on the bench as a hot, tingling sensation crept up my neck and face. This was probably the right moment to fess up about missing Juilliard's application deadline, but I was too chicken. "God," I said, pulling away from her, "we're idiots for being jealous of each other for all these years."

Violet started to nod in agreement but then realized what I'd said and shot me a confused frown. "What are you jealous of? You've made it crystal clear how much you dislike my career and the spotlight."

"That's one thousand percent true. All the money in Jeff Bezos's bank account wouldn't be enough to convince me to switch lives with you," I said. "But I'm not talking about your career. I'm talking about your relationship with Dad."

Her responding snort was chock-full of bitterness. "Trust me, that's not something to be jealous of. What you and Mom have, your bond with music? That's special. Dad and I just work together."

"No, you have Dad wrapped around your finger. Half of the time, I don't think he even knows I exist. I called him out after our fight, and he's been making an effort since, but for the past few years? Not at all."

"Dad's always been that way though. When we were kids, he practically lived at the office. The man thrives on work. It's probably his one true love," she said with a laugh, but there was no joy in the sound, just disappointment. "The only reason it seems like Dad and I have a special bond is because *I'm* his work now. If I could go back and change things, I never would have agreed to let him be my manager. It wasn't a healthy decision for our family."

"Yeah," I agreed. "Probably not."

"I'm sorry, Indie. If you want, I can fire him and find someone new so the two of you can spend more time together."

My immediate thought was to tell her yes, but then I realized this wasn't her problem to solve. "No, don't do that on my account. If there's one thing I've learned from this whole messed-up situation, it's that I need to take responsibility for my own actions. Same goes for Dad. He's the one who made the choice to prioritize work over family. If he wants to fix things with me, he needs to make the effort himself."

"You sure?"

"I am," I said, nodding decisively. "Also, you don't need to withdraw from your *Lady Phoenix* audition. I never should have asked you not to try out. That was unbelievably selfish of me, and I think you'll make a great Kelina."

Violet's eyes lit up. "Really?"

I grinned. "Yup, but once you get the part, you have to promise to invite me to set. I want to fangirl over all your costars and embarrass the hell out of you."

"Okay," she said, matching my grin with one of her own. "I think that can be arranged."

At the sound of approaching footsteps, we both turned toward the garden path. A couple passed by us on their way out of the party, but either they were too wrapped up in their own conversation to notice us or they couldn't see our bench in the shadow of the hedges.

Once they were gone, Violet cleared her throat. "So…I take it you and Xander made up?"

This time, I beamed at her. "Yep. I went to the studio with the intention of apologizing to you, but I ran into him, and we hashed things out."

"I'm glad. The two of you are good together. I mean, the guy wrote a song about you. What's not to love?" she said, bumping her shoulder against mine in a playful way. "And I adore the version you guys played tonight. It finally sounds complete."

"Yeah?" I asked, perking up in my seat. Ever since recording my part for Xander's song, I'd been nervous Violet would hate it. Hearing her say the opposite was a much needed weight off my shoulders.

"Definitely."

We lapsed into pensive silence. It didn't feel uncomfortable, but after everything that had been said between us, we both needed a moment to let the debris of our conversation settle.

"Our tree house is gone," I said after a minute.

"Huh?"

"The tree house in San Bernardino?" I clarified. "After our fight at New Edge, I drove back to see our old house because...well, to be honest, I don't even know why I did, but it's gone. Whoever moved in cut the tree down."

"Oh no! That's so sad," Violet exclaimed. "We had so many good memories up there. Remember when I decorated it like an Italian restaurant and pretended to be a waiter?"

I laughed. "Yeah, you made me be the customer, but the only thing I was allowed to order was spaghetti because that was all you could cook."

"Or what about the time we convinced Mom and Dad to let us have a sleepover out there, but in the middle of the night—"

"—that raccoon scared us half to death?"

"I think we woke up half the neighborhood with our screaming."

"We? Pretty sure it was *your* screaming that woke everyone," I corrected. "Not mine."

"Whatever," she said, rolling her eyes, but it was obvious from the twitch of her lips that she was biting back a grin. "You still take the cake for the most dramatic tree house memory."

"Do I now?"

"Remember what you did the day we moved from San Bernardino to Newport?"

A bark of laughter escaped me. "Yeah, I chained myself to the trunk in protest."

"And then Dad had to call a locksmith because you chucked the key into the woods and none of us could find it," she added, shaking her head in amusement.

God, when was the last time a conversation had flowed so easily between us? I couldn't remember, but sitting here and trading memories was the most like family we'd felt in a long time.

"Well, the tree might be gone, but we still have each other, right?" I peeked over at Violet, afraid of her answer.

"Always," she answered. "You're my sister, Indie."

It was only a few simple words, but suddenly a golf ball–size lump took up residence in the back of my throat. Turning away, I swallowed a couple of times in an attempt to clear it. Until she said it, I didn't realize how badly I needed to hear Violet call me that—her *sister*. Because before her career took off, being Violet's sister meant so much more to me than someone I shared parents with. It meant I always had a best friend. Someone whose shoulder I could cry on when I had a bad day. Someone who was in my corner no matter what. Someone who always knew how to make me laugh.

And I missed all of that so, so much.

"Indie, are you okay?"

I nodded even as a tear trickled down my cheek.

It was time to tell her about Juilliard. I'd bottled up my grief for the past three days, and I needed to get this off my chest. Now that things finally felt okay between us, I knew she'd help me through this grief. After her earlier confession, she'd probably be crushed by my news, but at least we could be heartbroken together.

"Hey, Vi?" I said quietly.

There must have been something off about my voice, because hesitation flickered through her eyes. "Yeah?"

"Please don't freak out, but...I missed the deadline for Juilliard."

"*What?*" she gasped.

"It was due the day we fought," I explained in a rush. "I know that's not an excuse, and I shouldn't have waited until the last minute, but after everything went down, I just sort of lost it and didn't realize what time it was until it was too late."

"Oh my God, Indie," Violet said, clutching the edge of the bench. "You should have told me straightaway."

"Why? It's not like there's anything you can do about it."

"Actually, there is."

Now it was my turn to be shocked. "What are you talking about?"

Violet smirked and brushed a long curl over her shoulder. "So you know how you wanted to take a tour of campus when we were in New York but all the time slots were full?"

"Yeah..."

"Well, I mentioned it in passing to Jewel Peck that weekend. Apparently her cousin is on the admissions board, and she said she could get us a private tour, but then you disappeared with Xander, so I never brought it up. I can't promise you anything, but she might be able to pull a few strings."

"Are you for real?" I asked as an inkling of hope rekindled inside me.

"Believe it or not, knowing me has some perks." Violet winked and pulled out her phone. "Let's see about getting you an audition."

CHAPTER 20

Violet waltzed into the music room as I coaxed a final note from the song I was working on.

"Wow," she said, halting halfway to the sitting area, a mesmerized expression on her face. "That was beautiful, Indie."

"Thanks." Not sure what else to say, I slid my bow into its holder. The spinner was getting loose, so I made a mental note to find a screwdriver and tighten it later before gently placing my violin into the velvet shell of its case.

Two days had passed since Violet's birthday party, and while we'd accepted each other's apology, things were still a bit awkward between us. Which was to be expected. I knew we might never be able to return to the same easygoing relationship we shared before *Immortal Nights*. Nearly five years of enmity were impossible to erase overnight. We were going to have to work at being sisters again.

"I've never heard you play that before." Her feet unfroze,

and she gracefully lowered herself onto the sofa. "What's it called?"

After shutting the lid, I snapped the silver latches into place. "Not sure yet," I told her.

"Wait." An astonished look returned to her features. "You *wrote* that?"

Wrote wasn't the right word to describe what I'd been doing. This was more of a battle than the idyllic state of creativity. Ever since helping Xander and Alec at the recording studio, the suggestion of a song had been swirling at the back of my mind, just out of reach. But unlike the melody for "Indigo Skies," which had come to me in a matter of seconds, I'd been teasing this piece out one note at a time. It was a frustrating process, but the awe in Violet's voice when she asked if the song was mine? That made my efforts worth it.

I offered her a shrug. "It's nothing. I'm just messing around. What's up?"

Suddenly reminded of why she was here, Violet broke into a smile. "I finally got a hold of Jewel. She said she'd be happy to talk to her cousin about your Juilliard application. No guarantee it will result in something, but it's worth a shot, right?"

"About that..." Tucking my bangs out of the way, I sank onto the leather cushion beside her. "Tell Jewel thank you for me but not to bother."

"What?" Violet's eyes went round. "Why in the world would you want me to do that?"

"Because I've been doing a lot of reflecting these past few days and, well—I don't think it's the right move for me."

"I'm sorry, but in what world is Juilliard not the right move for you? Have you heard yourself playing? You're incredible."

"That's not what I meant," I replied, flapping my hand dismissively. "I'm talking about using your connections to get me into school. This whole situation is my fault. I need to own my mistake, and I can't do that if you swoop in to solve the problem for me."

"Indie," Violet groaned, dragging a hand down her face in a dramatic, oh-come-on sort of way. "I understand you're trying to turn over a new leaf, but don't punish yourself by giving up Juilliard. This is your dream."

I hesitated, then said, "It is…and it isn't."

A breath hitched in her throat. "What's that supposed to mean?"

"The whole concert violinist thing. It's not that I hate performing—truly, it's really fun—but it doesn't excite me," I explained. "That was always Mom's passion, not mine, but she's such an inspiration to me, I guess my dreams got tangled up and confused with hers. I think that's why I struggled so much with my application. Part of my heart wasn't in it."

The room was quiet as she processed my confession.

"Okay," she replied, and surprisingly, her voice was full of acceptance. "What are you going to do instead?"

"I got into to the Academy of Cinema Makeup. Now before you freak out, the program only takes a year to complete, and I'm not even sure I see a career path in makeup, but this is something that excites me. I'm really, really good at it, Vi, and I want to explore that. Meanwhile, I'll have plenty of time to give my Juilliard application a good overhaul."

"But I thought you said you didn't want—"

"I'm going to apply for the composition program next year," I cut in before she could finish. "When I was at the recording studio with Alec and Xander and I got to create music instead of just playing it? That felt right. I'll have to compose two different scores if I want to get in, which is a little scary since I don't have much experience, but I want this."

Violet considered for a long time. "Well," she finally said, the corners of her mouth turning up into a dazzling smile, "based on what I heard when I came in, you're already halfway there."

☆ ♭ ♪

"I'm going to the grocery store to get snacks for later," Dad called over my music as he stepped into the garage. "Popcorn or ice cream?"

I stopped sweeping and hit Pause, cutting Diego St. James off midchorus. "Really? How is that even a question?"

I asked, setting the broom aside. When I got home from school today, Dad asked me to tackle the mess left over from my portfolio, so for the past half hour, I'd been tidying up my workbench. After dinner, however, the two of us planned on having a horror marathon. While it was still premature to call Dad a changed man, two Thursday movie nights in a row seemed like a good start.

He stroked his chin in thought. "Both?"

"The only acceptable answer," I said with a laugh. "Don't forget chocolate syrup and sprinkles."

Instead of heading for his sleek red Audi, Dad ambled over to me, a hand tucked into the front pocket of his jeans. "It's good to see you smile again, Indie. I was starting to get worried. You seemed pretty miserable last week."

"That's because I was miserable." I'd spent those days grieving. Not just for a dream I'd dedicated my entire life to but for the bond with my sister I thought was forever shattered. Now, however, I was thankful. Because every once in a while, the most effective way to fix something was by breaking it. Only then could you put the pieces back together in a way that made sense. "I'm fine now," I reassured him. "I promise."

"Because of this guy?" Dad asked. He dragged the metal shop stool out from underneath the workbench and took a seat. "Tell me about him."

My brows sprang up at his request. "Really, Dad? We're going to talk boys?"

"What's wrong with wanting to know some basic information about the person my daughter is dating?" As if to make a point, he crossed his arms over his chest like he had no intention of moving until I shared. "I'm not asking for his Social Security number."

"Okay, fine. His name is Xander, and yeah, he's one of the reasons." But not the only one. There were several factors contributing to my current state of mind: a fresh start with Violet, a plan for my future I was actually excited about, new friends, and a better outlook on life. I was happy now because I'd made the decision to be. "He's a musician."

"In the same band as Alec, right?"

Clearly Dad already knew the answer—he must have grilled Violet about the subject already—but I indulged him anyway. "That's correct."

"So he's pretty famous then." There was a glimmer of what looked like concern in his eyes.

"Yeah, I guess," I replied with a shrug, but Xander's fame was the least important part of who he was. To me, he was the boy with the most endearing, lopsided smile in the world. The boy who always put others first and hummed Hank Williams to himself when he was lost in thought. When I thought about Xander, I didn't think of Xander

Jones, lead guitarist for the Heartbreakers. I thought about the guy who, from day one, had always been there for me. "He's on tour right now, but he'll be back before Christmas. Maybe we could all have dinner together?"

This seemed to mollify Dad, because the anxious look faded from his expression. "That's a great idea," he said. "I can't wait to meet him. The distance must be so hard for you two."

It was, but as much as being apart sucked, we were getting really good at FaceTiming between the breaks in his hectic schedule. And when that didn't work, there was always texting. At least one good thing had come from Violet's career—all the time I'd spent alone had prepared me for this situation, and I knew Xander and I would get through the next eight months no problem.

"We're making it work," I told him.

Just yesterday, the sweetest package had been delivered to the house: a box filled to the brim with Mango Bite, a popular candy in India; a green alien plushy; and the first edition of *The Clockwinders Saga*, a comic about warriors working to stop an evil organization from changing the course of history by means of time travel. Apparently JJ had seen Xander reading *Lady Phoenix* and thought I might like the series.

"Good, I'm glad." Dad unhooked the sunglasses dangling from the collar of his shirt and slipped them on. "I should leave before traffic gets bad, but I'm curious to know what you think of my theme for tonight."

"Which is?"

"Wait for it..." Dad did an over-the-top drum roll. "Demonic possessions!" he exclaimed with jazz hands. "I pulled out *The Exorcism of Emily Rose*, *Insidious*, and *Paranormal Activity*, but if you don't like those options, we could always go with a classic like *The Exorcist*."

Before I could answer, my phone rang. It was an incoming FaceTime from Galaxy Rider, the first I'd received in days. "Those all sound great, Dad, but do you mind if I take this? It's Xander and—"

He gave a dismissive wave of his hand. "Say no more. I'll see you later, kiddo."

I scrambled onto the vacated stool and punched the Talk button. When my boyfriend's smiling face appeared on screen, I couldn't help but grin. "Hey, you! What's up?" Normally Xander called me from his hotel room, but today it looked like he was sitting in some kind of fancy lounge.

"Nothing much." His tone was casual, bored even, but I didn't believe him. Not when there was a mischievous glint in his eyes. "Just wondering if you want to hit up the archery range with me tomorrow?"

"Oh," I said, my shoulders sagging at his not-so-funny joke. *Ten more days*, I reminded myself. That was how long I had to wait until he came home. Not a long stretch of time when you looked at the bigger picture, but at the moment, it felt like an eternity. "You know I'd love that, but considering you're halfway around the world, I don't think that's a possibility."

His mouth quirked. "What if I just touched down at LAX?"

"For real?" I asked, unable to believe my own ears.

"As of two minutes ago." He changed his camera view, and suddenly I realized exactly where Xander was. Not a lounge like I'd first thought but on a private jet. Alec, who was sprawled across a sofa opposite him, waved at me, and farther down the cabin, I spotted Oliver and JJ relaxing in leather recliners.

An uncharacteristically obnoxious squeal escaped me. "Oh my God! Xander, that's—wait a minute." I frowned, confusion tainting my sudden burst of joy. "Don't you guys have a show tonight?" The second leg of the Heartbreakers' tour didn't wrap until December 20.

"We were supposed to," he said, flipping the camera back around so I could see him, "but we had to postpone some of our dates."

Well, shit. That didn't sound good. "How come?"

Xander released such an exaggerated, long-suffering sigh that his bangs fluttered off his forehead. He flicked them out of the way and said, "Just a classic case of JJ being an utter moron."

"Hey!" came a faint shout from the background. "I heard that!"

My grin was instant. "Now *this* sounds like a good story."

He shrugged. "There isn't much of one to tell. The hotel we were staying at has this huge, three-story staircase in the lobby. JJ thought it would be a good idea to slide down the railing, and his wrist paid the price."

"Why am I not surprised," I said, trying to contain a snort. I could picture the scene in my head as if I'd been there to witness it: Oliver egging JJ on as he mounted the banister; Xander muttering under his breath about being surrounded by idiots; JJ's lively cheers as he picked up speed; curious hotels guests watching as he flew out of control; a spectacular wipeout; and finally, Alec standing in the corner, earbuds in, pretending to have nothing to do with his bandmates. "Is he all right?"

"He'll be fine," Xander told me, his gaze flicking up in annoyance. "A doctor confirmed it's only a sprain, not a broken bone, but he can't play for at least a month. I figured I'd take advantage of my time off and come see you."

His answer made my heart swell. What had I done to deserve a guy as sweet and caring as him? "Then I suppose I should be thanking JJ for his stupidity?"

"I know you're a big proponent of thank-you cards, but

knowing JJ, he'd prefer an Edible Arrangement. Or a stripper. Your choice."

"Definitely a stripper!" I heard JJ call.

I wrinkled my nose at the suggestion. "That's a bit tacky for my taste. What about a singing telegram?"

"As long as I get to see you tomorrow," Xander said, the corners of his mouth jerking into my favorite crooked grin, the one that had stolen my heart, "I don't care what you do. I'll even spring for a sky banner."

"Then I'll be there," I told him, because nothing would stop me from seeing him tomorrow. Not even an alien invasion.

EPILOGUE

"I feel like an idiot," I complained, taking another small step in trepidation.

Violet, who had both hands firmly planted on my shoulders, guided me forward with care. "Don't worry. I won't let you trip."

"That's not the point." The blindfold she'd given me was itchy, and I hated not being able to see anything. "You know I don't like surprises."

When school let out an hour ago, I'd found Violet leaning against my car, her lips curved into a wicked smile. Dad or Lydia must have dropped her off, because I didn't see her sleek Mercedes parked anywhere. Without bothering to say hello, she demanded my keys, and then we were on the highway, speeding off to God knew where. I tried asking her questions but only got one response: if I wanted to know what we were doing, I'd just have to wait and see.

Things got even weirder when, thirty minutes into our drive, she tossed a scarf in my direction and told me to tie it over my eyes. I'd already surrendered to the situation at that point, so I figured what the hell?

Which was how I ended up here, wherever that was.

"Believe me," Violet said in an almost giddy tone, "you're going to love this one." Her grip on my shoulders tightened, jerking me to a halt.

"Can I take this thing off now?" I grumbled as my patience wore thin.

"No!" she exclaimed. Two seconds later, a door opened in front of us, its hinges squeaking in protest. "Okay, now I need you to take a big step up."

Oh hell no. "I'm not climbing stairs completely blind, Vi."

"You're not completely blind," she answered, giving my shoulder a light squeeze. "You have me."

"I'm curious. Was that actually supposed to make me feel better?"

"Would you stop being a snot for two seconds and listen to me?" she snapped. "We're almost there."

It was a shame my eyes were covered, because that meant Violet couldn't watch me roll them, but I sighed and took a step up. Then another. A sudden wall of AC smacked me in the face, and I felt Violet shuffle around me, the door screeching as it swung shut. I waited for something to happen, for Violet to help me forward or give me another instruction, but nothing happened.

Thirty seconds passed.

Sick of not knowing what was going on, I reached up to pull off the blindfold, but before I could undo the knot, someone moved in my direction.

"Violet?" I asked.

A pair of warm arms wrapped around my waist. "Try again."

I sucked in a sharp breath. "Xander?"

"If I kiss you right now," he replied, gently running the pad of his thumb over my bottom lip, "will these kill me?"

"Nope." I'd been making an effort to avoid eating anything Xander was allergic to. It was difficult, but at the end of the day, impromptu make-out sessions put my favorite foods to shame. "I had a dairy-free salad, an apple, and—"

He cut me off with his mouth. After not seeing him for two months, I melted against his body, sliding a hand up the nape of his neck and cradling it. Xander's lips were hot as they moved against mine and…wow. Just wow. How was it that every kiss with him felt better than the last? All I wanted to do was spend the rest of the day locked in his embrace.

"All right, lovebirds. That's enough," Violet called from across the room. "You can maul each other later. We have to get ready."

Ready for what? I yanked off the scarf and blinked a few times before realizing we were standing inside Violet's trailer. The one she used on the set of *Lady Phoenix*.

Back in January, she'd gone through two quick rounds of auditions before being cast as Kelina Stardust. Less than a month later, preproduction began. By that time, I'd forgotten all about her promise, the one she'd made the night of her birthday party. But Violet hadn't. When she brought me to the first table read, I nearly had a heart attack.

"What are we doing here?" I asked, glancing between Violet and Xander. Judging from the smirk on his face, he knew exactly what was going on. The two were clearly up to something, and I didn't know how I felt about my sister and boyfriend conspiring behind my back.

"We start filming the night battle for episode three today," Violet explained. "How do you feel about being an extra?"

"An extra?" I asked, her words not computing.

"You know, an actor who appears in a nonspeaking capacity, usually in the background."

"You want me to be in the episode?"

She nodded. "That's the idea."

"Me?" I repeated.

Xander and Violet exchanged looks. "I think you broke her," he said.

"Well, I guess it's a good thing she doesn't have any lines. You okay with yours?"

He pulled a folded-up booklet from his back pocket—a script. "Got them all memorized," he said, tapping a finger against his temple.

This shook me from my daze. "You're going to be in the episode too?"

"Violet felt bad about my fight scene being cut from *Immortal Nights*," he explained, "so she hooked me up with a guest spot. Hope you don't mind sharing the spotlight with me."

"Holy shit, we're going to be in an episode of *Lady Phoenix* together." It was hard to imagine that only six months ago, the two of us had met at Comic Con. Xander hadn't even heard of the comic back then.

"We are," he said, grinning at me.

"Are you nervous?" I asked as a sudden burst of anxiety shot through me. I knew it was silly to worry since I didn't have any lines, but my stomach was suddenly a fluttery mess.

"Me?" He scoffed. "Not a chance."

I rolled my eyes but smiled. Xander had always been a positive, self-assured person, but lately I'd noticed a new level to his confidence. Not in an off-putting, egotistical way but in a charming manner that made people pay attention.

I contributed a small part of this change to Oliver. Xander

told me that during the Asian leg of their tour, his bandmate had apologized, not just for what happened at Comic Con but for all the times Xander had been overlooked and shunted aside at events, and he promised things would change moving forward.

But the majority of the transformation came from his song. Right before JJ sprained his wrist, Xander had performed "Indigo Skies" solo at the Heartbreakers' concert in Tokyo. Multiple videos of his performance went viral, prompting Alec to release the song straight away. Besides the beginner's recurve bow Xander gave me, the best Christmas gift I'd received was watching a song I contributed to climb the music charts. Xander and Violet already had an interview lined up with *Alternative Press*, and they'd be shooting the music video around the band's tour schedule.

"Hey," I said, perking up as I remembered the news I'd read this morning. "Did you hear that *Rhythm of Your Heart* is getting published?"

Xander drew back and gaped at me. "That fan fiction? The one about me?"

"Yep."

He shook his head in disbelief. "Is that even legal?"

"If they change your name? Sure."

"But what's another guy name that starts with X? Xavier?" He scowled. "Because that doesn't sound pretentious as hell."

"Well, that's way better than Xylophone, which was the first X word that popped into my head."

"They can't name me after a dorky musical instrument. I'm the badass leader of a rebel group, remember?"

I let out a small laugh. "Pretty sure you don't get a choice in the matter, but hey, if the book does well, maybe it will get a movie adaptation, and you can play yourself?"

"They should cast The Rock to play me instead."

"Yeah, I can really see the resemblance."

"I don't know. I think he could pull it off."

"That's a nice dream, babe," I said, patting him on the arm, "but I wouldn't get my hopes up if I were you."

Hair and makeup only took an hour. Since I was an extra, there was no wild transformation into a Disney character, alien, or monster. I would be portraying a plain old human, and even though Xander was a guest star, he would be too. When I looked at our reflections in the mirror, I couldn't help but smile. Not only were the two of us living our best lives, but were together and happy, and wasn't that a dream come true?

Just as the hairdresser finished teasing my ponytail to soaring heights, Violet poked her head inside the trailer.

"Xander? Indie? You all done?" she asked. "We're ready for you on set."

ACKNOWLEDGMENTS

For a period of time, I wasn't sure this book would happen. I wrote it over five years ago, before Covid and my mother's cancer diagnosis. I've evolved so much since then, both as a writer and as a person, but one thing that hasn't changed is how grateful I am that writing books is my actual, real-life job. Not everyone has the opportunity to do what they love, so I will always be thankful to all the amazing people who help make this possible for me.

First, Jared. I always thank you last, so I thought it was about time that I begin with the most important person in my life. There are no adequate words in the English language to convey how much you mean to me. Thank you for your endless patience, support, and love.

As always, I'd like to thank my amazing agent, Alex Slater. Without your unwavering support, I wouldn't be writing the acknowledgments for my fifth book.

I've had the privilege to work with multiple editors on this book—Annette Pollert-Morgan, Molly Cusick, and Wendy McClure. Thank you all for believing in this story and helping me bring it to life. In addition, thank you to the wonderful team at Sourcebooks that made this book possible: Jenne Abramowitz, Jenny Lopez, Olivia Haase, Thea Voutiritsas, Brittany Vibbert, Jessica Thelander, Deve McLemore, Karen Masnica, Lia Ferrone, Delaney Heisterkamp, and Taylor Geldermann.

Thank you to my friend Rachel Mienke, for all the virtual brownies that inspired me when I was suffering from major writer's block and for loving Xander more than anyone else I know (with the exception of Indie); to my Wattpad readers who supported this story when it was a rough draft and have waited patiently for the physical copy; and to Dahra Gillen for helping me with Xander's food allergies.

Finally, endless thanks to Kelly Anne Blount. Kelly, not only did you help me with brainstorming this entire story, but you came up with the perfect title. I'm so thankful for your friendship.

ABOUT THE AUTHOR

© JARED KALNINS

Ali Novak was born and raised in Wisconsin and is a *New York Times* and internationally bestselling author of contemporary young adult novels. She started writing her debut book, *My Life with the Walter Boys*, when she was only fifteen. Since then, her work has received more than 150 million reads online. When she isn't writing, Novak enjoys traveling with her husband, Jared; binding fan fiction; and reading any type of fantasy novel she can get her hands on. You can follow her on Wattpad, Facebook, Twitter, Instagram, and TikTok @ authoralinovak.

sourcebooks fire

Home of the hottest trends in YA!

Visit us online and
sign up for our newsletter at
FIREreads.com

....

Follow
@sourcebooksfire
online